A BANGKOK VERDICT

THE OMEGA FILES QUARTET

BOOK 3

MIKE KINGSTON

MITRE
PUBLISHING

A BANGKOK VERDICT

The Omega Files Quartet

Book 3

Mike Kingston

Mitre Publishing

First published by Mitre Publishing, 2024

For more details see website:
omegafilesquartet.com

Published by Mitre Publishing
Cover design by Red Nomad Studios
Typesetting by Red Nomad Studios

ISBN: 978-1916873223

To my wonderful family: Margaret, Sarah, Mark, Miriam, Finnian and Ronnie, for all the love, laughter, joy and continuing inspiration.

Thailand was never a European colony, so even though Bangkok is very Western on the surface, deep down it's very Asian. It's quite enigmatic, and I like that. I can't get to the bottom of Bangkok, and I never will.

Lawrence Osborne

Heroin spread that soft blanket over everything. But once the blanket was ripped off, it took a layer of skin with it, leaving nothing but nerve ends screaming in the breeze.

Jerry Stahl

ALSO BY MIKE KINGSTON

The Omega Files Quartet

A Candle for Consuela

A Flyblown Solution

A Bangkok Verdict

A Covert Corruption

Novellas

Roots of Destiny

Forged in Fire

Shadows of Redemption

Legacy of Revenge

Read more about Mike Kingston at omegafilesquartet.com

PROLOGUE

Bangkwang Prison, a decaying concrete hulk on the northern edge of Bangkok, is Thailand's maximum-security jail. It houses around seven thousand inmates. Prisoners serving long sentences wear leg irons for the first three months of their stay. The remaining prisoners are on death row. Their leg irons are welded on permanently.

Each cell measures six metres by four metres, has a bucket in a corner and holds between twenty and thirty men. There is no running water.

The Chao Phraya River runs nearby, rendered lifeless by years of industrial pollution. Its water is pumped into troughs for the prisoners to wash in.

The locals refer to Bangkwang as the "Bangkok Hilton" and the "Big Tiger" because they say "it eats men alive".

Thailand has been a major drug through-route for decades.

The authorities have responded with tough sentences for anyone caught with drugs. Those found to be involved with drug smuggling are treated particularly harshly.

There are several hundred foreigners inside Bangkwang's walls. Most are convicted of drug smuggling. These are the drug mules. They tell stories of naivety, stupidity and bad luck. Some were drug addicts themselves and risked their freedom and their lives to help finance their habit. A few claim not to have been aware they were carrying drugs at all.

The penalty for attempting to smuggle heroin, cocaine, amphetamine or methamphetamine is death.

For Westerners, the death sentence is usually commuted to life in Bangkwang.

But there is no guarantee.

CHAPTER ONE

"Mat."

"Mat."

He heard the voice through a hangover haze.

"I've got to go," said Kathy.

Mat Cooper forced his eyes open and remembered.

Bangkok.

Khaosan Road.

Green chicken curry, Tom Yum Goong, Tiger beer. Back to Kathy's friend's place.

More Tiger Beer.

Kathy smiled, "I've got to get the train for Chiang Mai. You've got to get your stuff."

She sat on the edge of the bed and kissed his head.

"Lao, remember?"

He did. He nodded and smiled. Lao: Vientiane; Plain of Jars; Indochina. Hmong hilltribes. Another gap year adventure.

He dragged Kathy down onto the bed.

"No. No. No."

She laughed and pulled away.

"I've got thirty minutes to get the train. You'll have to wait. Ten days, OK. Don't be late."

He fell off the bed, staggered to his feet and held her.

"Have a great time. I'll get a flight from Luang Prabang and see you in Chiang Mai. Ten days,"

He shook his head, "Seems like forever."

She kissed his cheek.

"You'll have a great time. You know how much you've been wanting to get there."

He did.

Kathy grabbed her backpack and left.

Mat looked at the crumpled sheets. They looked so inviting.

His stuff was packed and ready in his room at the Siam Paradise Hotel.

He checked his watch. His flight was in three hours. Shit! The airport road was always a nightmare.

* * *

The receptionist at his hotel didn't look up.

The young Amerasian kid...? Kid? He was almost the same age as Mat, stared at him and shook his head.

What was it?

Mat frowned.

What did he want?

Bangkok's rip-curling humidity had kicked in. His head pounded.

He turned away. Just wanted to get his stuff from the bedroom and onto the minibus waiting outside, get his head down through the inevitable traffic jams and clear the fog.

The bill was paid. The door to the minibus was open.

He looked back.

The Amerasian kid had gone.

He got in and fell asleep.

* * *

Check-in was a cruise.

Immigration, no hassle.

Customs a stroll.

“Here!”

Shit. Too good to be true. What?

He forced a smile.

Customs official. Pointing at Mat’s daypack on his shoulder.

Mat placed it on the stainless-steel counter.

Two officers - sunglasses and tight green uniforms – one with an array of gold stars on his shoulders, watched intently from a nearby doorway. Their concentration was menacing.

The customs guy pulled a knife from a pocket.

“Hey!”

He sliced the top of Mat’s daypack.

White powder poured out.

Mat stared.

He looked up.

The officers had gone.

A telephone rang.

Feet clattered on hard floors.

He looked again.

White powder spread across stainless steel.

The moment his life changed.

He couldn’t breathe.

CHAPTER
TWO

January 2000
London

Dan Cooper leaned across the bed and grabbed the telephone.

Even years after the divorce, he still slept on just one side of the large bed.

A car's hooter resounded in the calm night outside his bedroom window.

His alarm clock shone out: 03.46.

A shaft of alarm sprang inside him. Early morning calls rarely brought good news.

"Mr Cooper?"

A cultured voice.

Detached.

Official.

He pushed himself up against a pillow.

"Yes."

"I apologise for telephoning at such an unsocial hour. I am calling from the Foreign and Commonwealth Office. Our

Embassy in Thailand has advised that your son Matthew has been arrested in Bangkok."

A pile of documents was stacked on a bedside table alongside a lamp, which he switched on before responding.

It was absurd and must be a mistake.

Another hooter drifted through the black night.

"Arrested. For what?"

"Possession of heroin."

Heroin! Dan's brother had died in New York of a heroin overdose. Mat no! Not possible.

A stray, dark image of his brother's wasted body flashed quickly before him.

He shook his head.

It *must* be a mistake.

"You must be wrong."

Later, the words seemed so lame.

"Your son is in Thailand?"

"He will be in Lao at the moment. He was flying there a couple of days ago."

"He was arrested at Bangkok's Don Mueang Airport."

His voice was incredulous. "Mat?" Saying the name prompted his son's face before him. He felt sick.

"Matthew Daniel Cooper," came the distant voice.

"Can I call you back?" asked Dan.

He replaced the receiver and turned to the full-length window dominating the wall of the apartment on Stanhope Gate. He felt displaced from the moment and almost fell to the floor as he left his bed. Pressing a button on the bedside table, he watched the blinds open and saw a couple of taxis waiting in the rank beneath the building.

A tremor of panic ran through him.

He shook his head again to clear away the words. It *would* be a simple mistake.

After calling directory enquiries and confirming the Foreign Office number, he picked up a dressing gown folded at the side of the bed. He slipped it on before making his way to the window. There were no more details. There was no mistake. Dan noted down the number of the Embassy in Bangkok and the name of a consular official, Fairbrother, who had visited Mat.

He immediately called the Embassy and spoke to Fairbrother. Mat was in something called the Police Interrogation Unit. He hadn't been charged yet. A quantity of heroin had been found in his possession as he was going through Customs to catch a flight to Vientiane, the capital of Lao.

Fairbrother's voice was cold and detached. Although any emotion for this moment was for Dan alone, the man's abrupt tone shocked him. Only much later did he understand why Fairbrother was attempting to distance himself from the consequences of his own words.

He replaced the receiver and checked his watch. It was five minutes past four.

The moment his life changed.

He stumbled against the toughened glass window.

Nothing had changed.

He pushed the window open slightly, and a blast of cool air seeped through the gap. A burst of laughter spiralled up from the street far below. He could almost convince himself that this nightmare would pass. He would wake, shower, get dressed, get the underground to his office, and start another day.

The laughter spiralling up from the street sounded more sinister the second time. He closed the window. The pile of documents fell to the floor beside the bed.

He suddenly thought of Róisín, Mat's mother. She had enough problems with her husband in hospital following a heart attack.

He went into a vast bathroom, quickly showered, and shaved before throwing on a pair of jeans and a T-shirt from an expansive wardrobe inside the dressing room.

As he was leaving, the telephone rang.

"This is Tim Taylor from the *Sun*..."

He slammed down the receiver and left the apartment.

CHAPTER THREE

Tony Tavinor replaced the phone. He didn't move; he just stared through a window as a young boy rode slowly past on a ramshackle bicycle. The boy called over his shoulder to an unseen friend, stood on the pedals, and sped away laughing.

Tavinor frowned in disbelief. Perhaps it was a mistake. They happened - a mix-up with names. The police sometimes confused Falang names. Bangkok police could, and frequently did, get things wrong.

The details were precise, though. He shrugged aside his doubt as a worm of suspicion scratched at his consciousness, the truth he failed to acknowledge until too many tears had been shed and too much anger dissipated. Only later, as he toiled through the Laotian rainforest, would he look back at the moment and wonder whether he should have sounded an alarm which might have prevented so much anguish and pain.

Matt Cooper's face flashed before him as he approached the door and looked across at the long stretch of sand outside their small cottage. Alisa shouted in delight as she jumped in and out of the Malacca Strait's gentle rolling waves. The ten-year-old girl waved at Tavinor as he watched, and Maria, sitting on the sand, turned, and looked toward him.

She waved and then frowned.

They had endured hard years together, and she knew him so well.

She stood and walked across the sand toward him.

Alisa jumped as a large wave swept up Penang's Batu Ferringhi beach.

"What is it?" asked Maria as she came to Tavinor.

"Mat Cooper has been arrested in Bangkok. Heroin."

Maria shook her head. "That's not true. Is it?"

He shook his head and touched her hand. "I have to go."

She nodded.

CHAPTER FOUR

As the taxi passed the dark, sombre chapel beside the graveyard at the end of Róisín's Hampstead Street, Dan saw a small knot of people waiting at the gate to the terraced house. Reporters! He was too late. Lights shone from behind the curtains in the front room.

Róisín had married the boss of an advertising agency five years ago. Dan asked the taxi driver to go to the end of the road and called her number on his mobile. The answerphone cut in. He left a message saying he was coming to the back door. He also noticed five missed calls from his ex-wife – from when he was in the shower.

After giving the taxi driver a fifty-pound note and promising another if he waited, he slipped into an alley running behind the houses before pushing through a stiff gate and making his way up a garden path.

Róisín waited at the open door.

The divorce hadn't been bitter. Róisín said she had just given up a battle she couldn't win and that she should cite

Atlantic Santos- his company - for adultery. He'd been too busy to notice anything was wrong until it was too late.

Bright blue eyes were red with tears. A white dressing gown hung carelessly about her shoulders. Her blonde hair, cut short, was tousled as it framed the precisely delicate features that still gave him pause - and occasional anger at his stupidity.

"Dan" The voice was soft and pleading." It is a mistake, isn't it?" They came together and held each other in the dark, silent night. He tasted the sleep on her skin as he gently kissed her cheek.

He couldn't answer the question and wouldn't risk joining in the tears. "Let's go in."

She made two cups of coffee. They sat on each side of a large wooden kitchen table.

"How did you find out?" asked Dan.

She pointed down the hallway toward the front door. "Reporters turned up about thirty minutes ago. I called you. Is it true?"

"What have they said?"

"That Mat's been arrested in Bangkok for smuggling heroin."

"I spoke to an Embassy official who's visited Mat. He told me it was possession."

He paused, took a sip of coffee, and lied. "He said Mat's fine. He's being held at something called the Police Interrogation Unit. He didn't know of any charges."

As he took another sip, he decided what he must do.

"I'm going out there tonight."

Róisín nodded. She wiped her sleeve across her eyes, and as she did so, he saw the flash of rage and determination that distinguished the woman he could not stop loving despite their separation. She still ran the punk music label – *PileUp*

Records - which they had set up together when they got married.

Dan thought he had no choice when, years ago, he had to get over to Brazil and Central America to save the family business after his father had a stroke. He spent too long contemplating whether what he had saved was worth as much as that he had lost.

A photograph of Mat sat on the shelf of a large dresser filling one wall. Leaning across, he picked it up and, as he did so, knocked the coffee over his jeans. He wiped the stain as he looked at the wide smile everyone remembered about Mat. The photograph was taken one year ago on his eighteenth birthday when they'd taken him to the River Cafe.

The telephone rang.

Róisín didn't answer it.

A voice came from the answerphone, a reporter from the BBC.

"They all want a photograph," said Róisín, again gesturing toward the front door.

"We can give them one to share. Mine were all taken in the break-in at my apartment a few weeks back."

"The police haven't found the stuff that was taken?"

"I don't think they're interested. I guess an old computer and a few photographs aren't top priority. Why anyone would want them..." He shrugged as the words stuttered into silence. He remembered one of the photographs and the expression of terror and excitement as Mat was poised at the door of a light plane, about to do a sponsored parachute jump.

"I'd come to Bangkok with you, but can't leave Ben." Her face brightened a little. "They think he'll be out of intensive care within a few days and that a bypass will put him right."

The man had been a superb stepfather to Mat. He had intuitively recognised that Dan and Róisín would remain close despite the divorce. He had never shown any resentment at their warm relationship. He was a decent and honest man - a member of Gentlemens' clubs that Dan would give his eyeteeth to avoid.

She paused and raised her voice. The fury that rarely strayed too far from the surface emerged. “This isn't Mat.” She shook her head. “Absofuckinglutely not. Get him out, Dan. Find out what's gone on and get him out of that place.”

She turned away and hesitated.

“You encouraged Mat” she paused. “He wouldn't have gone if you hadn't persuaded him.”

She was right.

Dan had been trying to forget that he'd talked Mat into taking a year out before going to Durham University. He didn't answer.

“It can't be true, can it?” Her voice had fallen as though she was disassociating herself from the words. “You know what Mat's like. He'd help anyone out.”

“No, of course, it's not true. There's no way that Mat would get involved. He may be good-natured, but he's not stupid.”

He realised he was now almost shouting. “Sorry.”

Róisín stood up. “You'd better get moving if you're going out there today.” There was a pause as though she was waiting for him to change his mind. “Are you sure you'll be able to get away?” There was uncertainty in her voice.

He nodded.

“I'll be over later with a letter.”

She passed him the photograph. “Can you deal with the reporters? I've got the negative. They can make their own copies. Please get them away from the house.”

He promised to try as she closed the door. The light went off. The garden was dark.

Mat was all that was left of their marriage.

* * *

The taxi driver sat listening to the early-morning news. He turned and opened the rear door of the cab as Dan approached.

As they pulled away, he called Rosa Aris, his company's Director of Operations and asked her to meet him at the office as soon as she could get in. She told him she was already there waiting for him, having heard the news. When he ended the call, he asked the driver to stop. They had reached the front of Róisín's house, where a line of reporters was sitting on a garden wall. They ran across as the cab stopped. Dan got out and faced them. A barrage of questions flew at him.

"There will be a press conference this afternoon. I'll have photographs of Mat for you then. If you hang on here, there'll be no conference."

He got back in the taxi.

"What's all that about?" asked the driver.

"My son's been arrested in Thailand."

The driver looked in his mirror. "Mat Cooper. It's just been on the news. I thought I'd seen you before. Dan Cooper. You've been on the TV, haven't you?"

"Occasional business programmes."

His tone of voice closed the conversation.

* * *

Rosa opened the door of their offices. Black hair tumbled over a bright red t-shirt bearing the name of Real Madrid Football Club. There was nobody he trusted more than the thirty-seven-year-old Spaniard. She was a one-time punk groupie whose boyfriend put her in hospital when she left him. Dan ensured she was kept safe until the boyfriend was locked away for four years and then persuaded and funded her to take a master's degree in business administration. Outside the office, they were close friends. Although the closeness had almost tumbled into passion many times, they eventually realised what could be destroyed was more precious than what would be attained. Genuine friendship and professional respect were the consequences.

They briefly embraced. There was little accent left in her clipped voice. The words shot out. "I heard the radio. Mat wouldn't get involved in anything so dumb. What have you found out?"

Her brisk tone invigorated Dan.

He outlined his conversations with the Foreign Office and Bangkok.

Rosa sat down on the long black sofa lining one wall. She took a notebook from a leather briefcase. "I can take care of the business. I've reserved you on a British Airways flight to Bangkok at nine-thirty tonight."

She looked surprised when he nodded. "I wasn't sure you'd go."

"Neither was I," he admitted.

"I've also booked a suite at the Shangri-La in Bangkok."

Dan leaned across and grabbed her hand. "Thanks. I haven't started functioning yet."

She returned his grip. Her voice was soft. "I remember you were there in my bad times, Dan."

Turning to the window, he swallowed and tried to calm the panic her words released.

"I've agreed to do a conference this afternoon for the media. With any luck, interest would have faded by then. Could you get the PR guys to sort out the details? I'll put out a statement giving the details of the arrest. I'll write it shortly. Invite all the nationals and get copies of the statement run-off. I want to try to get them off Róisín's back. She's got enough to cope with at the moment." He reached into his pocket and looked at Mat's photograph. "Get someone to do enough copies of this to go with the statement."

Rosa touched his arm. "Everyone will help, Mat's popular. Last summer, he was great. He made a lot of friends." She smiled. "He never once played the boss's son bullshit. Handled all the bollockings with a smile and an apology. He's tougher than he looks."

Dan found a smile. He knew his son had done some shifts in a few of the company's ninety-seven coffee shops to save up for his trip.

"He never said a word to me about anything he'd done. Or not done." Turning away, he made for the bathroom as panic surged again. The door closed. He looked in the mirror and closed his eyes when he saw uncertainty reflected on his face. He hunched over the toilet bowl and threw up. Then, he entered his office and sat down to put a statement together.

Rosa called, "The press conference is organised for three o'clock this afternoon at the Hilton, Park Lane. You could get home and change."

"Three o'clock. OK."

He walked from his office and handed over the statement he had crafted. "Could you get a few copies to spread around?"

"Philip Walton is coming along."

"Why?"

Rosa shrugged. "He's *your* lawyer, who knows."

* * *

Rosa turned to Dan as he waited in a small annexe beside the hotel's second-floor conference room. He had brought his suitcase and was ready to leave in the evening.

"It looks like you've got a full house."

He shook his head. "I was hoping for a big story to break and that we'd have an empty room."

The copies of Dan's statement were piled on a table at the front of the room. Mat's photograph was attached to each.

"I'll get these handed out," said Rosa. "I'll open the conference..."

Dan interrupted. "No. This is a personal matter. I'll do it alone."

She frowned. "What about questions? It could get out of hand if nobody's there to control things. I do know most of them," she snapped. "More than a few reporters out there may have their own agendas. You've not been gentle at times."

"Only when they write rubbish about this company. Anyway, I won't have the company involved any more than it has to be."

She didn't look convinced. "What about a personal interview afterwards with someone we can trust?"

Dan shook his head. "I'm doing this because I don't want the press corps camped outside Róisín's. That's it. I wouldn't be here otherwise."

Rosa's scepticism was undiminished. "It's dangerous, Dan."

He shrugged. He had nothing else to say. Rosa touched his arm. "Philip Walton is waiting."

Dan checked his watch. "We're due to start in a few minutes."

"That's what he's come about," said Rosa.

"OK, get him in."

Rosa grabbed her phone and told the solicitor to come to the anteroom. Dan could hear the commotion next door. Television crews setting up their cameras. Reporters talking in muted voices. An occasional burst of laughter broke through.

Philip Walton came in, a perpetual frown stuck to his forehead like a flag of convenience. “Dan, you must cancel this pantomime. What can you hope to achieve?”

Dan sighed and repeated his concern about Róisín, adding that it was also important to inform the Government that he expected it to support a British citizen overseas.

“You expect the Government to question Thailand’s legal system? If you claim Mat has been set up, you’ll get Thai backs up, embarrass both Governments and make negotiations impossible ...”

Dan leapt to his feet. “What the hell do you expect me to say? That my son’s guilty? For Christ’s sake, he would not deal in heroin. Therefore, he has been set up, and I’m his father, and I’ll bloody well say so!”

His voice rose in anger.

“And I don’t care if I get anyone’s backup. I know all about quiet diplomacy. It means no one says anything and some poor bugger is supposed to go quietly. Well, not this time. I’m going out tonight and not coming back without my son ...”

He stopped suddenly as he felt Rosa’s hand gripping his arm ever more tightly. There was silence in the conference room.

“Fuck,” he whispered and threw an accusing glance at Walton, who looked like he wished he could disappear as he opened his mouth to speak. Dan held up his finger.

“No more,” he snarled in a whisper. “I know you’ve got your job to do. You’ve done it.” He moved closer to the solicitor, his voice softer. “Thank you. I appreciate your concern.”

He picked up the remaining copy of his statement, threw his shoulders back and walked into the adjoining conference room.

The silence grew deeper as he sat at the only chair behind a table at the front where a mess of microphones and cassette recorders were waiting. Flashbulbs momentarily dazzled him as he read the statement explaining what he knew about Mat's arrest and his belief in his son's innocence.

One or two of the faces were familiar. Not many were friendly. Over the years, he'd left the PR to his staff and always regretted being persuaded to do the occasional in-depth interview. He only succeeded in coming across as angry and intolerant.

He sat back in his chair after he'd read the statement. The questions came uninvited from all over the room. Camera lights dazzled him.

"You're going to Bangkok?"

"This evening."

"What do you hope to achieve?"

"To prove my son's innocence and bring him home."

"How do you know he's innocent?"

"I know my son."

"Has he been involved in drugs before?"

"He's not involved now."

"Then how do you explain ten kilos of heroin being hidden in his backpack?"

He paused for a second. Ten kilos! How did they get information he didn't have?

"That's why I'm going to Bangkok, to find the explanations."

"Is your son denying the facts?"

"I'll be seeing Matthew as soon as I arrive. I'll find out the facts then."

"What was he doing in Bangkok?"

"Travelling during a year off before University."

"Did your son attend Archbishop Temple School in Islington?"

He didn't see the reason for the question. "Yes."

"The hotel where he was staying was in an area of Bangkok where drugs are readily available. Isn't that right?"

The pause was longer this time. He didn't know the hotel or area where Mat had been staying.

There was momentary relief when an authoritative voice came from the rear of the room. He recognised it from the television news. "Isn't it true that your company gave twenty thousand pounds to the Labour Party this year? Will you be calling on the Government to support your son?"

He didn't know they had given any money. He'd long ago refused to be consulted over donations, considering them a waste of money. He only agreed on a budget to be spent as the remaining directors decided.

"I expect my son to have the same support from the Government as any other person."

"Do you think he will get a fair trial in Thailand?"

This was getting dangerous. He stood up.

"When all the facts are known, Matthew will be found innocent of any charges. Thank you."

As he approached the door, a female voice came from the front of the room.

"Is it true, Mr Cooper, that if your son is found guilty of smuggling with intent to sell or of being in possession of over ten grammes of heroin, the penalty under Thai law is death?"

Flashbulbs exploded into his shocked face as he turned in the doorway.

The death penalty!

More questions were shouted at him. He didn't hear them as he staggered through the doorway and slumped into a chair, trying to calm the panic. His voice was barely audible. "The death penalty!"

"Pardon?"

He turned, shocked to see Philip Walton still sitting behind a table examining a pile of documents. “I thought I would wait,” the solicitor said by way of explanation.

“Is it true?” asked Dan.

Walton lowered his head. “I don’t know.”

“What a fuck up,” muttered Dan to himself. He looked at the solicitor, who was still glancing at some documents. “You were right.”

“I think you handled everything extremely well.”

“You know ...” He paused as the door opened. Rosa came in, her expression sombre.

“The photograph that will be used tomorrow will be me standing in the doorway like a rabbit caught in the headlights.”

Rosa spoke. “You didn’t hurt Mat, but keep away from the press now, Dan. It’s done now for the right reason. Forget it. There are more important things to think about.”

Walton cleared his throat. “I’m sorry to mention this. It may seem indelicate, but have you reviewed your will recently? I thought I should raise the matter as you are going to Thailand.” He looked uneasy. “You don’t know what you may face.”

Dan felt a sense of the absurd. Walton’s face looked so doleful he couldn’t help laughing. “Thank you, Philip. I needed some light relief.”

“It wasn’t quite true about the Labour Party money,” said Rosa. “We sponsored a conference on money laundering organised by one of their think tanks.” She held up a telephone message. “The head guy just called after seeing the press conference and expressed concern for Mat. He assured me that he would assist if at all possible. These matters are delicate, blah, blah.”

Rosa put the message away. “Róisín called. She’s on her way over. After that, I need to sit down with you for the rest of the day to ensure we’ve covered all the bases. I’ve spoken to everyone, and I'll have an updated report from each division when you're finished with Róisín. And you've had a mass of calls offering sympathy and support."

Róisín appeared in the doorway.

Rosa moved across to her, they kissed briefly on the cheek. "I'm sorry about Mat," said Rosa. "I'm sure everything will work out. I'll leave you in peace. You want me to get some food organised?"

"I couldn't eat anything," said Róisín. "A cup of tea, perhaps."

Dan nodded his agreement.

Róisín sat down. The resemblance to Mat was heartrending. Blonde hair, blue eyes and, although there was no sign of it now, a smile that sparkled and lit up a room. She delved into a large shoulder bag and came out with a letter and an Arsenal football shirt with *- 10 - Van der Shift -* written across the back of the shirt. Dan remembered the nickname Shifty given to Mat by some of the boys at his school. He'd forgotten why.

"I know it's stupid," said Róisín, but he's always wearing it. He only forgot to take it because it was in the washing when he left."

"Do you think this is our fault?" asked Róisín.

They fell silent as a waiter brought in a tray with two cups of tea,

Dan knew it was his fault. His devotion to the company, to his ambitions and little else.

"Fault. I don't understand. What are you saying?"

Róisín turned from his denial. "I'm worried. You remember the fuss at his school about a year ago. One of Mat's friends was excluded because of drugs. I'm sure the lad was Thai and went back home. It wouldn't have anything to do with that, would it? You know Mat's always been up for a dare."

Dan was silent. He remembered the question about the school at the press conference.

"Perhaps you should go away for a few days," he said.

Róisín frowned. "With Ben still in intensive care?" She paused. "Why do you say that?"

He told her about the reporter as she sipped at her tea.

She seemed to shrink in size. Her eyes closed as she slumped down on the sofa as though trying to hide. "I'm going to the hospital," she said eventually, pushing herself to her feet and dragging up her bag as though it was weighed down. "Call me as soon as you've seen Mat."

He walked to the door with her. "Of course I will."

"Don't let me down, Dan. Not again. Bring our son home. Please."

* * *

It was a long afternoon at his office in Canary Wharf with Rosa and the Managing Directors of the company's various divisions: Coffee shops, coffee and sugar plantations in Brazil and El Salvador, food manufacturing and a stake in an investment services operation.

The meetings finished. He was alone. In truth, he had barely registered what had gone on. Rosa had led him through the discussions.

A driver called. The limousine was waiting in the basement car park.

They slowed at a flurry of blue flashing lights just past Brompton Oratory. A young man, about the same age as Mat, sat leaning against a wall. His shocked face was covered in blood. Two paramedics were patching him up.

Dan checked his watch, and it was seven hours ahead in Bangkok. It was early morning now.

Mat would be sleeping in a prison cell - if he was sleeping at all.

CHAPTER FIVE

Parting from Maria was painful. Tony Tavinor felt desolate as he boarded the taxi outside their small beach-front house in Batu Ferringhi, Penang.

It was a twenty-hour journey to Bangkok, and he needed the time to adjust and find the resources needed to deal with what lay ahead. Leaving Maria's warm embrace was a tender sorrow. Their time together at Batu Ferringhi had been a solace that allowed previous struggles to drift away with the gentle tides of the Malacca Straits.

Only now did he know the release of contentment and the surge of adrenalin which had moulded the ex-soldier's life for so long. Confrontation was an anticipation to be relished. When he heard from a colleague from his time as a private investigator in Bangkok about Mat Cooper's incarceration, there was no hesitation as he threw some clothes into a back-pack and set off for Thailand.

Whoever had caused that boy to be thrown into the stinking hell that was Bangkok's prison system – a corrupt, vicious, and brutal open drain hidden from view behind high, secure walls – had miscalculated. They could not have known that Mat would be protected and by whom.

Mat had spent Christmas in Penang talking excitedly about his plans for his upcoming trip to Laos and the iconic Plain of Jars - Maria would look at Tavinor and smile as the boy would wax lyrical about *"the archaeological landscape consisting of thousands of stone jars scattered around the upland valleys and the lower foothills of the central plain of the Xiangkhoang Plateau."*

Tavinor said he must have got that from a textbook, Mat answered with a burst of laughter, "Of course."

It was archaeology that sparked Mat's imagination. Tavinor knew there was no way the boy would try to smuggle drugs. It was absurd, but then he had spent time when he was in Bangkok investigating drug routes, *"mules,"* and the background that allowed the billion-dollar trade to flourish. He knew that most flights to Western Europe carried mules that had secreted drugs either around or even in their bodies. They could be kids who had run out of funds, dupes suckered into doing a favour for a friend or lover, or others who were prepared to take the risk of being caught to make a few hundred dollars.

It was also true that Western nations pressed the Thai government to take action to stop the flow of drugs. That pressure was hammered down onto the police, and every so often, a mule was apprehended at the airport, and the police and government could demonstrate that they were tackling the problem.

Drug cartels funded police elements to ensure that the system was smooth and allowed the trade to continue uninterrupted. Occasionally, a victim would claim innocence, and Tavinor had met one or two in Bangkwang central prison that he felt had been set up, but, in most cases, they were just broke kids without the resources to challenge the police.

Sometimes, he had investigated where he was certain there was another reason behind an arrest - a sting to exact revenge – or an incentive to secure a business deal. Then the police would be paid off, and the victim end up in the "Bangkok Hilton."

However Mat had ended up in that stinking system. Tavinor would find the truth and destroy whoever got in the way.

The train pulled out of Butterworth station on the mainland after he had crossed from Penang on the ferry. He had booked both upper and lower seats in the second-class sleeper carriage to give him the undisturbed space he needed to prepare for the trials that lay ahead. The two lower seats pushed together to form a comfortable bunk, and he lay looking from the window as the train rolled on through a landscape he had known well from his time in Malaysia and Thailand.

Scattered settlements of concrete blockhouses, corrugated iron roofs of small neighbourhoods sometimes almost touching the sides of the carriage. Open-air cafes with wooden tables and plastic dishes featured occasional customers not bothering to look up from their rice bowls as the train moved past. Between the habitations, green forests competed with extensive clumps of palm trees gently waving in a half-hearted breeze. Groups of villagers would gather at track crossing points and watch as the eight wagons would labour slowly past.

As the train rolled through Thailand, he called a solicitor he had once worked with in Bangkok. The man would find out more details and make arrangements to visit Mat as soon as possible.

Then, after time had passed and he was ready for what lay ahead, the urban sprawl of Thailand's capital announced their imminent arrival at their final stop - Hua Lamphong station. He waited and watched the mayhem of backpackers, hotel and taxi touts amongst the frenetic energy that envelops a major station. He was in a place that had once been home for a while, and back then, he had been reluctant to leave - the crazy vitality of the place drew him in as he made his way through the cavernous main hall.

As he reached the exit, he stood for a moment, feeling the intense heat wash over him and then breathed in the smells of the place - jasmine, tuk-tuk fumes, sewage, grilled meat, smoky incense – a rich, unique cocktail.

He decided he would walk to the Shangri-La hotel. As he started, his phone rang. It was Ray Lancaster, one of his oldest friends and ex-colleague in the parachute regiment, from London, and Dan Cooper's security chief.

He flexed his shoulders the game was on.

CHAPTER
SIX

KAMCHAN Nirundorn was just over five feet tall and almost as wide. With his trademark bright blue suit, the appearance told a story of affluence and influence.

Tavinor had worked with the solicitor in the past. He knew the man was hard-working and would do as good a job with Matt as any lawyer in Bangkok. He also knew that self-interest was the man's abiding impulse, but to his credit, he never pretended it was any other way.

A high-pitched voice made positive noises as Nirundorn confirmed that he had arranged a preliminary visit to Mat later in the morning. He sat in the Shangri-La lobby and asked about Mat's financial situation.

Tavinor laughed. "Check out Atlantic Santos Holdings, Café Santos Coffee Shops, and estates in South and Central America. His father's business is one of the UK's largest private companies. Your fees will be covered."

Nirundorn nodded, reassured.

"So, we meet up with Matt briefly." A frown momentarily flashed across his face. "Major Prisit is running the case..."

Tavinor interrupted. "Prisit. Why the hell is he involved?"

Nirundorn shrugged. "Prisit is Prisit," he said.

"He's a psychopath."

The solicitor nodded. "And well connected."

"That's one way of describing his loyalty to anyone who pays his price."

Nirundorn closed his eyes and waved his hands as though absolving himself from the words just spoken. "We deal with the situation." He stood. "I will return at ten-thirty, then we leave for Mat."

Without another word, he left the lobby and exited the hotel.

Tavinor stood and walked to the tall, wide window overlooking the Chao Phraya River.

He knew Major Prisit and remembered a few years back finding two murdered Australian boys – the police officer had just laughed. Tavinor knew that the man had murdered the boys himself for a big payoff from one of the drug lords, Chao Thanarat.

Mat's situation had just got a whole lot worse.

* * *

Tavinor and the lawyer sat in the prison interrogation unit's stark, airless room. Their photographs had been taken at the entrance when they were finally admitted. Doors banged in the barren silence mixed with occasional angry shouts and cries of pain echoing along narrow, filthy corridors.

Mat was pushed violently through a door as it suddenly opened, revealing a small dusty square where an old man pointlessly swept dust into no particular order, every time he appeared to have mustered a small pile, a warder came and kicked it over. The man merely started sweeping again.

Tavinor waited as Mat fell into the room. He held up his hand as Mat started to speak with the warder gripping his arm. Prisit stood in the open doorway, watching the scene before him, his uniform clinging to his muscular frame. He stared at Tavinor, his glance malevolent, the contempt undisguised.

Mat's voice was frail, but Tavinor felt an unexpected strength as the boy spoke.

"Tony, I didn't do this." He looked around, his eyes pausing at Prisit whilst he looked back at Tavinor and touched a bruise under his left eye.

Tavinor nodded. He understood, but there was nothing he could do – not yet.

"I know you didn't do this, Mat. "He stepped toward the boy, but the guard pushed Mat away. "I will get you out of here."

He looked to Prisit and nodded toward the bristling figure who remained in the doorway before turning back and slowly repeating the words. "I will get you out of here."

The repetition lent anger to his determination. He continued. "One question. Where were you staying before you were picked up?"

The guard grabbed hold of Mat and started to pull him back through the doorway. Mat grimaced at the fierce grip digging into his arm. Tavinor leaned forward, taking hold of the guard's hand and forcefully releasing it from Mat's arm. He looked toward Prisit while he crushed the guard's hand. Tavinor reached into a pocket with his free hand, drew out a US$100 note, and offered it to Prisit.

"Siam Paradise Hotel, Rham Buttri Road," said Mat,

Tavinor released his grip from the guard and spoke to Prisit.

"Thank you, Major, for all your efforts."

Prisit snatched the note and nodded to the guard, gesturing for Mat to move through the door.

"We will be back, Mat."

He looked toward Prisit. "We will be back."

He bowed toward the police officer, holding his hands together as though in prayer.

* * *

They sat in the hotel lobby. A waitress came carrying a tray. She knelt on the carpeted floor and placed two coffee cups on the table.

Nirundorn coughed as Tavinor watched the waitress move elegantly across the lobby. He turned to the solicitor and smiled. "I forgot how much I love this place. So beautiful, alongside the worst of all our desires."

"Yes, yes," Nirundorn didn't bother to disguise his impatience. "How did you know the boy had been picked up? There has been no announcement yet, together with a self-congratulatory speech from a minister."

"I'm living in Penang. I had a call from Lynne Kramer..."

The solicitor interrupted, "Of course, you worked with her at that investigative agency. They would have heard as soon as he got picked up. They have their informers at the airport." He paused, "and Kramer is still plugged into the circuit. So she would have heard soon enough."

"In Chiang Mai."

"Of course. She sends work down to her old colleagues. Transfers from the drug unit in Chiang Mai to Bangkok. No shortage of them."

Tavinor waited as Nirundorn continued.

"I understand the agency is still thriving, although one or two original operators have departed."

"And Kramer is still active but had enough of Bangkok."

Nirundorn paused and then nodded. "Closer to Chao up there, I suppose. She always kept a close interest in his activities."

Tavinor was surprised Nirundorn was aware of what he always considered Lynne's obsession with the drug dealer.

The solicitor continued. "He's a powerful force now. Fingers in many very lucrative pies. He is still loved among the Hmong people in Laos and keeps a base there. Near Hongsa, I believe. Most of his businesses are run from here, though, in Bangkok. Hotels, telecoms, brewing, foodstuffs, nightclubs. Big business, very, very powerful. Dusit Sombat, an accountant, controls everything. He was at Chao's right hand during the so-called "secret war" in the seventies. Chao sent him to the US and a business school when the Pathet Lao took over in Laos..."

Tavinor interrupted, "The communists?"

"Of course. Chao took himself off to Burma, Thailand, and Chiang Rai and eventually returned to Laos a while back. Set up laboratories in the Golden Triangle and still controls the drug trade. He runs the army and the police in the north. Nothing moves without his approval. It's the dirty money that drives the legitimate businesses."

"Could he be involved with Matt Cooper?"

Nirundorn raised his eyebrows and spread his hand as though powerless. "Not for me to know. Not yet, anyway."

He stood. "Send me Cooper's flight details, please. I'll keep an eye on it and meet him up at the airport this evening. He is booked in here?"

Tavinor nodded.

CHAPTER **SEVEN**

Films flickered against the ceiling from personal video screens. Stewards wandered quietly around the shrouded first-class cabin of the flight to Bangkok.

The time didn't drag. It was worse than that.

Each moment sucked the certainty from Dan Cooper.

Whatever he was experiencing was outside anything he could understand. There was no yardstick to measure this misery. There was no reassurance that the nightmare would end. He'd lost control. None of the usual points of reference applied.

Staring vacantly at pictures of '*Exotic Asia*' in the airline magazine, Dan remembered a couple of business trips in the past to Malaysia and China. The abiding memory was heat, humidity and long-winded speeches.

He tossed the magazine away and tried to find something interesting in one of the films being played out on his screen. The only picture he saw, though, was Mat's face looking desperately toward him, seeking help. What chance was there of his being able to help his son? The dark silence in the cabin was no easy companion. A vacuum filled with Mat's spiky blond hair topping off the smile, which gave an excuse for just about anything; the laugh which threw its pleasure around you, infecting you in its innocent delight. Images drifted into blackness - he felt himself sinking into an aching despair that gripped his body.

The time didn't drag. It seized up.

He ceased to function. Desperate for the hiatus to end, he clung to the sense of being nowhere, suspended in time, dreading, yet desperate, for the moment he would see his son. When he and Róisín had fought, Mat had always been the peacemaker. Jumping between them, his hands outstretched shouting - 'NO!' - he remembered the little face, so concerned, trying desperately to bring them together. It was always the same. Róisín angry that he was always away after his father's stroke. She was left to run their punk music company, *PileUp Records* and care for Mat while he was often out in South America and El Salvador trying to keep the family business afloat. Sometimes, he couldn't get back for weeks at a time, and even if he was at home, he often arrived back too late to see Mat. Their son only heard the anger and weeping denunciations. What he understood, Mat tried to reconcile, not realising the fault lines were too well-hidden and, in time too deep.

Perhaps they should have tried harder.

He knew *he* should have tried harder.

He flicked through the video channels and paused at the nightly news from the UK. An item on a murder trial ended, and a photograph of Mat suddenly flashed onto the screen before switching to his press conference. He dragged off the headphones and turned from the display. The airline meal he'd eaten a few hours ago tasted sour.

He called over a steward and asked for a large brandy.

He rarely drank alcohol.

It tasted fierce as it burned its way down his throat.

He asked for another.

After he finished the second glass, he closed his eyes. Mercifully, sleep came.

CHAPTER **EIGHT**

After returning to the Shangri-La, Tavinor started calling some of his old colleagues from back in the day when he worked in the city as a private investigator after more than ten years in the Parachute Regiment. That was a few years ago, and as Nirundorn had told him, many of his one-time colleagues had left Thailand, but he met up with a couple who remained when they came to the hotel for lunch.

They knew about Mat's arrest and were as sceptical as Tavinor.

"No one takes drugs into Laos. Perhaps a few joints they'd forgotten about, but heroin, no way. Someone wanted to shove a firecracker up that boy's arse. You working the case, Tony?"

Tavinor told them about Mat, his father Dan Cooper, and their friendship with Tavinor. He asked about Lynne Kramer.

"She's up in Chiang Mai. We have tried to get her back, but she won't have it. Had enough of Bangkok, she said. Do you remember those two kids who ended up dead in Lamphun? She worked that case with you, didn't she, Tony?"

He nodded. "The Aussies, they went missing, and we spent

about a month searching for them until their bodies turned up."

"She bailed after that. Prisit wasn't it? He slotted them for Chao Thanarat. The Aussie kids thought they were smarter than the locals. Bad mistake."

"Are you sure it was Prisit?"

"That's the word, but what the hell. He's not gone down for it, has he? Too well protected, I guess. Lynne's doing some freelance shit for the DEA up there, and she's always had a hard-on for Chao. He's up in Chiang Rai and across in Laos. Dusit Sombat runs the business down here. It's big time now."

The lunch ran on, Singha beer mixed with reminiscence and laughter, stories told and embellished, characters gone but recalled. Eventually, they left. Tavinor returned to his room. He checked Dan Cooper's flight and found out it was delayed.

Throwing on a pair of shorts, an old t-shirt, and battered flip-flops, he made his way out of the hotel and passed the clique group of black limousines to the tuk-tuks waiting by the access road.

He covered his face with a handkerchief as his tuk-tuk careered through fume-filled traffic. He laughed as he bailed out in the mayhem of backpacker central – KhaoSan Road. He realised he had raised the average age by more than a few years as he walked slowly through the sharp tang of marijuana fumes, one of the area's distinctive flavours spreading from around Thai massage parlours, bespoke tailors, open fronted cheap knock-off clothes shops, and bars with widescreen TVs showing various films of which *The Matrix* and a new *Star Wars* seem to feature pretty strongly. Restaurants spreading over the pavements had young "pushers" offering up fancy pictures of meals as they enticed the punters to sit and spend their gap year funds.

He turned into Sol Rham Buttri. The Siam Paradise Hotel

opened up to the narrow road. An open-air bar with around a dozen tables was situated in front of open doors leading to a lobby and a wide reception desk. A bank of computer terminals and monitors was situated to one side of the reception area, all occupied as young kids banged away at keyboards.

He paused and looked through the open doors before moving toward the reception desk. As he did so, he felt the note of alarm which always sparked when a threat was present. He paused, turned and encountered a forehead covered in a heavy plaster, eyes as tiny black holes, a ponytail, goatee beard and a suspicious expression.

Words spat out an insincere question. “We can help you?”

Tavinor looked around at the activity surrounding them. The bar was half full, the computers crowded, and three people were waiting at the reception desk.

“Why do you ask?”

Tavinor moved to the reception. A plaque behind the desk stated the hotel was owned by *Gilbourne Overseas (Caymen) SA Incorporated*. He memorised the name.

Two security guards approached him from a door behind the reception area. He turned and faced the distrustful gaze that fell on him from the figure that had stayed just behind him. Two hands gripped his arms. He span and quickly ripped them away, snapping one of the guards’ wrists as he jerked it from his body. A gasp of pain sprang into the warm air, and he looked at the other guard as the man moved toward him. Tavinor just shook his head. It was enough; the man stopped. A photograph lay on the floor, it had fallen from the guard holding his wrist. Tavinor recognised his image from the Interrogation Unit that morning.

A faint smile hovered on the scarred image as Tavinor paused on the pavement and looked back. The man’s scrutiny was undisguised.

* * *

He called a friend in KL when he went to his hotel room. The man agreed to send the details Tavinor requested as soon as he could locate the information.

He next called Lynne Kramer.

The woman didn't do pleasantries. She always said she never saw the need. "I wondered when I would hear from you," she demanded. "Did you get up to Bangkok?"

"I did, I'm here now, and thanks to you, I saw Mat this morning..."

The stern voice interrupted. "It was him then? I wasn't one hundred per cent sure, but the name was the same."

"Yes. It was Mat. Nirundorn arranged a preliminary meeting. His father, Dan Cooper, is coming over this evening."

"You told me at Christmas his company is worth a bundle."

Tavinor agreed.

"Then Nirundorn will try to hang onto the case. He's OK as long as you don't get into hand-to-hand combat."

"You're right. He was a convert when I explained Mat's company was one of the UK's largest private operations. He's meeting Dan at the airport this evening."

Tavinor paused. He hesitated to tell Lynne about Prisit. Her memories of that man might decide her not to get involved, and he wanted her assistance.

"Can you get down here? I'm going to need help with this thing."

"No. I have a dumb falang picked up for possession. I'll sort that out today, I've just got to find out if he has access to funds to pay his way out. More importantly, I've been asked to check out a couple of suspicious deaths. Two kids about Mat's age were alleged to have been involved in an accident. The parents don't believe the story the police are telling. They are good friends of mine, so I have to check it out. That's for tomorrow."

"And after that?"

"Tony, it's Bangkok. I got out of the place. I have work here. You can deal with this. It's got to be a crock of shit, hasn't it."

"Are you still freelancing for the DEA?" Tavinor had read that the USA's Drug Enforcement Agency had recently appointed a new station chief.

"It pays the rent."

"Chao Thanarat?"

"He's rarely seen, although he did make an appearance a few weeks ago."

"OK, I'll keep in touch."

The line was disconnected without another word.

CHAPTER **NINE**

Indistinct shafts of light fell through an evening blue sky onto waterlogged paddy fields. Dan looked from the 747's window as it descended into Bangkok. Suddenly, as though a switch was thrown, the precision and clarity of each colour sharpened and lengthened into a dramatic rainbow tracing around the sky, touching earth somewhere beneath the juddering plane.

The sharp beauty cut like a knife. Dan needed no reminder of what Mat would never see or experience again if he screwed up. He checked his watch. They were almost two hours late. A delay was caused by an instrument that went "technical" just before take-off.

That seemed a lifetime and a culture shock away.

The figure holding up a sign reading *"Dan Cooper"* had a thick moustache and teeth which looked like they'd been hammered in on a drunken night, noticeable when a broad smile emerged as Dan nodded in his direction when he turned into the arrivals hall at Bangkok's Don Mueang Airport. He rushed over and grabbed Dan's small case, which he insisted on carrying even though it was on wheels. Gesturing toward an exit door, the smile was sustained while elbowing a path through groups of touts trying to sell taxi rides, hotels, and anything else money could buy.

Dan pulled down his tie, undid his collar and slipped off his jacket as soon as he exited the terminal. The heat and humidity gripped him as he paused and watched the greeter rushing toward a grey Mercedes waiting in a non-parking zone. A policeman wearing a white mask covering his mouth and nose was leaning in a rear window and talking to someone in the back seat. He eventually saluted and walked back along a row of cars, shouting and gesticulating toward a taxi which had stopped in the middle of the road. Dan breathed deeply, trying to get some air into his lungs, before following the gestures of the driver, who had placed his case in the limousine boot and was waiting by the rear door, which he swung open as Dan approached.

Tony Tavinor had said that Kamchan Nirundorn was well-connected. The image matched the description. The solicitor's smooth face snapped into a broad smile of greeting as Dan slid into the seat alongside the diminutive figure holding out a dry hand, soft fingers loose, little substance or definition. Dan pulled on his jacket in the fierce blast of air-conditioning. Nirundorn wore a royal blue silk suit that shone out like a warning beacon. His voice was high-pitched, singing a soothing message as the car exited the airport. They paused at a tollbooth and, as the lawyer talked, Dan looked from the car at an urban sprawl featuring unfinished concrete blocks, aspiring multi-storeys and an occasional splash of bright colour when a temple interrupted the unremitting suburban streaks of grey-stained concrete. They ground to a halt, traffic stretching into a chaotic distance.

Dan had clung to the hope that a mistake had been made and would have been put right before he landed. The belief grew as he passed through immigration - perhaps Mat would be waiting for him.

He sat in silence for a few moments, absorbing the disappointment.

Nirundorn's sing-song voice suddenly cut through his meditation.

"Two days! Did you say Mat has been in custody for two days?"

The smile broadened as Nirundorn checked his notes. "Oh, yes! He was stopped at the airport whilst flying out to Laos at eleven in the morning two days ago. He has been in police custody since that date." He looked up. "He is fine, Mr Cooper. A strong boy."

"What the hell does that mean?"

A momentary frown disturbed the smile. "He has been resolute that he knows nothing about the heroin."

"He wouldn't know anything about it. He has never touched drugs," snapped Dan.

The shrug in response dismissed the notion as irrelevant. "Of course." There was a pause. "We accept facts, Mr Cooper."

"OK." Dan tried to drain the anger from his voice. It would get him nowhere, especially in Asia, where he knew anger was pointless and self-defeating. "Run through the facts."

Nirundorn looked down at his notes again. "Your son was stopped at Customs at the airport as he was about to board a flight for Vientiane in Laos. Ten kilos of heroin were found stitched in the lining of his backpack. He was detained at the airport, transferred to police and taken to the Police Interrogation Unit, where we will meet him tomorrow. Major Prisit in charge of the case. Experienced officer. As I say, your son claims he knows nothing about drug."

"Why weren't we told of the arrest earlier?"

"Normal procedure, Mr Cooper."

Dan was silent, looking out of the window at another traffic jam.

"Rama Four road," said the Thai, with pride, as they crept along a dual carriageway.

"Ten kilos stitched into a small backpack. That doesn't seem possible."

"The police like to exaggerate. It makes them look better. It may have only been one or two kilos, but it grows to ten or twenty kilos by the time they reach the Interrogation Unit. The court will take that into account."

Dan paused before asking. "Is it true that a conviction may mean the death penalty?"

"Smuggling any amount of heroin with intent to sell is punishable by death penalty."

Dan struggled for air and opened the window but only let in a blast of heated gasoline fumes. Gasping in the polluted, sodden air, he closed the window again. Eventually, he found sufficient control to force himself back against the seat.

"The death penalty!" His words were barely audible.

"Rarely carried out," came the response. The lawyer found a wide smile as though striking the first triumph in the case.

"Rarely?"

"You must not think of such things. There are ways that matters can be ordered in Thailand. We speak with Minister. It OK. We resolve."

"I've read about Thai prisons."

Nirundorn shrugged. "We do our best. Reputation worse than reality." He smiled and touched Dan's knee. "Newspapers exaggerate." He shrugged again.

"Can we make an application for bail?"

The smile broadened. "Of course. We make application."

He leaned closer. "No bail. In drug cases, for amount your son picked up for, no bail." There was a pause. "Not normally."

"Normally?"

"We must consider these matters carefully, Mr Cooper. You must be tired."

"I can sleep when my son is released."

"Of course."

"Are we going to the embassy? I've arranged a meeting."

Nirundorn held out the palms of his hands. "Regrets, Mr Cooper. Delay of your flight...? Everyone has left the embassy." He pointed at the telephone between the front seats. "They call me. See you tomorrow."

Dan sighed in exasperation as Nirundorn spoke again. "As I said, there are ways that matters can be resolved in Thailand."

There were things left unsaid in the little speech that followed. The soft, round face nodded toward Dan as though he should understand what couldn't be said. He didn't. As Nirundorn carried on speaking. Dan turned him off. He wouldn't listen to words of deals and pay-offs.

Mat was innocent.

* * *

Nirundorn dropped him at his hotel, promising to return the next morning and that he would confirm the time later. Dan passed between statues of two enormous red elephants, their gilded golden tusks reflecting the massive chandeliers hanging in the cavernous teak-lined lobby of the Shangri-La Hotel. He walked across to vast windows overlooking the Chao Phraya River and a swimming pool ringed by palm trees.

"Mr Cooper," a sober-suited Thai stood with his hands behind his back, a badge on his jacket indicating he was an Assistant Manager. "Welcome to the Shangri-La. We can complete any formalities in the Siam Suite. Your case has already been taken up."

He guided Dan toward a bank of lifts across from the reception desk.

The river viewed from the twenty-fifth floor was a mayhem of activity. Boats criss-crossed the wide waters, their wakes painting an abstract picture. The suite had a large bedroom, lounge and massive bathroom. After filling in a couple of forms, the assistant manager advised him, with his head bowed, that a car and driver were at his disposal and a valet who could be called by pressing a button alongside the telephone. He did so.

A young man showed up inside a minute.

"This is Bapit. From Chiang Mai, a beautiful city in the north of Thailand."

Bapit, young, bright-eyed, dark hair shining in the lights, brought his hands together and bowed toward Dan.

"Get coffee," ordered the Assistant Manager and Bapit rushed away.

The coffee came shortly as Dan sat and looked over the river. Frenetic activity clashed with his cocooned silence. There had been little silence in his life. It was disturbing. He felt he should be doing something. This wasn't his territory. He was alone and scared, even though he could barely admit it. All the support structures he relied upon were six thousand miles and twelve hours away. The notion of coming to Bangkok was quixotic and probably absurd, but once he announced his decision, he was committed, and he grasped onto that commitment. The silence grew steadily more oppressive, his thoughts finding little focus. Nirundorn's relaxed objectivity provoked him. It was because the Thai lawyer had failed to express his faith in Mat's innocence. To expect that was absurd, but nevertheless, a feeling of betrayal persisted, exacerbating the isolation. His eyes closed for a moment.

* * *

Tony Tavinor sat in a corner of the lobby, waiting for Dan Cooper's arrival. He had found out that the man's flight was a couple of hours late, and in that time he had made his way to the Siam Paradise Hotel.

Dan entered the lobby and walked across to the windows overlooking the river. Tony watched Cooper, shadowed by one of the Hotel managers. Although he looked the same, he was diminished from the man Tavinor knew from London. A dark woollen suit hung loosely from his slight frame, kept in shape by long-distance cycling and still throwing himself into the mosh-pit at his and Róisín's *PileUp Records* company's punk gigs. Dan had resurrected the family business after it nearly went under. He now oversaw the Café Santos coffee shop chain with more than ninety outlets, factories in the UK, coffee and sugar plantations in Brazil and El Salvador, together with an interest in a financial services operation. The company was one of the country's largest privately owned corporations.

But, here, in this place, he looked lost as he followed the manager across to a lift, which stopped at the 25th floor.

Tavinor waited to allow Cooper to settle into his room and accept the truth that he had no doubt Nirundorn would have passed on. A truth that would take time to absorb and recognise. Cooper must understand that he was in a different culture, where rules he had previously understood no longer applied. Only when he grasped that realisation could he help his son.

After he eventually finished his coffee, he picked up the telephone on the table beside him.

* * *

When the telephone rang, Dan realised he'd fallen asleep. He felt exhausted. Nirundorn confirmed that he would collect him at ten the next day to visit Mat.

The phone immediately rang out again.

Tony Tavinor was downstairs. The voice was clipped, devoid of any sympathy. He met this man when he helped Dan deal with Adolfo Guzman. He was intimidated by him. There were no excuses from this moment on.

"I'll come up." Tavinor's stern tone invigorated and unnerved Cooper. If he felt exhausted, so what, the voice demanded of him. Get over it – Mat was stuck in a Bangkok cell, and he needed to keep his shit together to get him out.

There was a knock. Dan stood straight, threw his shoulders back and made his way to the door.

CHAPTER
TEN

Tavinor looked through his window at the early morning traffic moving through the river.

The Siam Paradise Hotel ownership details had come in during the night. He sent them to Lynne Kramer and then waited for the call.

He felt certain that bait would be snatched as soon as it landed.

The phone rang. He held it away from his ear to reduce the volume.

"Did you know?"

He didn't respond.

"Did you? Is that how you figure you drag me into this."

"I went to the Siam Paradise yesterday. That's where I got the company details. I was made as soon as I got to the hotel. There's only one place I could have been picked up. When I was at the unit, our photographs were taken, and I noticed one of the prints was with a guard at the hotel."

"Tavinor, what the hell else haven't you told me?" Kramer paused. "And no names. This line is not secure in this place."

"OK. You remember the Australians at Lumphun, that SOB who did the man's dirty work. He was there at the unit when I saw the boy. He's running the show. I figured he may still be working for the man. That's why I had the place checked out."

Kramer interrupted. "Who worked the magic there? Who traced the company through all the offshore blind alleys."

"A friend in KL."

"He knows his business." A brief silence fell until Kramer continued. "We need to talk. But I still can't get away. I have to check out two deaths. Get the first flight. I'll meet you at the airport."

The line was disconnected.

* * *

Dan was in the Fountain Café looking across toward the river with an untouched plate of fruit in front of him.

Tavinor sat beside him. "I'm going up to Chiang Mai."

"Why?"

"I heard about Mat before you guys, through a friend in Thailand. Lynne Kramer, she's a PI based in Chiang Mai. She stayed with us in Penang for a few days before Christmas. She met Mat then. I worked with her in Bangkok when I was over here before. She's smart and tough. She has to be to survive the business she's in. Her father was American, and her mother was Thai. Got a law degree in the US and then worked in the police over there for a spell before coming back."

"Why?"

"What do you mean?"

"Why did she come back," asked Cooper.

Tavinor shrugged. "No idea. Some of the American guys she worked with said she was on the fast track with the police in the States. Then, her mother was killed in a car crash, and she ended up over here. I worked with her in Bangkok, and then she relocated to Chiang Mai."

"So why are you going up there?"

A blue silk suit hurried past the buffet as he asked the question. The solicitor Nirundorn bustled in.

He nodded at Tavinor and then turned to Dan. "Mr Cooper. We go. Time changed."

Dan looked confused, "Why?"

Nirundorn's broad face broke out into a disingenuous smile. "Because they want to make life difficult. Welcome to Bangkok." He gestured hurriedly. "We go." He pulled at Dan's arm.

Dan nodded to Tavinor as he followed the solicitor out of the hotel to his limousine, waiting at the entrance. Tavinor went to the concierge and asked him to book a seat on the first flight to Chiang Mai.

* * *

"The two cars pulled up outside a large concrete building, dominating a narrow street alongside a rubbish-strewn river, fronting the enormous, forbidding structure. Dan didn't speak to Nirundorn on the journey as they crawled slowly through morning traffic jams in the solicitor's car. It was all Dan could do to control the rising wave of nausea, which again threatened to render him incapable.

Three small, barred windows on the ground floor scarred the isolated building. The driver came round and opened Dan's door. The air hit him like a hot sponge. He walked back to tell the driver following in the hotel car to wait as, after the visit, he would be going on alone to the British Embassy. He asked him to hold onto the bag containing Mat's football shirt and Helen's letter. Nirundorn had advised him to make the appropriate arrangements before taking them in for Mat. He didn't understand - then - what the lawyer meant.

Nirundorn shepherded him up steep steps toward two thick, forbidding black metal doors. He moved slowly, body running with sweat, staining his shirt. The lawyer pushed a bell on the wall. A cover eventually slid across an opening in the door. Two eyes scrutinised them. The cover closed. They waited. Dan pulled out his handkerchief, wiping his face and trying to dry his back, both soaked in sweat. Eventually, one of the doors swung slowly open and two silent guards, rifles slung across their bodies, gestured them inside toward a window in the wall of the airless lobby.

The smile never left Nirundorn's face as he spoke in Thai at the window and handed over passports. Dan heard Mat's name. The lawyer then guided him along a corridor. Dull yellow institutional paint peeling from walls and ceiling, dark brown, dirt-encrusted floor tiles curling up at their edges. Voices echoed from invisible corners behind closed doors. A mounting sense of panic accompanied Dan as he felt the horror of confinement.

They turned into a small room with a tiny, barred window cut high in the wall. The door slammed behind them. A lock turned. Dan stretched up and glimpsed through the window at a small dusty square surrounded by low, windowless buildings. They sat silently on plastic chairs in oppressive humidity for over an hour until footsteps sounded outside.

His stomach turned.

The door opened.

He made a muted sound that came from a sorrow too deep for understanding. It was primitive, as old as conception, as inexplicable as the moment he had held this child in his arms and Mat had screamed his way into life.

He rushed toward his son as he hobbled into the room. A gasp of horror and anger came when he saw the bruises on Mat's face and the heavy iron manacles around his wrists and ankles. They would have embraced. They would have kissed on the cheek, as they always did, without inhibition or reserve. He was halted barely a metre from his son. A gun pointing at Mat forced him to halt. A guard stepped in front of Dan. Sunglasses and cold indifference gave out a chilling image. The voice mumbled something Dan didn't catch.

"Mat..." It was all he could find to say. Normal greetings dried in his throat. They were too trite and absurdly inadequate.

"Dad. I'm OK." The words came too quickly.

"This is Major Prisit," said Nirundorn, gesturing toward the officer in front of Dan.

Prisit stepped aside but held his arm out so Dan couldn't reach Mat. The uniform was tight on the blunt figure. It seemed a miracle that the straining material didn't split apart. Dan smelled cheap aftershave. Mat forced a smile toward his father, who looked more closely. Bruises had darkened on his left cheek. An angry red graze stained his forehead.

They sat on two plastic seats fastened to the floor on either side of a chipped table bolted to the stained floor. Prisit leaned between them.

"Who did this?" Dan's angry voice demanded as he pointed at the bruises on Mat's face. Nobody moved or answered. It was as though he hadn't spoken.

Mat held up his hands in a gesture of reconciliation. "Dad. It's OK, I can hack it."

The anger fell from Dan's voice. "What happened, Mat?"

"I don't know. Honestly, I have no idea. I think my daypack

was taken apart and restitched while I was out of the room for the night."

"It's OK, Mat. I'll get you out of here. We can get bail."

"There's no bail. Forget it. But someone set me up." he pointed at Nirundorn. "I've told him some stuff."

Prisit's voice cut through. "OK. Finish."

"No!" shouted Dan.

"Finish." Prisit waved his hand dismissively at Mat, and two officers grabbed his arms and pushed him back out the door.

"Mat. I'll be back tomorrow," shouted Dan as he saw his son stumble and fall to the ground. The door slammed.

He turned to Prisit. "If he gets any more injuries, someone will pay for it." The lawyer's hand pulled at his arm, dragging him toward the door. Prisit pointed toward the exit. There was no expression on the smooth, unyielding face.

"Come," said Nirundorn.

Dan couldn't speak for a few minutes as they sat in the hotel car's sudden blast of cold air-conditioned air.

"You are seeing the Ambassador?' asked the lawyer eventually.

Dan nodded.

"Ask him to contact the Interior Minister. Ensure no obstacles to regular visits."

Dan agreed. He couldn't speak.

Eventually, Nirundorn insisted that they meet later at the hotel. As he returned to his car, the solicitor passed over a press cutting.

Dan pushed the cutting into his pocket as he told his driver to wait, and he stumbled across to the riverbank. Tears and sweat poured down his face. His shirt was soaked.

Holding on to the bent metal support of a fence that had long ago disintegrated, he looked at dirty brown water flowing slowly between banks of accumulated rubbish. Suddenly, his eyes caught the plump, bloated limbs of a naked baby floating slowly past, face down, its head covered in thick black hair. He closed his eyes and turned away. Nothing had prepared him for this. He jumped back from the road as a police car blasted its hooter at him. Major Prisit was sitting in the passenger seat. The sunglasses stared straight ahead.

CHAPTER ELEVEN

His driver dropped Dan off on Wireless Road at the entrance to the British Embassy compound. A statue of Queen Victoria looked on with appropriate solemnity as Dan tried to brush away the stale traces of that bastard prison building.

An embassy security guard escorted him down a corridor, with a wooden floor polished to a high shine and teak chairs lining the walls. He was shown, with elaborate courtesy, into a waiting room opposite the Ambassador's office. A picture of Queen Elizabeth II hung on the wall, and a few British Magazines were carefully arranged on a low table in the middle of the thickly carpeted floor. A toilet door was situated in a corner. He felt dirty. Stains of sweat, tears and anger had dried in the air-conditioning of his car. He threw cold water over his face and did the best he could with his grey woollen suit, white shirt, and tie - completely unsuitable for the searing heat and humidity. He noticed that few people wore jackets. Nothing could rid him of the stench that seemed to have followed him from the Interrogation Unit.

He opened the door and waited.

A burst of laughter from across the corridor broke the quiet hush which seeped through the elegant setting - an echo of the earlier meeting broke into his mind - keys jangling, boots marching on dirty concrete floors, and desperate shouts breaking through the embassy's subdued urbanity.

He shook his head, trying to clear the memory.

He looked up as a discreet cough came from the doorway.

"Mr Cooper?"

A groomed figure stood in the doorway. Dan felt the grime rise through his skin, the creases standing out in his battered clothes as he responded to the greeting.

The voice was assured. "I'm Henry Fairbrother, an assistant to the Ambassador. We spoke on the telephone the day before yesterday. Sir David will be with you in a moment." Dan felt Fairbrother's glance, assessing him - calculating and shrewd.

Two figures laughed as they came out of a door across the corridor. One wore a uniform similar to Major Prisit but with more stars on his shoulders.

"'Who's that?" asked Dan.

"Khaosai Svetsreni, Chief of Police," said Fairbrother. "Excuse me for a moment".

Fairbrother approached the Chief of Police and spoke quietly to the stocky, dark-haired figure. Svetsreni looked across to Dan. The scrutiny was blatant, undisguised. Was it intimidation? Why? The man's glance had meaning. So, what was Fairbrother's role? Was all this accidental? Amidst the fear that rested in his stomach like a cancer, he felt the stirring of raw anger. He was being played and had no idea what the game was about. Not yet.

Fairbrother gestured for Dan to follow as he led the way across the corridor and into an expansive office with carpets still deeper than the waiting room and a long window shielded by blinds shutting out the sun's glare.

A tall figure, even more immaculately dressed than Fairbrother, moved briskly from behind an immense wooden desk. He smoothed short grey hair before holding out his hand toward Dan.

"Sir David Laurence," the face assuming a momentary sadness. "I'm so sorry to hear of your son's predicament, Mr Cooper. Please," he gestured to a dark chair and sat beside Fairbrother on the opposite sofa. "I understand that you have spoken with Henry. Such a worry for you." Dan noticed him glance at a card that Fairbrother had placed discreetly on the arm of the sofa, "that Matthew faces this ordeal. We will do all we can to assist."

"What *can* you do?" asked Dan.

Laurence leaned back on the sofa. Fairbrother followed suit. "Obviously, we cannot presume to interfere in a friendly sovereign state's legal system." He leaned forward. "I know you wouldn't expect that."

You know that, do you, thought Dan, you pompous shit. *Like fuck I wouldn't,* he wanted to shout. He remained silent.

Laurence continued. "But of course, we will do all we can to see that," he glanced at the card again, "Matthew is treated correctly, that his rights are protected and that legal proceedings are handled properly and promptly." He leaned back again.

"I would appreciate it if you could make representations about regular legal visits for his solicitor, together with myself."

"You have my assurance."

He gestured as though granting Dan another opportunity to speak.

"My son has been attacked."

There was silence. Laurence looked toward Fairbrother, who leaned forward and spoke. He was dismissive, holding out his palms. "These things are so difficult to verify, facts unable to establish. Regrettable, but in the heat of an arrest." He made a vague sign of helplessness. "Perhaps Matthew was over-excited. It's perfectly natural."

It was Mat's fault, then! Dan paused as he realised this place would offer him and his son nothing. At least nothing that could disturb genial diplomatic relations. Only much later, when he recalled this meeting, did he recognise the duplicity that manipulated the carefully controlled agenda.

"He was assaulted."

Fairbrother nodded and, after waiting for a moment, spoke again. "I understand. We could protest." His voice became harder. "You have to ask whether that would be in your son's best interest. He is, and may remain, in police custody for some time." He paused, his voice severe. "You understand me, Mr Cooper?"

He did, of course he did.

The Ambassador spoke. "You're using Nirundorn. A good man. He knows his way around. I will speak with the minister concerned to ensure that your son does not wait an inordinate amount of time before any trial. That can be a problem. There has already been a degree of publicity surrounding the case. Despite all you may hear, the legal system is generally reliable."

"Reliable?" asked Dan, not bothering to hide his scepticism.

"It doesn't always pay to be judgmental." Laurence stood. "We are often more successful the quieter we speak. You understand, Mr Cooper." He held out his hand. "If you'll excuse me." He gestured to Fairbrother, who was standing alongside him. "Please do not hesitate to contact Henry if we can assist further." He moved toward the door and ushered them out.

Nothing was offered, nothing achieved. Dan felt only that a

ritual had been completed. He heard Fairbrother speaking. “We’ll talk to the Ministry and try to ascertain the current state of the investigation. Call me if I can be of further assistance.”

Further? Thought Dan. Further than fuck-all!

Fairbrother handed over an elaborate business card. The embassy’s address was printed in silver raised letters, along with Fairbrother’s name and a mobile number but no job title.

A group of children were laughing and playing in the gardens. One of the little girls waved at him. She hid her face behind her hand when he tried to smile in response. The heat hit him again as he watched another traffic jam crawling to nowhere.

CHAPTER **TWELVE**

Chiang Mai airport was chaotic – a 747 from Japan had arrived not long before, and the terminal was clogged up with tour operators looking for their clients and clients trying to return the favour.

Tavinor skirted the mayhem and saw Lynne Kramer waiting beside a battered VW as he left the building.

She looked the same as he remembered from about nine years back. Dark hair framing a beguiling fusion of east and west. She had been lucky to take the best of both cultures with a confusing mixture of bright blue eyes standing out on an image redolent of mysteries of oriental desire. She looked slight, a white t-shirt hanging loosely over a pair of jeans, and almost fragile, but Tavinor knew that deceived. She was tough and abrasive. Many people taken in by the sensual attractions that spilled from her appearance underestimated the woman. They rarely made the same mistake twice.

A few years back, just before Tavinor left Thailand, they had jointly investigated the case of two Australian boys – youths - who had gone missing. Lynne became close to the families, and it was only after two months of fruitless investigation they received a tip-off that the bodies were dumped not far from Wat Chaiyasit Tharam, about one hundred kilometres north of Bangkok. Lynne had wept when she saw their bodies thrown in the back of a cart left in some waste ground behind the temple.

They dug a bit more and found they had got in too deep with associates of Chao Thanarat. The boys were nineteen and stupid. More digging made them certain they had been picked up by the police in Bangkok, held during the time she had been searching for them and then executed. Major Jaran Prisit headed the police unit that had picked them up.

She left Bangkok after that and settled in Chiang Mai. She hadn't forgotten that case, though, and certainly not Prisit.

Tavinor remembered plenty of talk about why she had left a stellar career in the police in the US, but no one had yet unearthed that story.

Lynne wrapped her arms around Tavinor and kissed his cheek before entering the driving seat.

He threw his backpack into the back of the VW.

She looked across at him. "I'm so sorry about Mat. This is one crock of shit."

He nodded.

"I wanted to get you up here because I have some intel you have to see. I had to agree not to copy it or take it to Bangkok. It's from a friend in the DEA - Drug Enforcement Administration - and I promised I would get it back to him later today."

"Are you still working with the DEA?"

"Pays the rent, as I said.."

"So what's the deal up here?"

"The deal?"

"You work for the DEA, doing what? Anything else?"

She laughed as they slowed and turned onto a road alongside a waterway, "The Mae Kha canal. They're trying to clear the crap and make it a tourist attraction."

"Are you a tour guide now?"

"It's a thought."

She pulled over at the side of the road." I haven't the time, Tavinor, to tell you what's happening up here. You'll have to wait till I've finished. You can bail out and meet me later at my apartment or shut the fuck up and let me get on with my work. I have a couple of deaths to investigate and a cop who wants to meet. Two kids were allegedly killed in an accident, their families are good friends of mine, and I said I'd check out what happened. They think the police investigation is a snow job."

"OK, deal," he said. "I'll keep out of your way until you're ready."

They passed several military bases as they made their way to the accident site.

"HQ of Thai army Fifth Special Forces regiment," said Lynne as they passed an extensive army base and approached a large warehouse just off the main road.

They pulled over, and Lynne took what appeared to be a police report from a large bag on the floor.

"This is where it happened. A witness claimed the kids on a straight run supposedly suddenly swerved across the road and went headfirst into one of the lorries that had just left the warehouse."

She got out and walked across the road. "It makes no sense. The report claims the kid had been drinking and that they were laughing and messing about just before it happened. Even so!"

"Any witnesses?" asked Tavinor.

She pointed at the unit. "Employee."

"Convenient." He looked at the large unit as an articulated lorry emerged. *Global Harvest International Distribution* was emblazoned in red and yellow letters on the side.

He picked up a few labels scattered on the path alongside a tall fence surrounding the unit and pushed them into his pocket.

"OK. I need to speak with the parents," said Lynne as she returned to her car. "They live in Pa Daet across the other side of the city."

* * *

An hour later, Lynne emerged from a modern apartment block.

"OK. She held up a folder. This is serious shit. I'll tell you when we get back to the apartment. I'm meeting a contact", she checked her watch, "in twenty minutes." She revved the engine, "he won't wait."

Lynne parked by the Roong Ruang hotel just down the road from the Tha Phae gate one of eight gates in the city wall built to keep out the Burmese a few centuries back.

She ran on the path alongside the moat surrounding a wall, shutting away the traffic noise, and turned into a bustling street, rushing past a 'coin laundry', one of the many 'massage' shops, and then into a bar next to a tattoo shop.

The cop was out of uniform. He had an empty beer glass in front of him and looked suspiciously behind Lynne when she pushed through the swing door.

"Sawadi", she wai'd and smiled toward the cop who, almost hidden in a booth, was out of uniform. He returned the greeting, and she gestured for two beers from a waiter leaning over his newspaper at the bar.

Lynne had cultivated many contacts in Chiang Mai. Cops, street dealers, suppliers, always working quietly, never making a noise. The contacts rarely came as friends - usually as purchased commodities.

This man had been the latter but had, in time, become a

friend, but Lynne knew there was always a limit to friendship here. Self-preservation always came first in the murky Thai world of drug-infused corruption, but she had helped support his son's education and paid for his wife's treatment for a serious lung disease.

"I checked out the report you asked," he said quietly when the waiter moved away. "The two boys were just back from Bangkok. It was an accident on the Mae Rim road. They were knocked off their mopeds by a lorry. The report said they had been drinking. No autopsy. Too quick. Not normal."

He took a sip of beer and shook his head. "Cremation too fast."

"Why?"

He shook his head again and looked down at his beer glass, refusing to catch Lynne's eye.

"They worked in Bangkok Hotel."

"Chao's Hotel," responded Lynne.

The eyes darted around the empty bar in panic. "Not say that name."

He quickly finished his glass of beer and looked up whilst placing a file on the table. "I go."

Before Lynne could speak, the man had leapt to his feet and exited the bar.

She sat back down and opened the file. It was a statement from the mother of one of the boys. It confirmed what the woman had told Lynne, that the boy had never had a drink and intended to become a monk. He was only working to support his sister, who had cancer. A separate piece of paper had a woman's name printed beside that of the Orchid Hotel and beneath them another name - *Chris Ralston.*

A tuk-tuk dropped her off outside steps leading up to the wood-lined lobby of the hotel. She went to the reception desk and gave the name printed on the paper. The receptionist pointed to a *World Travel Service* booth across the lobby.

She said, "Not here today, tomorrow. Two days here."

Lynne thanked her and immediately went down the steps to the Huay Kaew Road. She waited patiently at the roadside and then set off to the narrow, grass-covered central reservation. As though remembering something, she turned and retraced her steps. A single security guard watched her from the doors to the hotel, but there was no attempt to follow. She hailed a tuk-tuk and returned to the Roong Ruang Hotel. Tavinor was inside nursing a coffee.

"Get in. We'll go to my place."

Lynne Kramer lived on Nimmanhemin Road near a medical offshoot of the university. As she made coffee in a small kitchen, he resisted the temptation to open a folder lying on the table. He knew Kramer's sensitivity at any attempts to interfere in her activities, and she had earned the right to control her research.

After placing the mugs on the table, she paused and held up the statements of the mothers of the two dead boys. "The boys worked at a hotel in Bangkok." She paused. "The Siam Paradise."

Tavinor let out a note of astonishment as Kramer continued.

"There was another boy that went to Bangkok and worked at the hotel, according to the family." She checked her notes. "They think his name was Chris Ralston, but they knew nothing about him."

She moved across, opened a drawer in a wooden cupboard, extracted another folder, and brought it over.

"You asked about my work with the DEA. They've just appointed a new Special Agent in Bangkok due to the volume of heroin hitting the East Coast. It went up as far as the White

House, so they're ratcheting up the investment and relocating resources up here."

She paused. "The target is Chao Thanarat."

"He was only one of many wannabees when I left."

"That's right. A Burmese kingpin was killed in the late eighties. It was the wild west for a while, and it was about then you went off to Angola. All the cartels were fighting for the action. Chao got his Hmong guys back together and wiped out the opposition. He then bought up the army and police and destroyed any opposition. The DEA has had a hard-on for him since '89 when he killed one of their guys together with his wife. The agent got a bit too close. Then, he was nearly out of business when an extradition request came in from Australia. I'm not sure how, but he got out of that. He reorganised his business, particularly the distribution and invested the proceeds in clean businesses. We can't get near him. He's too well protected and knows our moves before we've even thought about them. He is a major investor in Telecoms; hotels, the Siam Paradise is one of about thirty hotels, most of them pretty high-end, the Siam Paradise is one of only two or three low-rent joints left; car hire; he owns the airport here, Chiang Rai and Udon Thani; and he has just bought out one of the major banks. It's all run from Bangkok now by his accountant, Dusit Sombat. Ownership is opaque, hidden behind offshore companies and trusts – Chao's name is kept out of it. The drug money finances all his operations. Sombat is smart, but Chao runs the show when push comes to shove. All the details of pay-offs and kick-backs end up in Laos, where the Thais can't get near. His HQ is located in Hongsa in Sainyabuli."

"You know it?"

She shook her head. "Very remote."

She held up her empty mug. "Another?" He nodded.

"OK."

She returned from the kitchen. "This is why I got you up here. Chao rarely leaves his estate in Chiang Rai. But a few weeks back, he made his way down here. All the bells and whistles went off, and he was shadowed every step. He ended up at the Orchid Hotel – which he owns."

She held up a computer disk.

"One of my contacts lent me this, but I must return it to him this evening. It's an audio of a meeting he had at the hotel. The quality is poor because he knows we watch him, normally we get nowhere. We were lucky a de-activated unit was in the room where he had the meeting. We thought it was dead, and obviously, it didn't get picked up by Chao's guys. It unexpectedly sparked up and gave us this. It's the undoctored version."

She played the disk through her laptop. It mostly consisted of static and just a few words. Tavinor only heard the words *Cooper, Itinerary, Hua Lamphong* and *Vientiane*, and the rest was electronic mush.

When it finished, Lynne spoke, "It was worked on and the rough version that emerged claims that whoever this is with Chao is asking for his assistance. The target is Cooper, and there's an itinerary. He needs to be picked up to put pressure on someone, who and why wasn't clear. Cooper, is arriving at Hua Lamphong station and leaving from Don Mueang Airport. That's about it. Chao never speaks, but then he rarely speaks. He just nods or shakes his head."

"Who is the guy he's meeting with? Any photographs?"

Lynne shook her head. "I don't know. My contact doesn't have clearance if there are any images." She paused. "The man flew down to Bangkok. I do know that."

Tavinor nodded. "So? You coming back down there with me?"

She gestured toward a holdall on the floor. "Let's go."

CHAPTER **THIRTEEN**

Dan Cooper looked spellbound from the window of his suite at the sky populated by random bursts of bright red flashes, interspersed with reflections played out in a cool orange as the sun raced below the horizon. The shadows of the buildings opposite his hotel lengthened across the Chao Praya River, still frantic with activity, the wakes of boats interspersing in a clashing kaleidoscope. The dramatic beauty only gave him a brief pause from the bloody day that had unfolded.

The emotion that wrecked his body caught him by the throat and left him gasping for air as he recalled Mat's expression as his son had stumbled away back to ruthless incarceration. The memory of the prison visit plunged him almost beyond resolution. What he had imagined had been way off the reality. Tony had tried to prepare him by insisting he imagine the worst he could conceive - but his imagination had failed him. He had inhabited a world of euphemism and synthetic aspiration for too long. Desire disguised as need and unable to understand the difference.

This was raw and elemental, and he understood that he

had to endure and understand it, or he would lose Mat because of his own inadequacy. One of the recent speeches he had heard at a conference referred to business as a "battlefield". He had enjoyed the metaphor as he bathed in the glow of achievement on the top table. Such absurd conceit. How many years had he strutted with that illusion, only to suddenly face this harsh reality and not know how to react? Instincts he had discarded needed honing in this world as he struggled, unprepared and hauling the polluted baggage of another place.

He turned to the telephone as it rang and noticed the press cutting Nirundorn had passed him yesterday.

He asked the lawyer to come up to his suite. He read the first few words of the article from the "*Bangkok Post*":

"Karen Marie Sucher, who was controversially granted bail after being accused of drug smuggling, has not shown up for a hearing at the Supreme Court..."

He opened the door. The man's smile was too wide, his suit too bright, and the handshake he offered Dan as though he'd never met him before was too weak. They sat down in the enormous lounge. Dan fell silent, looking again from the window whilst the valet poured two coffees. A tug, low down in the water, struggled ponderously through the river, hauling eight barges.

He turned back to the lawyer when the valet left.

"Do you think Mat is guilty?"

The lawyer's voice was dismissive. "What is that to do with me? I am his lawyer. I help him. I'm not a Judge, Mr Cooper."

"How do we prove Mat's innocence?"

"Mr Cooper." A weak smile came on the well-tended face. "Mat had heroin in the lining of his daypack. There's no question it was his daypack. He doesn't dispute fact. There's no question he was carrying it. There's no question it was heroin.

So there's no question that he is guilty in the eyes of law. Let me ask you question. Which fact have I got wrong?"

Dan couldn't answer.

"You want to fight case, Mr Cooper. That good. So prove that Mat not know heroin in backpack." The smile disappeared. "How you do that?"

His eyes held Dan's.

The question came again. "How you do that?"

Dan didn't know. That was the goddamn-awful truth. He didn't know. Eventually, he responded. "We find out who *did* put it there."

Nirundorn nodded. The voice was dismissive. "Yes, of course, and we find the witness who put it there and make sure the judge will believe witness."

"Mat said he told you what happened before he was..."

Nirundorn interrupted. "There are ways to help your son's release at right time. We make plans."

"What do you mean?" demanded Dan.

Nirundorn deflected the question as he pulled a notepad from his case. He started to read. "He'd come up from Singapore a few days before, staying at Siam Paradise Hotel. He was away at night and returned the next morning to pick up his bags. Went to airport, stopped by customs after he'd been through immigration. Heroin found in the lining of daypack he was taking on plane."

"Where's the Siam Paradise Hotel?"

"Sol Rham Bhuttri by Khaosan Road. Where young backpackers stay. Cheap guesthouses and restaurants.

"I need to see my son without that goon running the show."

The lawyer stood and walked to the window. He waited before turning back to Dan and speaking slowly. "I understand you are successful man in your country, Mr Cooper. Wealthy?"

He nodded as though agreeing with himself. “We believe, above all else, that respect is very important. You lose respect when you shout. It no good showing anger.” He smiled and shook his head. “You understand that if you shout, you may win argument, but you lose because respect is forfeited. It is important for your son. You win, but he suffer.” He paused. “Major Prisit is a proud man.”

“He’s a thug.”

“Perhaps, Mr Cooper. He also holds your son’s life in his hands.” He placed his hands together and gave a slight bow. “When we meet in Thailand, this is how we greet each other. It is called a wâi. You understand? You place your palms together and bow so that your index fingers touch your nose.”

Nirundorn sat down again.

Dan gritted his teeth. He tried to stop his anger from pouring out. “I still need to see my son without that thug running the show.”

“OK. One hundred dollars for one hour.”

“No one else in the room so that we can talk? I take his mother’s letter and present in?”

A smile flickered on the lawyer’s face. “I’m sure.”

“So that’s how it works?”

“That’s how everything works. You don’t get angry, you smile, you pay money. You get what you want. Mat gets quiet life.”

“When?”

“Tomorrow morning. I pick you up at ten o’clock again. Bring cash. OK?” He placed his hands together and waited until Dan reluctantly returned the gesture.

As he left, Nirundorn pointed at the press cutting beside the phone. “Contingency, Mr Cooper. Contingency.”

Dan looked through the window after the lawyer had left, and evening had raced into night. The sky was dark, and the city's lights spread in front of him, highlighting the snake of the river as it wound its way into the distance.

He called Róisín's number.

"I've seen Mat this morning." He said as she answered immediately. He tried to hide any emotion. "He's fine. It's not as bad as I expected. How's Ben?"

"I'm Mat's mother, Dan. Don't bullshit me."

There was no point in sharing the misery. Róisín could do nothing.

"He's OK, I promise. Sends his love."

"Did you give him my letter?"

"Tomorrow. I was only in for a few minutes today, but it will be longer tomorrow. I saw the Ambassador. He was helpful."

"Helpful?" Róisín didn't disguise the scepticism.

"As helpful as Ambassadors get, I suppose."

"Ben will be out of intensive care shortly. Shall I come over? He thinks I should."

"Let me get things sorted first. I'm going in with the lawyer again tomorrow. He knows his way around. There's a lot of legal work to be done. But you get over here whenever you're ready."

"You don't have to protect me.

He did, or perhaps he needed to for his own sake. He wasn't sure which.

"Why should I do that?"

"Because of who you are." There was a silence before Róisín spoke again. "How are you holding up?"

He paused and breathed deeply. "I haven't been so exhausted for years. It's probably jet lag."

"You think?" she responded.

They said goodbye. Róisín knew him too well to fall for his

reassurances, but she was also devoted to Ben. Dan didn't know what she would do.

He dragged himself across the room and looked in the wardrobe. Woollen suits. They were too heavy, too hot and too formal, but he felt he had to have the look, at times, to show intent in this place. Jeans and a T-shirt wouldn't always be appropriate. He called the valet and asked him to arrange to have the suits he had already worn cleaned for the next morning.

He wanted to get out of the hotel. Somewhere other than the interrogation unit or the embassy.

"How far is the Khaosan road?" he asked the valet.

"Thirty minutes. Take car." He smiled, "Tuk-tuk outside hotel quicker."

"Tuk-tuk?"

The valet gave the sign and sound of a motorbike. Dan realised that a tuk-tuk was one of the three-wheeled motorised bikes with a seat attached at the rear that he'd seen buzzing and smoking their way through traffic jams, generally adding to the pollution.

A couple of tuk-tuk drivers leapt to their feet when he came down the slope from the hotel. They were parked up by a money exchange booth.

"Where you want to go?"

"Siam Paradise Hotel. Rambuttri Road."

"OK. OK," shouted one, wearing an elaborate pair of red sunglasses with only one lens.

"How much?" asked Dan.

"How much you want to pay me?" the driver laughed.

Thirty minutes drive, he thought. "Three hundred?"

The driver looked at his fellow driver. They both laughed. "OK, Mister."

Dan fell into the back seat as the bike veered across the road.

"Where you from?" asked the driver, turning round as they stopped at a set of traffic lights.

"British," he echoed after Dan replied. "Marks and Spencer. Cold there, eh? David Beckham." The lights changed, and they rushed forward until hitting the rear of the next line of traffic. The driver pulled a dirty handkerchief over his mouth. "Pollution. Bangkok very bad."

Dan agreed. He could almost cut the fumes.

"You want to go to nice tailors. Nice clothes. Good price," the driver shouted as he swerved. Dan began to refuse. As he did, he remembered his heavy trousers sticking to him. He agreed.

He emerged from the "nice tailors" an hour later, having ordered two lightweight suits that would be delivered to his hotel in twenty-four hours, costing a fraction of what he would have paid in London. All in all, he thought he must have gone crazy.

Saville Row, it wasn't, but what the hell? He was in Bangkok, not London.

The driver gave him back one hundred baht when Dan handed over the fare outside the Siam Paradise Hotel. He laughed. "No. You good man. Tailor gives me money. You pay too much."

Before Dan could reply, the tuk-tuk left a trail of exhaust fumes along the street and disappeared round a corner.

It was like visiting someone else's dream. Rock music poured from speakers above a dark wooden unattended reception desk at the Siam Paradise Hotel. The desk was covered in small statues of the Buddha. Faded chinese watercolours hung on a gloomy paint-peeling wall behind the desk. A dozen ceiling fans stirred the air sufficiently to disturb the leaves of a few scattered and dejected plants distributed amongst tables full of youngsters drinking, talking, and studying travel guides. A line of computers filled a far wall. A sign read INTERNET - E-MAIL.

He could feel Mat holding court at one of the tables, laughter echoing, pleasure mingling with shouts of hilarity. Shorts, sandals and t-shirts, as uniform - no surprise, it was what Mat wore at home anyway. A few pens with *Siam Paradise Hotel - Hospitality in the City of Angels* stamped on the side were scattered around the tables. He pocketed a couple as souvenirs.

A gang of dogs suddenly tore into each other just outside an open-air bar overlooking the road. A young woman sitting by a travel desk glanced over at him. He looked away into the ceiling, the fans continuing their desultory efforts. He sat at one of the tables on a terrace and ordered a Singha beer. A smell of spices drifted from a kitchen at the end of the bar. When it arrived, he sipped the cold beer and noticed a couple playing chess at the next table. She was blonde and petite. He caught her bright, inquisitive eyes, looking him over, smiling as though she knew him and then turning away. Dan looked at the board. Her bearded, long-haired opponent, hunched over the game, had lost. He just wasn't good enough to realise it yet. A young waitress sat at the table and started talking to the girl whilst the beard's concentration continued on the board.

"Ah, shit." The chess king went over. "One day, Lizzy, I'm going to beat you. One day, I promise."

Lizzy smiled. "Not in this lifetime, Tim boy." The laughing accent was Australian.

"She always beats you," said the waitress nonchalantly before standing up and wandering off amongst the narrow line of tables.

Dan didn't realise that he was staring at the couple. He

could see Mat so clearly. The pain surged through him. He grabbed at the beer.

The young man's voice broke his preoccupation. "You play?"

"Sorry. Yes, occasionally."

"Perhaps you'd beat her for me. Just once. Then I'd die happy."

"Buy you both a beer?" asked Dan.

"Free country," said Tim, pulling a chair by their table indicating for Dan to join them whilst shouting at the waitress for three beers.

A waiter came over with the fresh bottles. He had a ponytail and a small goatee beard, turning slightly grey. His eyes were tiny black holes under a forehead covered in a heavy plaster. His expression was suspicious.

Tim drank from the bottle and waited, watching the waiter until he moved away. "Shit. I can't stand that son of a bitch."

"He's always listening. Watching," said Lizzy. "Sometimes you come out of your room, and he's just standing there."

"You know the place pretty well?" said Dan.

"Bangkok?" asked Tim.

"This hotel."

They looked at each other with a suspicious glance.

"I guess. I'm sorry - again. My name's Dan..."

Lizzy gasped and interrupted him. "I knew it. You're Mat's dad. I thought I recognised you. He showed us a picture of you when we were pissed the other night."

He gritted his teeth as he felt his forehead break out with sweat. A few minutes passed as the distress receded. Lizzy leaned over and put her hand over his white knuckles.

"There's no way Mat would have done it."

"I know."

"Have you seen him?" asked Tim.

He nodded, wiping his forehead. "How did you meet Mat?

Lizzy answered. "Kathy's a friend of mine from Melbourne. We met up with Mat in Singapore after he'd been in Penang for Christmas. They came up here a couple of days before us. Kathy's gone trekking up in Northern Thailand for a couple of weeks. They are due to meet up in Chiang Mai. She won't know anything about it yet."

"How's he doing?" asked Tim.

Dan paused. He wiped his forehead again and breathed deeply, trying to calm the feeling of nausea. He noticed the waiter almost hidden behind a plant just beyond their table.

"OK. Dumb question," continued Tim. "It was a crazy fucking few days here..." He fell quiet as the waiter wandered past their table again. "... sorry, I just don't trust that guy. There was a rumour on the morning Mat was picked up. Someone saw it happen at the airport, but we didn't figure it could be him. For Christ's sake, who smuggles drugs into Laos? So when we heard it was him, we couldn't believe it. Shit, no way was Mat into that."

Lizzy continued, "Someone must have set him up, but I don't understand. Why?"

Tim interrupted. "Then, an ancient Yank stormed in a few days back, just after Mat was picked up, and took this place apart. He was crazy. Well over six feet, thin as a rake, white-haired ponytail. He picked up one of those chairs," he pointed to a couple of heavy wooden planter chairs, "and smashed it on the reception desk. He was screaming in Thai."

Lizzy took it up again. "There were these three kids from up north who used to do all the odd jobs. They showed up to hear what the noise was all about. This guy went to one of them, grabbed him by the arm and dragged him away."

He pointed to the waiter. "He tried to stop him. The yank got him by the throat, pushed him over the bar, smashed a beer bottle over his head and screamed at him to tell some guy called Chao fucking Thanarat that he would cut his fucking heart out if he ever came near his boy again. The kid went with him. The other two boys were gone within a couple of hours. Back to Chiang Mai, we were told."

"Chao Thanarat?" questioned Dan.

He hadn't noticed the waiter standing almost next to the table. The movement was almost imperceptible. A hand came out and knocked Dan's beer over him. He leapt up as cold liquid poured down his legs.

The waiter was alongside. "Sorry, Sir."

Dan felt his arm being gripped as he stumbled whilst getting to his feet. Another Thai, heavily built, sunglasses, appeared alongside. Together with the waiter, they marched Dan through the lobby. No words were spoken as they each took an arm and pushed him forcefully into the street.

He looked back.

Lizzy and Tim's table was empty.

He walked in a daze. Sweating, fear-ridden disorientation enveloped him in the cloying gasoline-rich heat. He fell into a seat at a small pavement café a few minutes walk away and ordered a beer and some food. The chilli in the soup scalded his tongue, setting his mouth on fire - he coughed and spluttered, grabbing at the beer in front of him. It was his second.

He didn't drink beer.

He didn't get scared either - he was scared now.

He drank more beer.

After finishing his drink, he found a tuk-tuk driver at the end of the street.

"Shangri-La Hotel."

"Two hundred baht", said the driver.

"One hundred," responded Dan.

"OK."

CHAPTER **FOURTEEN**

Dan waited in the lobby. His head was thick from the previous night. Tony Tavinor had called earlier, back from Chiang Mai, and they agreed to meet when Dan returned from seeing Mat. He had Lynne Kramer with him and had booked her into the hotel. A waiter came over and indicated that Nirundorn's driver was outside. Dan grabbed an envelope with a hundred-dollar bill inside, together with Helen's letter and present, and made his way through the foyer.

Nirundorn shook his hand again as he got into the car. The smile was still wide, the suit a slightly duller blue.

He pronounced in triumph as Dan handed over the envelope. "You get thirty minutes alone with Mat."

"You said one hour."

The lawyer shrugged. "Nobody in the room."

"That article, the *Bangkok Post* - Sucher," said Dan, "the one who jumped bail. What are you suggesting?"

"Suggest nothing, Mr Cooper. Information - information."

Dan frowned, there was more to it. Nirundorn turned away.

They took the same route as the previous day. The same roadside stalls. The same traffic jam.

When they reached the Interrogation Unit, Nirundorn waited outside the door of the small room. Dan entered and listened as footsteps clattered along the corridor. Prisit did not comment as he looked into the room. The lawyer handed over the envelope and bowed. Nirundorn pulled some papers from his briefcase and sat in the corridor as the door was locked. Over an hour later, the other door to the inside of the Unit came open. Mat hobbled in and grabbed at the table as a guard pushed him violently forward. As Dan made to protest, Mat looked up and shook his head. Prisit waited in the doorway as the guard moved to a corner of the room.

Dan pointed to the guard. "I was told we would be alone," he said to Prisit, who immediately marched in and grabbed Mat's arm, manhandling him back toward the door.

"OK!" Dan shouted. "OK."

Prisit turned and stared through the sunglasses. Dan's chest tightened, his fists clenched as he saw the grip close tight on Mat's arm, fingers digging into the skin.

Eventually, Prisit thrust Mat forward again and slammed the door behind him.

"Dad."

The still, almost silent voice was filled with a mixture of fear and relief. Dan put his arms around his son. The trembling body seemed so fragile. After a moment, a harsh voice shouted at them, and the guard gestured for them to sit down. Their hands gripped on the table, and the guard brought out a gun and hammered it down next to their hands - Dan understood. He placed a five-dollar note next to the weapon. The guard snatched it and resumed his seat in the corner.

"I didn't do it, Dad."

Dan hesitated. Looking into his son's eyes, he nodded. "I know."

The words came quickly. "No. You mean you don't believe I did it. I understand, but it's not you I have to convince. What I'm saying is that somebody did this to me. They went to the trouble of taking my backpack apart, filling it with a bag of heroin and then restitching it. I didn't even notice, it was so good."

"Do you have any ideas who it could have been?"

"There were three young guys always who worked in the hotel. They were pretty friendly, though. And a very weird, scary manager."

"The Siam Paradise?"

"Yes. They had keys to all the rooms and knew I would be out all night."

"Where?"

"With Kathy. An Aussie girl I met. She was leaving for Chiang Mai by the early train the next day and was staying over for the night near the station with some friends she was going up north with. We intended to meet up about ten days later after I got back from Laos. I only went to the hotel in the morning to pick up my gear."

"So what happened then?"

"I got there about ten o'clock after seeing Kathy off. Grabbed my bags and headed out to the airport on the minibus." He paused, "I remember an Amerasian kid who seemed to be attempting to tell me something. I didn't understand what he was trying to tell me."

"Was he one of the three who hung around the hotel?"

Mat nodded. "I think so, but I was too knackered to notice. Went through immigration and got stopped at customs. They were waiting for me. It wasn't a random search. My daypack was slit open. They knew what was there.' He breathed deeply. 'Jesus, Dad, that was scary. I almost shit myself when I saw the powder. They knew it was there. How did they know? You read about shit like that, but it doesn't happen to you. Not in real life. It was like I was at the movies. But in it, not watching."

He stood up for a minute, breathing deeply.

The guard stirred in the corner. He had fallen asleep in the stifling heat, his head dropped back to his chest when Mat sat down again.

"After they found the stuff, all hell broke loose. An officer came in and started shouting. Prisit was already there watching, with another guy, stars on his shoulders, a senior guy. About half an hour later, Prisit brought me here."

"We'll find out what happened."

His son's voice was censorious, as though giving a rebuke to a child. "This is Thailand, Dad. They do things differently out here."

Dan smiled at the mild rebuke. "I'm learning," he gestured to the sleeping guard.

"I figured." Mat returned the smile. It soon disappeared.

"Have you upset anyone?"

"Come on, Dad. You know me."

Dan leaned down and handed over Helen's letter. Mat read it and then looked up at Dan, his eyes full of tears, voice shaking as he spoke. "Give Mum my love." He leaned closer. "Don't let her come out here." He swallowed. "Not now. Not yet." He closed his eyes. A tear rolled from one corner. "If it all goes wrong, that's different." He stopped and forced out a smile. "So where's the shirt?"

Dan brought out the football shirt.

Mat laughed and held it up. "Cool. The star man. Shifty."

"Why did they call you Shifty at school?"

"Who knows how nicknames come about." His face briefly lit up with a wide smile. He held up the shirt.

Dan hesitated. 'All this has nothing to do with the boy excluded from your school, does it?'

A flash of anger passed across Mat's face, quickly replaced by a smile. "That's Mum talking. Willi's here working for his dad and making a fortune on the stock market. He was caught smoking a spliff, that's all. The school overreacted. He was coming home anyway."

Dan felt a stab of fear as his son looked into his eyes. He felt Mat's hand gripping him tight. "This has nothing to do with me, I promise you. Get me out of here, Dad."

Mat must have noticed Dan's onrush of panic. He continued. "I mean, do your best. I can hang on as long as I know you're doing everything you can."

"You know I will." He hesitated. "Have you heard the name Karen Sucher?"

Mat looked confused. "The women have a separate prison. Why?"

Dan shook his head. "Something Nirundorn mentioned. Forget it."

They stared at each other in silence. The door banged open. Prisit shouted at the guard, who jerked back to life and leapt across, grabbing Mat's arm.

"I love you, Mat. I'll move heaven and earth. See you tomorrow."

His son was bundled from the room. Prisit followed. Mat turned at the door. "I love you too, Dad." The football shirt was wrenched from his hands and thrown to the ground. Prisit stamped it into the dust. The door slammed.

Dan made his way from the room and along the corridor.

"I'm going to the British Embassy again," he told Nirundorn, still waiting in the corridor.

Dan told his hotel driver to get him to the British Embassy. He noticed that the Bangkok Post press cutting lay on the seat. He asked the driver about it.

"Mr Nirundorn put it," said the driver as they set off.

Dan read the article again. *Bangkok Post* - dated 10 June 1995 - headline on the second page:

Australian Drug Dealer jumps bail.

"*Karen Marie Sucher, who was controversially granted bail after being accused of drug smuggling, has not shown up for a hearing at the Supreme Court...*'

He put down the press cutting he had already read when they pulled up at the Embassy. Nirundorn was sending a message. Information only – he didn't think so. The embassy receptionist insisted that neither the Ambassador nor Henry Fairbrother was available. As she finished insisting, Dan noticed Fairbrother walking past the doorway.

"Mr Fairbrother," he exclaimed and made his way toward Fairbrother. The receptionist stood and motioned to a security guard who rushed over and took Dan's arm.

"It's OK. I'll handle this," Fairbrother insisted, drawing Dan to one side. "Security has to be tight." He looked at his watch. "How can I help?"

"I wondered whether the Ambassador has been able to speak with the Minister?"

A trace of exasperation entered the smooth tone. "It's best to arrange a meeting before dropping in, so to speak. However, as you're here. The Interior Minister has assured us that the legal process will be expedited. I understand that there are few obstacles in the way of a speedy trial. He has allocated Justice Vyraj to the case, and I can assure you he is notoriously independent and incorruptible. You couldn't have a better Judge."

"Thank you," said Dan. He made to leave.

Fairbrother moved off down the corridor. The security

guard came closer. Dan felt the receptionist's scowl as he returned to the car.

* * *

Tony Tavinor sat in the lobby. Dan paused as he saw the man's companion.

A beguiling mixture of West and East. American father, Thai mother, he recalled Tavinor telling him as he tried to shrug aside the sudden and unwanted desire grabbing hold of him as he took in the black t-shirt and short white skirt hiding a sensual body. The feeling seemed like a betrayal of his son lying in a stinking cell.

She gave a cool smile as he approached. "Lynne Kramer," she said softly.

Tony Tavinor watched as Lynne Kramer unconsciously - or so he thought – wove a spell about the man. He observed Dan trying to suppress his initial astonishment - a private investigator could not look this slight and elegant. He'd seen it before, but the sudden glimpse of Lynne's tough edges, when revealed, also never failed to surprise him.

When the coffee arrived, Tavinor told Dan about Chao's meeting.

"So, who was meeting with Chao?" asked Dan.

"We've I've no idea, yet. We need to find out."

"And when he left Chao?"

"Went to the airport, flew down here, to Bangkok. We'll get the agency to find out his movements. They can access CCTV coverage at Don Mueang. Then try to see where he goes, who he meets."

Kramer nodded. They'll need to throw some money about." She looked at Dan. "Is that OK?"

He nodded and stood up. "Let's continue in my room."

Dan waited until they sat down on the expansive sofas scattered about the substantial lounge before he spoke. "So Mat's arrest was all arranged, just as he claims. OK, I have heard the name a few times, and now, for some reason, he is involved, but who the hell is this Chao Thanarat?"

Kramer looked at Tavinor. She started, "I'll give you the short version. General Chao Thanarat, born eighth December nineteen thirty-two. He is ethnic Hmong born in a Hmong village named Nonghet in Central Xiangkhuang Province in the northeastern region of Laos. Joined the Royal Lao army supporting the French military after the end of the second world war when the Japanese had invaded Laos."

She paused and looked around. Although he had never discovered the reason, Tavinor knew of Lynne's preoccupation with Chao. Dan listened, engrossed in the story of a time and place he had scarcely heard about.

Lynne continued, "Then the French were thrown out of Indochina by the North Vietnamese in 1954 after the battle of Dien Bien Phu. The US got involved just after that. Chao was recruited by the CIA in nineteen fifty-nine and eventually placed in command of a CIA "secret army" in sixty-two. Secret because the details were never disclosed to the US Congress. The "secret war" was waged with the assistance of massive aerial bombardment and regular supply flights to the "secret army" by Air America, a commercial airline fronting for the CIA, which flew in food and ammunition to mountain helipads cut out of the jungle.

"Sacks of opium grown by the Hmong villages were smuggled out of Laos on the same Air America flights and delivered to a clique of South Vietnamese generals in Saigon. That's how so many GIs got addicted and then took the habit home when they got demobbed. The trade funded the CIA activity and

Chao's army, with the complicity of senior CIA operatives. This was so the US government did not have to provide funds, which would have made the details public.

"Chao even set up a heroin laboratory at a secret US CIA base at Long Tieng. At one time, this was claimed to be the busiest airbase in the world. Then, the US bailed out in seventy-five after they had left Vietnam. Chao left most of his men and thousands of Hmong refugees on the runway at Long Tieng to be captured by the Pathet Lao communist forces."

She stopped speaking, and her eyes filled with tears.

Dan made to interrupt but she gestured him to silence. After a few minutes, she continued.

"After that, Chao cosied up to the warlords in Burma, particularly a guy called Khun Sa. After Khun Sa left the scene, Chao reorganised parts of his Hmong army and ramped up his heroin dealing, destroying any opposition to his operations in the eighties. From the early nineties, he began to buy his way into legitimate businesses. Dusit Sombat, his accountant, set up the current matrix of companies – mostly off-shore and hidden from view in tax havens. An extradition request from Australia in the early nineties nearly finished him. Nobody knows how he got away with that, but the word is he bought his way out.

"He's almost untouchable now with assets right through Thai society, politics, police, army – nobody can get near him."

She shook her head.

"He's an evil motherfucker, and as I said, that's the short version." She fell silent.

Dan eventually spoke. "And now he's involved in Mat's arrest and imprisonment. Why?"

The worm of suspicion that had bounced around Tavinor's mind since he heard Mat had been picked up made its presence known. He looked across at Dan. The man was no fool. He would be thinking the same. Nevertheless, nothing they did now could change the past.

Lynne spoke, “I’m away to the agency, Dan, then I have to go visit a friend this afternoon. Come with me.”

She stood and left the room.

CHAPTER FIFTEEN

Dan struggled to keep pace with Lynne Kramer as they walked from the hotel through Oriental Pier food stalls and hawkers selling boat trips on the river. At least he felt cooler in the cotton trousers of one of the new suits delivered the previous night.

"Lynne, what's the point of this? I'm not some bloody tourist," snapped Dan.

"And I'm not some bloody tourist guide. Have you got your passport?" She carried two plastic bags full of books and packets of food.

"Yes, I've got my passport, as you asked."

Dan watched as she cut through the chaos and crowds on the jetty. She was wearing jeans, a black T-shirt and sandals. He shook away the desire which coursed through him, clashing with the irritation at being treated with such condescension.

A succession of boats came across to the pier from amongst the large fleet of craft busying themselves on the bustling river. Eventually, Lynne pointed to a long, crowded boat surging toward them through the choppy waves. A succession of whistles came from a boy situated at the rear of the craft, a bizarre communication to the driver far away in the bow. The boat touched the pier, and a crowd of passengers jumped across the narrow gap. Dan jumped aboard to the accompaniment of more shrieking from the whistle, which then let out a long blast as the boat pulled away.

"What is this?" Dan asked after Lynne handed over twenty baht to a young girl who passed across two tickets from a cylindrical machine.

"The Chao Phraya Express," answered Lynne as she marched down some steps, under a wooden roof, to the front of the boat.

Dan hesitated and looked about the crowded craft. It was full of what appeared to be shoppers loaded down with bags and a large block of saffron-robed monks taking up almost a quarter of the space, offering an abstract splash of colour. He made his way forward and sat next to Lynne in the front seat, looking over a riverbank lined with beaten-up apartments - chickens and ducks in cages on damp wooden verandas - interspersed with wide stretches of carefully tended gardens surrounding spectacular golden temples and palaces.

"How long were you with the police?" he asked.

"About two years after law college." Her expression was angry. She put her hand on his arm. "OK. Mr Cooper. Let me tell you something." She looked round. Nobody was interested in them. "If you want the truth, I thought you were another Falang whose stupid son thought he could come over here, do what the hell he liked and get away with it. I think the prisons here suck, but I also detest what the drug trade has done to the country. But I'd met Mat, and that set me on wondering."

She wiped away some water that had sprayed up from the river onto her cheek. "Opium has been a part of hill-tribe life for centuries, here and in Laos. Used as medicine, in rituals and to suppress appetite when there's no food. In Nineteen-thirty, there were over six thousand government-regulated opium dens. It only became lucrative in the sixties and seventies when the Vietnam War was on and opium was converted into heroin. The Americans established the trade, and the economy became dependent on the business. Instead of the hill tribes growing a few acres for their own use and selling a bit to the lowland tribes whilst putting the rest of their land to food, they were forced to turn over most of their land to opium. So, there's malnutrition, and the region is run by warlords and drug dealers who buy who and what they want, including the army, the police, regional and sometimes national government. The biggest is Chao. The Westerners who feed the demand have corrupted the country. That's why I detest them."

Her expression was vibrant as she launched into another attack. "The prisons are full of idiots serving life sentences for acting as mules. They should get a slap on the wrist and be thrown out. But the traders, the dealers, and the major operators are above the law, own much of the country and are never called to account. Across in Burma, they own the country and the army and are the law."

She paused.

Dan didn't respond.

The river throbbed with all manner of vessels. Long-tailed boats buzzed through the brown water, sending spumes of spray high into the air; ferries crisscrossed the river from bank to bank; powerful tugs slowly churned their way through the centre of the channel, towing heavy, low-in-the-water barges tightly lashed together with thick fraying rope. A woman sat with her feet trailing in the water on one of the barges while scrubbing away at her washing before laying each item on the deck to dry in the remorseless afternoon sun.

She turned away. "What I've heard doesn't add up."

The monks alighted together, floating away, a silent saffron cloud drifting into one of the temples.

A young boy slept on a seat beside the driver perched on a chair high above the floor so that he had a clear view of the river ahead. He kept pushing at the connections to a fan, which occasionally flared into life, throwing a cool draught onto the sleeping child.

"I'm arranging a meeting for you. So you understand this place a bit more."

Lynne Kramer retreated into herself. She barely acknowledged Dan's presence, occasionally shifting on the hard wooden seat as they hit the wash of another boat and spray flew into the air beside her, depositing a few more drops onto her face. The river widened as it slipped beneath a six-arch bridge supported on concrete pillars. Beyond the bridge, the activity on the river eased in intensity. The apartments on the banks became bigger and more luxurious.

As they pulled into one of the piers, at which they stopped every two or three minutes, accompanied by more frantic whistling from the stern, a large motor yacht cruised majestically past. The name Horizon was only slightly smaller than that of the SHANGRI-LA HOTEL, which was emblazoned in the centre of the hull.

Dan pointed at the boat and jerked Lynne from her reverie. "Wouldn't it have been easier to have caught that?"

The glance in his direction was not far from contempt or pity. He couldn't decide which.

"This isn't a pleasure cruise," snapped Lynne.

"Then what the hell is it?"

"Hell is exactly what it is!" The clipped tones of a schoolmistress. "Get used to it." She turned sharply away from Dan as they carved their way past a military base with over a dozen dark green landing craft strapped to the Embankment.

Eventually, Lynne and the few passengers who remained after almost an hour stood up. The sign on the Pier read *Nonthaburi*. They disembarked and marched from the boat past a white clock tower. Dan struggled to keep pace as they skirted a line of market stalls selling fruit, sizzling sticks of meat and drinks resting on large slabs of ice. He stumbled against a kerb almost slipping to his knees as he avoided a dog crossing in front of him whilst Lynne took a road on the left. The dog had three legs. It limped away. An older woman looked up at Dan as he grabbed onto a road sign to keep himself upright. She squatted on the pavement, cutting up pineapples and slipping the pieces into cellophane bags. A young girl carrying a school bag bumped into him as he brushed down his shirt, wiping the sweat from his forehead. Her hands came together, and she smiled in apology. Dan looked up. Lynne was out of sight. He reached the corner and saw the slim figure striding away.

He started along the street and stopped, suddenly realising what this was about.

He didn't need this. Sweat ran down the back of his neck, soaking his shirt as he broke into a run. A figure in a white watchtower at the corner of a high wall leaned on his rifle, observing him. Dan felt the eyes scrutinising him.

"Lynne!"

The figure ahead stopped and waited just as she was about to turn into a gateway.

Dan was breathless as he reached the stern figure.

"What the fuck is this about?" He pointed at the forbidding wall topped with barbed wire running along the street and dotted with watchtowers.

Lynne pointed at the name in gold lettering above an iron

gate through which two silhouetted figures examined them. The letters read *BANGKWANG CENTRAL PRISON.* "This is where Mat could spend most of his life if we fail him." She turned. "Now we've got someone to visit. Give me your passport."

A sign on the gate read *VISITOR REGISTRATION.* Lynne took their passports to a desk behind which a uniformed woman reached for a form. Lynne handed over their passports and said they wished to visit Steven Ross in Building Six. At the same time, she handed over a note on which she had written the name and building in Thai.

"That's who we're visiting," she said as the woman filled out a form. "Steve Ross."

The form was handed over; the woman waved her hand toward the prison across the road.

"Who is he?" asked Dan as they crossed the road and followed a sign which led round the side of the gate and alongside a high unpainted wall topped with coils of barbed wire. A tremor of fear insinuated itself through him as he got closer to the wall.

"He came out here for a holiday from Denver. He ran out of money at about the same time as his mother had an accident and needed an operation the family couldn't afford. Agreed to carry ten k's of smack to Paris. It would have paid for the operation. He tried to pull out at the last minute, but it was too late." She paused. "He didn't have a wealthy father."

They walked through a thick wooden gate. Lynne offered the bags to the guard for inspection.

"Room one-one-three for books," came the instruction.

Lynne knew the route. They made their way down a dark corridor, through a wooden door into a stifling room scattered with desks and khaki-uniformed guards sitting around talking. One of them beckoned Lynne.

"Name of prisoner in books?"

She nodded.

"OK. Leave on desk."

The books were emptied out of one of the bags.

"Will he get them?" asked Dan as they retraced their steps back to a large, solid wood and iron framed gate. A guard again searched Lynne's remaining bag. Dan noticed it contained fruit, biscuits, coffee, milk powder and cigarettes.

"The guards here are pretty good. About this anyway."

After the search, Lynne handed the bag to Dan. "You take this."

A gate opened, and they moved along a path cut into a large rectangle. In the centre, a drive ran through a well-stocked garden to another massive, locked gate. Flowers leant a bizarre contrast to the grey depression of the buildings running either side of the rectangle. Lynne walked past a desk staffed by a guard. A sign read *WELFARE*. Behind a desk were packets of food and drink.

"You can buy food here or bring it in," said Lynne.

They continued along the pathway beside a line of wooden benches in front of an opening covered with iron mesh and thick bars. Beyond that was a gap of about four feet and then the same mesh and bars arrangement.

An older couple, alongside a woman making desperate efforts to keep three young children quiet, sat silently on one of the wooden benches. They looked across the gap at a prisoner, his fingers entwined in the mesh. Occasionally, he would shout across the divide.

Dan turned away.

"This side's for Thais. Over there for foreigners." Lynne gestured across the other side of the rectangle. They made their way around, handing the registration form to a guard sitting at a desk. He pointed toward one of the benches.

"They take about half an hour to fetch him," said Lynne.

"Was this necessary?"

She paused and looked around. "Necessary? Possibly not. But I thought you needed to know how it feels. You can always return to the UK and get on with your life. I'll do what I can. I know Tavinor will as well, but your son's life may depend on you. That's why you're here – so you understand and can't say later that you didn't realise."

Dan fell silent. He found it hard to speak, looking along the other benches. About ten black prisoners were shouting across to their visitors. Lynne followed his glance. "Nigerians mostly. There's a fairly large contingent. Used as mules by the dealers and shopped to the police when convenient for themselves." Shouting echoed around the rectangle. Dan breathed deeply and tried to regain some composure.

"How long has Steve Ross been here?"

"Eleven years."

"What happened to his mother?"

"She died. His father can't afford to visit. He's only made it over once."

As he answered, a fresh-faced boy, looking no older than Mat, came up to the bars and shouted across.

"Lynne. Good to see you." He pointed to Dan. "Hi, I'm Steve Ross."

"Dan Cooper."

"Dan, eh. I guess you're from good old England with that accent." He laughed and then continued as he clicked his fingers together. "Mat Cooper. Right! Lynne's showing you the animals in the Zoo. A bit obvious, wasn't it? On the way to Laos. For Christ's sake, you may as well try to smuggle ice to the North Pole. Someone wanted that boy. That right, Lynne?"

"It's a bit strange," she replied.

Dan could only see Mat behind the bars, his fingers reaching through the mesh.

"Strange, and some. Laos survives on opium. Nobody but nobody would take drugs into Laos, Dan. Your son has been set up."

"I left some books for you," said Lynne, pointing to the bag. "Cigarettes, fruit, biscuits and coffee as well"

"Lynne, you are a saint." He turned to Dan. "This woman is a saint, Dan. I'd have died in here years ago if it wasn't for her. Keep your son away from this place. Find a way, any which way you can, but keep him out. I'll tell you about Bangkwang. You have to buy everything. You want to get in a dormitory without twenty-four beds crammed together, mattress to mattress, you pay for it. You want a locker, pay for it. You want anything more than a bag of cockroach-infested rice and a cup of water at meals, pay for it. Soap, cleaning, showers, clothes, towel, pay, pay, pay, pay. You cross any of the guards, you get your head kicked or stuck in the hole for a month or two, and I promise you nobody comes out of the hole without their brains scrambled. You don't want to see your son like this, Dan. You know how long I'm doing?"

Dan shook his head.

Steve Ross paused and wiped his forehead. "Fifty years. So you have to make out or top yourself. You understand me. If Mat gets in here, you're dead. He can't spend his life wishing he could have his old Dad put his arms around him and take care of him. This is the best it gets, shouting through bars across a four-foot divide."

He gestured toward the inside of the prison. "This will be his life, and you ain't in here, so you ain't nowhere. What books you got, Lynne?"

"A few novels and a Spanish dictionary."

"Great. I'm learning Spanish, Dan, so when I get out," he

laughed, "I'll be sixty-eight. Then, I'm going down to Mexico and living on a boat. I saw a film in here where a cat did that after he escaped from a prison. So when I get there, I'll speak the language, and I pull the Mexican chicks."

He stopped. His face fell, and his voice suddenly became very quiet. Dan could barely hear him. "Keep Mat out of here, Dan. Find a fucking way," He looked at Lynne and shrugged an apology before turning back to Dan, "You know what I'm saying. Keep him out of this hole. I'm full of bullshit because you have to be to survive."

"Have the Embassy visited?" asked Lynne.

"Came a couple of weeks back. Nothing to say is there."

Lynne and Steve shouted at each other for over an hour, talking about family and friends who had visited over the years. Dan remained silent. A bell rang.

"That's all, folks," shouted Steve Ross in a fake Mickey Mouse voice. "Good luck, Dan. Thanks for everything, Lynne. I'll see you when you next make it."

"A few weeks if everything works out.'" Lynne waved as Steve Ross disappeared through a door back into the prison.

"You take the bag to the guy at the desk and collect the registration form. Then take your passport, bag and form to that welfare counter there." Lynne pointed across the rectangle. "They'll check it over and give it to Steve."

Dan did as instructed. The bag and passport were passed through a hole in the wall. He waited for about five minutes before his passport was returned.

Lynne was standing behind him. "Let's go."

A large sign by the gate revealed that there were almost five thousand two hundred inmates and over six hundred and fifty foreigners in the prison.

Dan retraced his steps from the prison. He wanted away. There was nothing to say. He hurried across the road away from the bloody wall, barbed wire, and bastard watchtower. A bus driver waiting at a stop paused from reading a paper and looked across as he rushed past. He went back to his paper. Dan wiped his face with a handkerchief.

He made for the ferry.

A cordon surrounded him - of silence - of anguish.

He couldn't look beyond this moment or see anything but utter despair.

A shout of concern came as he stepped out onto the road. A taxi screeched to a halt, the bumper just touching his leg. He didn't see it or feel Lynne take his arm and lead him to a ferry about to leave.

What was fifty years - if not the end?

He stumbled as he reached a seat on the ferry, setting off with a blast of whistling from the stern. Two monks sat in front of him. He stared at the colour of unintended irony, denial leading to fulfilment. He leaned forward and touched one of the saffron-coloured robes that fell down the back of the chair.

The monk turned, uncertain.

Dan looked back to Lynne. "I understand why you did it, Lynne. I'm not sure I needed it, but I suppose there may come a moment when the memory lends a perspective."

He stared from the boat when they arrived back at the Oriental Pier.

There was nothing more to say.

He went to the hotel.

He went up to his room.

He collapsed on the enormous bed. He closed his eyes but only heard boots clanging on hard floors, keys jangling and harsh voices drowning out desperate shouts.

The telephone rang.

The receiver almost fell as he grabbed it.

The voice was english public school and Oxford or Cambridge: cut glass.

"My name is Kumat, Thaksin Kumat. I may be able to assist you concerning your son."

The man said he was coming to Bangkok the next day. "You will want to check out my bona fides, Mr. Cooper. Please do so and call me back. We should meet." He gave Dan a number.

The phone went dead. Dan stared at the phone when the call ended. What was that about? He called the valet for a coffee and got hold of Nirundorn. He asked if he knew a person called Thaksin Kumat. The solicitor had never heard of him. He promised to call back.

CHAPTER
SIXTEEN

After introducing her to Nirundorn in the lobby, Lynne Kramer followed in the hotel car as they set off for the prison unit.

Nirundorn turned to Dan when he joined the solicitor in his car.

“You asked me about Thaksin Kumat. It is Colonel Thaksin Kumat of the Fifth Special Forces Regiment. His father is Chief of Defence Forces – as high as it goes in the Thai Army. His uncle is the permanent secretary to the office of the Prime Minister. He is as connected as possible in this country. He is a heavyweight, Mr Cooper. Why did you ask me about the man?”

“I’m having lunch with him today.”

Nirundorn. “I’m impressed. Why did he contact you?”

“He said he may be able to assist with Mat.”

“Then I suggest you listen very carefully to what he has to say.

Mat was already waiting in the room when Dan came in alone, leaving the others in the corridor.

They embraced.

Dan smiled. "You look great."

Mat grinned. "*Great*, Dad, don't overegg it, but I had a shower, some decent food and no hassle. What have you pulled?"

"I'm not sure it's anything to do with me."

"Then you don't know a guy called Kumat?"

"Kumat?"

"One of the decent guards said that a guy called Colonel Kumat had contacted Prisit. He knows someone who knows someone who's something in the interior ministry. That type of thing."

Dan told Mat how his lunch appointment with Kumat came about. He was just relieved that his son looked human again. He told Mat about Lynne Kramer.

"Go for it," said Mat. "We need all the help we can get."

Dan hesitated before speaking again. "They've appointed a Judge for the case. Name's Vyraj."

Mat looked frightened. "Is that good?"

"By all accounts, he's honest and incorruptible." He moved on quickly. The thought of a trial scared them both."

"Shall I get the others in?"

Mat nodded.

They filed in. Dan introduced Lynne Kramer. Mat's face broke into a wide grin as they sat around the scratched, unsteady table. His son turned to Dan.

"I know Lynne, we met up just before Christmas at Tony's place in Penang."

Dan nodded. He had forgotten.

Lynne's soft voice filled the momentary silence as a bizarre sense of normality filtered into the stagnant heat. Dan felt the perspiration soaking into his shirt, trickling gently down his face as Lynne pulled a notebook out of her pocket. He looked at the three figures, all breathing the same air and sharing the same space, but one of them would remain; one would be unable to walk through the door and taste freedom. Mat, almost certainly the most innocent, would be unable to set foot outside the walls. He suddenly felt lightheaded by the absurdity of the situation. He gripped the table and heard Lynne's voice calming the intensity.

Nirundorn nodded to them and said he would leave them and meet back at the hotel.

"Mat," she said. "I need you to remember everything from when you arrived in Bangkok until your arrest – every detail. Are you up to that?"

Lynne's voice was gentle but firm. She left no doubt that Mat had to be up to it.

She continued after Mat nodded his agreement. "How did you arrive?"

"We took the train from Singapore through Malaysia."

"Who's we?"

"Kathy, she's from Melbourne. We met up in Singapore after I'd been in Penang for a few days. With Tavinor and Maria." He turned to his father. "You sent me a few emails."

Dan nodded.

Lynne interrupted. "You knew where Mat was?" she asked Dan.

Mat smiled. "He made me do an itinerary when I left, and I updated it every week or so by email to say how things were going."

"You kept the details?" asked Lynne.

"Of course. I was interested in how Mat was doing," Dan replied.

"OK. So, you arrived at Hualamphong Station. How did you end up at the Siam Paradise?"

"We figured we'd stay around the Khaosan Road. Some of

Kathy's friends were near the station, but we fancied the Khaosan Road and were offered a ride."

"Who offered you the ride?"

"Three guys from the hotel. They had a picture of the room, and the location seemed OK. They only wanted one hundred and fifty baht for a double room and shower. It was a steal, and we got a free ride over there."

Lynne looked up from making notes. "I want you to go through this in detail. The train pulls into the station. What were your plans?"

"We had the names of a couple of hotels we'd got from the Lonely Planet, and the idea was to get a tuk-tuk over to Khaosan Road and see which one we liked best."

"So, you came off the platform and made for the exit. Toward the line of taxis and tuk-tuks?"

"Yes, to the right of the platforms. Then these three guys came over ..."

"What do you mean came over? From where?"

Mat paused. "No. I don't know. They just appeared in front of us."

"Had you seen them speaking to anyone else?"

"No."

"But you noticed the other touts that were around. Trying to sell taxi rides, hotels, all the usual stuff?"

"We avoided them."

"There were other backpackers on the train. I assume you had backpacks?"

Mat nodded.

"OK. So, you agreed to go to the hotel. How did you get there?"

"They had a minibus waiting in front of the station."

"They take anyone else or just you two?"

"Just us."

"And you get to the hotel. I guess you decided to stay?"

Mat rubbed his face. "The room was great. We couldn't believe how good it was, especially when we compared it to Kathy's friends' places, which we saw later. The shower and toilet were clean, the room was great, and," he looked at Dan, "it only cost around three pounds. We grabbed it. Later, we found we paid way less than others at the hotel."

"What about the three guys?"

"They worked around the hotel. Cleaning, behind the bar, reception, changing light bulbs, that kind of thing."

"You ever see them go out to the station again?"

"I can't say for sure. Not as far as I know."

Lynne paused. "When you were back at the station, did these three guys split up and spread themselves around the other kids or did they all make for you and Kathy?"

Mat looked over at Dan and then back to Lynne. He shook his head slowly, his voice betraying his growing unease. "They stuck with us."

"Tell me about them," said Lynne, head down, writing rapidly in her notebook.

"They were from Chiang Mai. Told us they had been in Bangkok for a few months working in the hotel. One of them was an Amerasian. Father was American. He told us he'd lived in Washington for a few years as a kid, I remember now, I think his name was Chris."

"How did they get their jobs at the hotel?"

"Worked in Chiang Mai for the guy that owned the Siam Paradise."

"What did they do in Chiang Mai?" asked Lynne.

"In a packing station, vegetables, dried fruits, spices, stuff like that. Global Harvest."

"So, you got to know them pretty well?"

"They liked talking and were always around."

"What happened on the last night?"

"Kathy was going north by an early train, and I wanted to see Laos. We were intending to meet up in Chiang Mai in ten days. She was staying the night with some friends in a hotel near the station and I went over with her."

"Why didn't you check out of the hotel?"

"I was going to, but the manager said I could leave my stuff in the room and collect it the next day. They said the hotel wasn't full."

"Was that true?"

Mat paused. "I don't think so. I was a bit surprised. I'm sure they were turning people away. I didn't make anything of it. It just saved me dragging my stuff around."

Lynne carried on writing.

Dan asked, "Was the manager the guy with the ponytail and beard?"

Mat looked surprised. "You've been over there?"

"Just for a drink."

He felt Lynne Kramer's irritated glare.

"Yes," said Mat. "It was him. Weird guy, scary."

Lynne jumped back in again. "So, they knew you would be out all night?"

"I came back about nine and took the hotel minibus to the airport."

Lynne closed her notebook. "Tell me about the airport."

Mat repeated what Dan had heard earlier.

"You make any enemies out here?" asked Lynne after Mat had finished.

"How could I in a couple of days."

There was a silence.

"Laos isn't a drug run, is it?" asked Mat.

Lynne looked at the ceiling. "No."

"So why?"

"At the moment," Dan felt Lynne's enquiring glance fall on him, "I've no idea."

Lynne stood up and shook Mat's hand. "I'm done. Has anyone from the Embassy been over?"

"A buttoned-up Consul. Gave me a lecture, and that was that."

Lynne made her way to the door, "I'll wait outside."

"She seems pretty switched on," said Mat as the door closed. "I can handle this. Just do the business out there for me, Dad." His expression was crestfallen. "If only I'd been a bit more streetwise."

Dan closed his eyes. He didn't want to leave his son. His voice was quiet in his confusion. "It's not about that, is it? Something else is going on."

"You know you mentioned the Sucher case yesterday."

Dan nodded.

"One of the guys here knew her. She carried a bag for her boyfriend, a Thai she'd met up with in Ko Samui. It's claimed that she's had to have plastic surgery in Switzerland and change her name."

"She's not serving a life sentence, though."

"Who's to say," answered Mat as a guard entered the room. "There's no visits tomorrow. Some inspection is happening." They stood and embraced. Dan waited as the manacles were put back onto Mat's ankles, and he hobbled away across the courtyard.

The room was empty.

Dan stared at the doorway.

Everything seemed empty.

Another door banged along a corridor. Keys jangled, he heard the harsh clatter of boots against concrete and wiped the sweat from his forehead. Mat was tougher than Dan had realised. He had come over to support his son and give him hope, but instead, Mat gave him conviction and encouragement rather than the other way round. An old man shuffled through the door, ignoring Dan, aimlessly sweeping the bare concrete floor. Dan snapped out of his reflections and joined Lynne, waiting in the corridor. They made their way to the car.

"You think he's OK?" asked Dan as they settled into the car on the way back to the hotel.

"OK?" She shook her head. "No one's OK in that place. But you should be proud of how he's handled things so far. Make no mistake, though, the unit is rough, and Prisit is one vicious mother. Someone set Mat up. The question is, why? Three guys meet him off the train. Professional job on his daypack. It's an investment, and I don't see that Mat has the history to justify it. Unless you and he are keeping something back."

Dan shook his head. "No. What you see is what you get with Mat. A young kid who enjoys life or did anyway. There are no hidden angles."

"It was you I was thinking of," continued Lynne. 'Interesting that the three guys worked in Chiang Mai. That's the base for Chao Thanarat's heroin operations. Handles at least a couple of thousand tons of opium every year."

Dan Cooper called to Kumat to confirm lunch as Kramer flicked through her notebook as they sat in a traffic jam, the heat-laden air buzzing with mopeds and tuk-tuks. Her voice was irritated when she questioned Dan about the visit to the Siam Paradise Hotel.

Dan ran through what had happened.

"Dumb move," said Lynne. "I'd rather you left the comic-book heroics alone. I prefer some subtlety."

"So the Siam Paradise is Chao's hotel."

"Of course. I thought you knew." She paused and turned to Dan as they pulled up at the Shangri-La. Her scrutiny was intense. "Mat's itinerary! They knew what train he was on and the details of his flight to Vientiane. They recognised him at the station. Think about it."

"I was the only one with his itinerary. It was on my computer..."

She interrupted, "Was?"

"My computer was stolen."

"When?"

"A few weeks back."

"Shit. You'd better work to find out what the hell happened to it. Have you told me everything? Someone's gone through a lot of trouble, time, and expense to put your son in that place. Why, Mr. Cooper? You haven't got much time to answer that question."

He stared at her. It couldn't be connected, could it? Not here. Thousands of miles away. It had to be something else.

"Mat's a victim." Lynne continued. "I do not doubt that now. His story hangs together. I didn't know Chao was involved when I first heard."

"Is that relevant?"

"It is for me," she said with an intensity he didn't understand – not until much later. She gave no explanation.

"You think we can find anything to help him in court?" asked Dan.

Her voice was irritated. "That's what we're working on, isn't it?"

Dan paused and changed the subject. "Why did you come back to Thailand from California?"

"My mother died. I decided it was time to see where I was born."

"Bangkok?"

"Udon Thani."

"Why did you leave Thailand?"

A flash of irritation crossed her face. 'What is this, an interrogation?"

"I'm sorry." He shrugged. "I'm interested. It's nothing more."

"OK. My father died - was killed - when I was ten. The place was in turmoil. His brother in California helped us settle over there." A note of finality in her voice stopped Dan asking anything further.

Nirundorn was waiting in the hotel lobby. Lynne went to her room. "I have to speak to Tavinor."

"You tell Mat about Sucher?" asked the solicitor when they sat down.

"I have mentioned it."

"Trial could be soon now Judge has been appointed. You are wealthy man, Mr Cooper, I think." he leaned close, "I do not want to meet you every few months when you come to Bangkok to visit Mat."

The remark hung in the air. Dan didn't know how to respond.

"Talk to Mat about bail. As a contingency. If everything else fails."

"Possibly."

The smile vanished. "Mr Cooper, you think it easy to arrange?"

"Yes, Mr Nirundorn. I think at the right price, it is easy to arrange."

The eyes narrowed, and then the face resumed its wide smile. "You got a good sense of humour, Mr Cooper. Let's hope Mat laughing when it's all over. You understand nobody gets found not guilty. Mat hasn't come up with any reason why this should happen. We have nothing. Mistake, perhaps, but believe me, Mr Cooper, we have no case and soon your son on trial."

The words shook Dan. He'd tried to hide from the truth. It was the only way to survive.

They didn't speak again.

Lynne Kramer came down. She told Dan she was going over to meet up with Tavinor. He was at the agency's offices trying to locate whoever had met with Chao in Chiang Mai.

She sat down. "So, tell me about your computer."

"Stolen from my apartment.

"Any investigation?"

He nodded. "Ray Lancaster, my security chief, is checking it out. Tony knows about it."

"OK, I'm going to meet him now. We need to follow that up, fast."

CHAPTER SEVENTEEN

Colonel Thaksin Kumat was waiting in the lobby when Dan went down at lunchtime. He was taller than most of the Thais Dan had met, with a face that appeared to have been polished with fine sandpaper, shining in the bright hotel lights. The appearance was completed by an immaculately pressed black silk suit, white shirt and MCC tie.

MCC tie! Dan couldn't believe it.

Kumat gave a self-effacing bow as Dan felt the soft feel of a handshake, which managed to be firm yet almost sensual, so malleable was the smooth skin that held him.

"You're a member of the MCC?"

The smile that came was wide, but the impression persisted that more was concealed than displayed in the response. "I had a trial for Middlesex while at university. My father is a member."

"You studied in England?"

"Law at Cambridge before Sandhurst." He led the way toward the lifts. "Shall we try the Shang Palace."

Kumat was greeted by name and elaborate deference at the

third-floor restaurant. They were shown to a table overlooking the river.

"They know you here?" asked Dan.

"I come occasionally."

"Is your rank from the Thai Army?"

A measure of pride shone on Kumat's face. "Fifth Special Forces." He picked up the menu. Dan's appetite had disappeared somewhere across the Bay of Bengal on the flight from London. It seemed an age away. He let Kumat order.

As they waited for the food, Kumat asked Dan to run through the details of Mat's arrest. He nodded at regular intervals but without interrupting.

"Thanks to you, Mat's conditions at the Interrogation Unit have improved considerably," finished Dan.

"I did very little. Merely mentioned the situation to a relative. I understand that you have Kamchan Nirundorn representing your son. I wonder if you would object to me speaking with him?"

Dan didn't object.

The food arrived. Dan picked at noodles, fish and chicken. He was certain it was as superb as Kumat elaborated, but the mixture of fear and excitement that, perhaps, this man could somehow obtain Mat's freedom was too overwhelming.

Kumat wiped his mouth and looked at the empty bowls. "You do not eat enough, Mr Cooper. It is necessary to keep your strength up. You cannot help your son if you are weak."

They took the warm towels offered by a waiter. Kumat leaned back and rested his towel on his face. After almost a minute, he came forward again, took away the towel and looked closely at Dan.

"You want your son out of that place, Mr Cooper?"

"Of course. Why are you helping, Colonel?"

There was a pause. Dan felt Kumat's eyes focused on him. The glance was intimidating.

"Let's say no more than we have a mutual interest in having the matter resolved. I am no more than a conduit, Mr Cooper. I hope I can help."

He stood. The matter was resolved, and although Dan felt himself slipping into a dark obligation, he didn't care as long as Mat walked free. The consequences would have to follow. He could live with that. He hoped.

"So, Mr Cooper," continued the smooth voice, "we get your son out." He checked his watch. "I have to leave. I shall be staying in Bangkok whilst I deal with this matter."

He checked his mobile phone.

"I am not available tomorrow. Could we meet the following day, with Nirundorn. I trust that is convenient."

Without waiting for an answer, he stood and bowed before walking quickly through the tables.

Two waiters rushed to open the door for the upright figure.

CHAPTER EIGHTEEN

After Kumat had left, Dan called Róisín and told her what was happening. He left out the meeting with Kumat because he wasn't sure where that would end up. A taste of arrogance and self-interest hovered around the man, causing Dan to hesitate before he raised any hopes.

Tavinor and Lynne Kramer called up from the lobby when they returned from the agency.

He made his way down and related what Kumat had said.

"What's his angle?" asked Lynne.

Dan shook his head. "A conduit, mutual interest, he claimed. I don't know what that means." He sighed. "If it gets Mat out..." The sentence remained unfinished, but his uncertainty was apparent.

"Let's see where it leads." Said Tavinor. "If it's genuine, grab it, get Mat away and fuck off out of this country. In the meantime, I've spoken to Ray Lancaster about the theft of your computer."

"Who's Ray Lancaster?" asked Lynne Kramer.

"Dan's security chief, he was with me in the army for ten years."

He looked at Dan. "He's been pushing the police, but no one is interested. An old computer and a few photographs don't get the juices flowing..."

"Whoever picked up Mat must have had access to his itinerary, which was on that computer. Is that right?" said Lynne.

"It is," said Dan.

"So we need to know what happened with that information."

Tavinor said, "'The management company of your apartment block have come up with the night's video. Ray has identified a stolen car that was used. He's following that up. I've told him to use whatever resources he needs to find out who was behind the robbery. We need to know who did it and what happened to the stuff they took. Ray knows we need results fast."

"OK."

Lynne spoke, "There were four flights from Chiang Mai to Bangkok following Chao's meeting at the Orchid. We've got someone at the airport trying to get hold of the surveillance camera product. I'm afraid it means going through various levels of the security outfit out there, so it will take a while, but we should get something soon. That's assuming they have it. Not all the kit is maintained as well as it might be."

The concierge approached Dan after Lynne and Tavinor had made their way to their rooms.

"You have two visitors, Mr Cooper."

He pointed across the lobby.

It was the two Australian kids he had met at the Siam Paradise - Lizzy and Tim.

"How did you find me?" Dan asked, sitting them down and calling over a waiter. "Beer, tea, coffee?" he asked.

"We phoned around," grinned Lizzy. "We figured you weren't staying in a Khaosan Road hostel."

They settled on three beers.

"You still at the Siam Paradise?"

"We left the same night you were thrown out, but that's not why we came."

He paused as the drinks arrived, together with a bowl of nuts and potato crisps.

Tim grabbed a handful of nuts before he spoke. "You remember we mentioned the American who went crazy and dragged one of the kids away. I recalled after you left that his name was Magach. He said to "tell Chao that Magach will cut his fucking heart out if he ever came near his boy again".

"I don't know if it helps,' said Lizzy."

Dan sat back. "Magach. I've never heard the name. But...." He spread his arms, "Who knows what's important in this crazy business," and checked his watch as Lizzy grabbed another handful of potato crisps.

"You want to eat something other than nuts and crisps?"

"Here?" said Lizzy.

"Unless you've somewhere else you'd like to go."

Tim looked around the enormous lobby with a broad smile. "I guess here will do, mate!"

"What do you fancy?

"Italian," came Lizzy's urgent answer. "I've been over three months without a decent pasta, and for someone with the surname Paparelli, that is painful."

Dan called over a waiter who had just collected a tray of coffee cups from a table. "Is there an Italian restaurant in the hotel?"

"Angelini's, just across the lobby."

"You beaut," shouted Lizzy and jumped up. "Let's go."

Dan smiled and momentarily closed his eyes. He realised

why Mat had fallen for her friend. Her enthusiasm temporarily alleviated the wretched feelings that had dominated him since he arrived in Bangkok.

After they'd eaten their way through the menu and drunk two bottles of wine, Dan noticed Lynne Kramer exit the lift. He called over and asked her to join them.

After introducing the Australian couple, he asked, "Have you ever heard of a guy called Magach?"

Lynne Kramer looked like she had received an electric shock even whilst shaking her head and claiming she didn't know the man.

Dan watched carefully.

The meal ended.

He watched as Lizzy and Tim piled into a tuk-tuk and careered off down the road, leaving a trail of exhaust fumes behind.

Dan said, "Let's talk in my suite."

"So, who is he? You know him – Magach. I could tell."

Lynne Kramer shook her head." I don't know him. But he's real. In the world of the blind, as the saying goes, the one-eyed man is king – or the man who says he has one eye – that's Magach."

"According to the kids, he dragged a boy out of the Siam Paradise and warned Chao not to go near him again. You think this could be the third boy? The one who may be able to tell us what happened with Mat and the backpack."

"That's possible. I'm back to Chiang Mai with Tavinor tomorrow to see if we can locate the third boy – who he is and where he is. Of course, if the boy is with Magach, then we have a problem – he's been here since around sixty-five – thirty-plus years – he might be in Thailand or Laos. He won't be found if he doesn't want to be found.

“But let’s see where we get in Chiang Mai. Before we get up there, though, I arranged for us to meet someone who was around at that time. Before we go to Chiang Mai tomorrow, I’ll let you know where and when.”

CHAPTER
NINETEEN

Lynne was over at the agency.

"The unit is closed," she said. "Get out of the hotel. You'll do no good sitting there. The place will suffocate you. You need a clear head to help your son."

He walked from the hotel down to the jetty and stepped onto a narrowboat waiting for business. The boatman tried to make conversation but gave up after a few abortive efforts. He took Dan to the Damnoen Floating Market. They drifted alongside boats filled with bananas, pineapples, mangos, mangosteens, and lychees. He didn't refuse as much as he didn't notice. Time passed him by.

When he returned, Tony was waiting in the lobby. They left the car on the main road and followed the driver's directions toward a small alley. Pimps with menu cards offered him anything he'd ever imagined sexually and one or two things he hadn't. Crowds of dark-haired girls beckoned him over - smiling, beautiful faces, over-acted disappointment as he passed by.

An ornate black door with a coat of arms and shield looked

heavier than it was as it opened from the gaudy seediness of Patpong Soi 1 into a world where time moved as though in a different dimension - the *Bar Catalonia*.

A long, highly polished teak bar ran the length of the quiet room, and deep, battered leather chairs were scattered about the wooden floor. A Spanish flag hung above the bar, behind which a woman, whose wrinkles stood out like a relief map, followed his entrance with undisguised scrutiny. Her eyes narrowed until he came closer, and suddenly, a wide smile broke out and transformed suspicion into welcome.

"You want Hank, eh?" A curious guttural expression came, which Dan didn't understand. She waved impatiently toward a corner where he saw Lynne gesturing them over, sitting beside her was a figure who reminded Dan of westerns he used to watch on television at a friend's house when he was a kid. He stood as they approached. The tall oak-stained barrel of a man belonged on a prairie somewhere, wrestling cattle, breaking bones. His handshake was as strong as Dan expected. The voice was smooth and robust as rye whiskey.

"Lynne's been telling me about your son, Mr Cooper. Sounds a bum deal for the kid. My name is Hank Aldrin."

"Thank you. It's Dan, please."

Aldrin called over toward the bar. "Marilyn. Bring us a bottle, honey."

"Marilyn?" asked Dan.

"After Marilyn Monroe. She was a looker in her time."

The waitress came closer.

He chuckled, although melancholy touched the laughter. "Those times were a few years back. A few years and a world away."

He poured four large glasses of Jim Beam bourbon from the bottle the waitress left on the table. "Cheers. Good health, and good wishes to your son, Dan. I hope I can help you, but I'm not sure how. Lynne says that you want to know about Chao Thanarat." He emptied the glass in one shot and poured himself another before pulling a photograph from his pocket and handing it to Dan. It showed four men. Three were obviously Westerners - two in fatigues, and the fourth was Asian. He turned it over, four names were written on the reverse:

Chuck Ralston - Magach - Chao - Aldrin

"I'm at the end there. That little bastard next to me is Chao. It was taken in the early sixties when he was in a Lao Royalist Special Forces Unit. We..."

Tavinor looked up, "Who's we?"

"The company, the CIA. We ran the show in Lao. We were told to recruit from the hill tribes in the north of Lao to fight the Pathet Lao, the underground communist army, and the North Vietnamese who were backing them. It was called Operation Momentum. Chao was one of the leaders of the Hmong tribe. They were ready for it. The name Hmong means "savage warrior."

He downed another glass.

"Vietnam was in turmoil, so the conflict in Lao was kept secret. We got no money. Congress wasn't let in on the war. We first ran it from Udon Thani in Thailand and then from Long Tieng, an airbase we set up in Northern Lao. I say we, but I was mostly based in Udon. It was Magach who was over in Lao. He created Long Tieng and signed up Chao."

"So where did the money come from?" asked Dan.

"From the early sixties, Chao did deals with the Burmese warlords. Many of them had come across from China after Mao took over. They ran their own private armies and funded them with opium. Chao bought the opium and converted it into heroin. He even had a laboratory in Long Tieng at one time. Air America was the company's own airline, and they would run weapons up there and then take the heroin back to

Saigon. That's where the money came from, in suitcases full of US dollars. Some of the Viet generals sold the smack on and made a fortune. The biggest market was the GIs and US Army in Vietnam, and when that fuck-up ended, Chao was dropped in the shit. The US didn't want to know him, so he set up a base in Lao, at Sainyabuli, kept his contacts with the Burmese Generals, started his own heroin laboratories up on the borders and supplied the US, European and Australian markets."

"He's still doing the same?" asked Dan.

"Yes. He had a setback in Ninety-three when an Aussie dealer dropped him in it. He got arrested but bought his way out."

"Bought his way out?"

"Word was he paid off the police chief for Chiang Rai. Evidence was lost. The Aussie got deported, Chao walked."

Lynne came in. "He set about eliminating the competition. Murdered about seven of the top operators and their families, blew up their houses and laboratories and then made an exclusive deal with the Burmese. Once he got the supply side set up, he transformed his distribution. He bought up the Northern Thai Army and police. Nobody's completely certain what he owns and doesn't own, but it's not hit-and-miss anymore. It was estimated a few years back that he was supplying at least half the heroin which hit the US eastern seaboard and at one time seventy-five per cent of the UK market. He's the law in Sainyabuli. Bought out the local Laotians long ago."

Aldrin continued, "Sombat runs his operations in Bangkok. He was a sergeant in Chao's army. Young kid, worked his way up because he was more violent than the rest. His speciality was cutting off the heads of captured Pathet Lao, sticking them up on bamboo poles and organising a dance around them. Chao promoted him and then sent him off to business school when it all ended. He's no fool and was already looking to the future."

Dan picked up the photograph. "Who are the others?" he asked.

"The stocky, dark-haired guy at the end is Chuck Ralston. He was a raven ..."

Lynne interrupted. "Ravens were forward air controllers. They flew little Cessnas over enemy lines."

Ralston stared directly into the camera with a dazed expression on his face.

Aldrin continued. "Crazy bastards. Not many survived."

"And the one in the middle?" asked Dan.

The tall figure in the centre with his arm around Chao looked extraordinary. Extravagantly angular, there seemed to be no round edges to the rugged figure as he looked down his hook nose into the camera with an expression which seemed to suck in the air around him.

Aldrin raised his glass and drained it in one gulp. "Neil Magach - arrived in Asia in fifty-nine when he was twenty-one and hasn't left. Can't quit the jungle." He tapped his head. "Not here. He'll never leave. Gone bamboo. That's Magach. Craziest bastard in the world."

Aldrin drained his glass and continued.

"Ralston saved Magach's arse when the man got caught behind the lines after the North Vietnamese launched a surprise attack. Magach had a couple of minutes left before he was captured. Ralston heard Magach cursing everyone on the radio and took off for him. He landed his Cessna on a track, and Magach jumped in as they took off. Ralston flew back to Long Tieng with a smashed kneecap when a shell caught them just as they were taking off. He didn't say a word till they landed but walked with a limp from then on.

"Chuck got caught up with a hooker from just along the

road here." He waved toward the door. "Bought her off her pimp and married her. Magach was best man. Chuck and his family went back to the States for a few years, had a kid and then came back working with the Drug Enforcement Agency. The DEA, Chuck, got close to nailing Chao. He was killed with the hooker, his wife, in Chiang Mai in eighty-six. Magach swore revenge. He doesn't forget. Fourteen years is no time."

Aldrin filled his glass again. The bottle was empty. Aldrin called for another. They drank in silence. Dan was lost in the story. He'd almost forgotten where he was, lost in the bizarre history he briefly looked round the quiet bar. A few customers had wandered in, one or two with young Thai girls in their laps, most of them staring silently at their drinks.

"Food, you want any food," Aldrin burst out laughing. Speciality of the house - SOS. This either means "shit on a shingle" or "save our stomachs", depending on who you ask. It is a mush of chipped beef, mixed with milk and gravy, slapped on toast."

He looked around, and they all shook their heads. "Good decision. The Air America jockeys used this place between missions up to Long Tieng. Most of them didn't last long."

He pointed above the bar. "There's a room up there where the spooks used to hold their clandestine meetings planning missions in Lao."

He fell silent and finished another glass.

"Chao should have been put away years ago," said Aldrin, eventually breaking his silence and staring into his glass. He continued, his voice emotional and starting to slur. "It was May fourteenth, Nineteen-seventy-five at Long Tieng. The whole fucking place was collapsing. Around ten thousand refugees crowded onto the airstrip. We were overwhelmed. Chao was getting out. He couldn't tell his people, or they'd have strung him up. An American USAID worker tried to commandeer a chopper to get a group of injured refugees to hospital. Chao shot him. First in the leg, he then planted two bullets in the poor bastard's head. The chopper took off. He was away to Thailand, leaving his people behind. Magach was in the chopper. He watched Chao murder the poor bastard. The guy had a local wife and kid as well."

Aldrin abruptly rose unsteadily to his feet. He emptied his glass again. The waitress shouted something in Thai. Aldrin sat down.

"Look at us all. Washed up old bastards. Can't go back to the bloody States. The place is a fucking cesspit. So we stay in Bangkok and relive the only memories that are worth jerking off over." He stood up again. "Got to go. Get your son out, Mr Cooper, any which way you can. No one comes out of Bangkwang with their head straight." He staggered to the bar and kissed the waitress. A blast of pop music filtered in as the door opened, and Aldrin swayed through it.

"Is he for real?" Dan asked Lynne.

"As real as it gets in his world," she replied. "This place has been his domain for almost two decades, like a lot of Americans that can't face going back. They came out to fight a war and never went home. Don't belong anywhere."

"And what he said about himself and Magach?"

"By all accounts, it was a crazy time. Magach is almost a mythical figure to some of the old guys. He never surrendered. You never know if the stories about him are true or part of the mythology."

"What type of stories?"

"That he used to decapitate prisoners and drop their heads over enemy lines. When a diplomat came up-country to recall him to Vientiane, he flew him up to China in a chopper, held him by his ankles and threatened to drop him. When his reports about enemy casualties were questioned, he ordered his men to cut off enemy casualties' ears and attach them to his reports. Then, when it was over, he disappeared into the jungle. He could still be there now."

Dan described what Tim and Lizzy had told him about the scene at the Siam Paradise Hotel.

"Thanks for this." He leaned down, "I don't know how it helps Mat, but..." He breathed deeply, shook his head and looked about the room again. A few older men with young Thai girls hanging on their arms had drifted in.

"What the hell am I doing here?" continued Dan. "Why the hell is my son locked up in that stinking, fucking dump with a psychopathic warder threatening to destroy his life? Why? What's happening? I've just heard about a war that happened thirty-odd years ago, and what the hell has it got to do with me... or Mat? For fucks sake, he wasn't even born."

Tavinor had remained quiet while Aldrin was speaking. "That was history, interesting. But does it help us?" He paused. "Mat said the boy at the Siam Paradise was called Chris and had lived in Washington for a few years. Magach dragged this boy out of the hotel and warned Chao to get his hands off the boy. Magach owes Chuck Ralston, who Chao murdered. We have to get back to Chiang Mai and find this third boy; everything points to him as Chris, likely Chris Ralston. If it is him and he's with Magach, we must find Magach. This Chris could be the one person who can help Mat. If he's willing, that is."

His telephone rang out, he stood up when the call finished. "The guys at the agency have come up with something. He nodded to Lynne. "Let's go."

They both left.

Dan wandered across the room and put some money on the bar.

"No. No. Mister Aldrin pays. You no give money," insisted the waitress.

"For you," shouted Dan as he reached the door. The heat hit him like a warm towel when he left the bar. Neon lights flashed in his mind. Smiling figures came at him from all sides. "You want lady, boy. Make you happy, happy. Nice and clean." He caught a snatch of a song by Bruce Springsteen. He never had time for music. He never had time for anything.

"You want massage, boss? Nice massage. Bangkok massage. Clean girls. Make you real happy."

"Mr Cooper."

He felt a gentle tug on his arm.

"The car's this way, Sir." It was the driver.

He allowed himself to be guided back to the car and slumped in the back seat. The Vietnam War was a film. Dramatic photographs. Vietnam wasn't a place it was an event. Something that moulded the world and all seen on the nightly newscast. Nothing to do with him. He closed his eyes.

"Mr Cooper." He felt a gentle tug on his arm. "We at hotel, Sir."

Dan opened his eyes wide. He looked around him.

Bapit, the valet, was exiting his room. He looked round, his eyes widened when he saw Dan. A sudden blast of fear disappeared behind a wide smile as he bowed. "Checking room, sir," He rushed away.

CHAPTER
TWENTY

It was 03.40 on a caffeine-sustained night. Lynne Kramer and Tavinor were trying to stay awake while staring at a monitor showing airline passengers moving along a corridor of Don Mueang's domestic terminal.

"There!"

Tavinor shot out of his chair, halted the playback, and slowly reversed the process. Passengers jerked backwards in a bizarre, clumsy dance.

He stopped it again and pointed at the monitor, his finger hovering over a figure looking up toward the camera and quickly pulling an *NYC* baseball cap over his face.

"Who is it?" asked Lynne Kramer as Tavinor fell back onto his chair.

"His name is Craig Pollard." He paused. "He's why Mat is sitting in that cell."

"Explain."

"I first encountered Pollard in Northern Ireland back in December eighty-six. He was with an outfit called the Force

Research Unit, which ran informers in the Provisional Irish Republican Army - the Provos. To cut a long story, his tout had been outed as a British informer, and a squad headed up by a top Provo named Kelly went to pick him up – "interrogate" him, which almost always ended up with a bullet in the head. After the tout was slotted, Kelly found Pollard hiding under the stairs. A gun was placed against *his* head, but the gun jammed, and he got away with it. Pollard went crazy. He went after Kelly, who had almost killed him, never got near him but murdered the man's twelve-year-old brother and another kid instead. He was rapidly shipped out of Belfast and kicked out of the army. He subsequently served time for assault and has ended up as a director of a company in the UK called Ludlow Holdings."

He stood. "We're going back to the hotel. I need to tell Dan. Now."

He strode out of the office, and Lynne rushed behind.

It was 04.30 when the taxi dropped them at the sleeping hotel. An assistant manager rushed over as they entered the lobby.

"Telephone," demanded Tavinor. He called Dan's room. "We're coming up. Lynne and myself. Now."

He replaced the receiver and gestured to the lifts. The assistant manager ran ahead and called a lift. "We want coffees in the Siam suite," barked Tavinor as the doors opened.

Dan was waiting at the door. He had thrown on a pair of shorts and a T-shirt. He didn't speak as he gestured them into the lounge. He checked his watch. "Quarter to five. Nothing good comes calling at this time."

Bapit, the valet, came in with a tray of coffee. He looked at Dan. "Can I get you anything else, sir?"

Cooper shook his head. Lynne moved over to the door and let the valet out, slipping him a hundred baht note as he left.

"So?"

Tavinor watched the valet leave and then spoke quietly. Looking about the room, he said. "I'll get some guys over to check this suite out."

He paused.

"Pollard met with Chao in Chiang Mai."

Cooper frowned. "Pollard? Why? What the hell is he doing over here?"

"I'm guessing he brought over Mat's itinerary."

"And gave it to Chao?"

Tavinor nodded.

"I don't get it..." Cooper suddenly fell silent. His voice stuttered. He turned to Lynne Kramer. "The two boys that were murdered worked for Chao. He owned the hotel where Mat was staying. Prisit was at the airport when Mat was arrested. You've always said he works for Chao." He fell silent again and then turned to Tavinor. "Pollard met with Chao." He paused again. The silence deepened along with the shock on Cooper's expression. "It's Mayer. Why is Chao helping him?"

Tavinor nodded.

Dan stared through the window and barely heard Tavinor and Lynne Kramer talking alongside him.

"Tony has told me about this Pollard. The guy met with Chao. Who the hell is Mayer?"

Dan didn't respond.

There was a silence. "What the hell are you two not telling me?" asked Kramer.

"Charles Mayer is the Chairman of Otterburn-Fuller, a bank in the UK. He's also a director of Ludlow Holdings with Pollard," said Tavinor.

Cooper turned to her. "Mayer claims I owe him ten million."

She stood and walked across to the large glass window overlooking the river.

"And neither of you two geniuses thought this was worth mentioning until now. What is this money? What's it about?"

Dan answered, "Mayer financed the transhipment of two hundred thousand landmines from the UK to East Timor, where they were going to be used by the Indonesians to oppress the local people..."

Tavinor interrupted, "I blew up the warehouse where they were stored."

Dan resumed, "And Mayer's family bank lost ten million, and he came to me to repay the money."

"I don't get it, why you?"

"I helped Tony, and I guess I'm the man with the money."

"So, you told him to take a hike?"

Dan nodded. "A few times." He hesitated. "And Mayer," he paused again, "or someone who finds Mayer useful has asked Chao to help recover the money." He paused again. "But why would Chao help? What's in it for him?"

"I could take a guess, looking at Chao's business and how quickly Ludlow has expanded," said Tavinor.

"Heroin? Fuck, are you sure?"

"No, of course, I'm not sure. But one of the problems with drug dealing is money laundering. Perhaps Mayer helps out." He shook his head. "But that's for another time. Now we need Mat out."

They sat in silence until Kramer broke the spell. "So, what now?" She looked at Dan, "You pay the money and Mat walks?" She shook her head. "How do you think that will work? The Thais can't admit they fucked up. According to them, he had ten kilos of smack in his backpack. They can't suddenly turn round and say - *oh, sorry, we got that wrong, it wasn't him, or we've tested it, and it turns out it was talcum powder or some other shit.* No one will volunteer to stand up and spout that bullshit."

Her fists were clenched as she walked back to the table. She suddenly leaned down to Dan. "I heard Nirundorn talk about the Sucher option?"

"Bail?" asked Dan.

She nodded.

"You think he's involved. Nirundorn? That he knew about Mayer and the money?"

Tavinor spoke. "I called Nirundorn from Penang. He didn't know anything about Mat. I'm sure he wasn't bullshitting. In any event, what does it matter? What other options are there,"

He turned to Lynne, who responded, "If you're right, how else do we get Mat out?"

Tavinor snapped, "We prove he was set up."

"The third boy?" Kramer shrugged. "And what can he say? What would he be willing to say? He'd be signing his death warrant. Chao would see to that. No witness, no chance. Mat goes away for fifty years or more." She turned to Dan, "You come over to Bangkwang every month or so."

She sat down.

Dan was silent. He looked beaten, having to accept that he was responsible for his son being locked away. For having possibly destroyed the boy he loved so much. He could have paid Mayer. He should have paid Mayer.

Tavinor leaned in, "OK. Enough. The bail option has to be kept alive. If it ends up being the only solution, we have to go for it..."

Lynne interrupted, "Not we. It's Mat who has to agree."

"Of course, you're right. So, that option is kept open until there's nothing else. But we have the third boy possibility as well. So, we go and find him. Of course, that's not certain if he's with this guy Magach, but if we locate him and he agrees to give evidence, then the next step is to keep him safe and alive to give evidence. And then agree to keep him secure after he gives his evidence."

"And Nirundorn?" asked Dan.

"He knows the case. There are no guarantees whoever we get. I say we keep him."

Dan nodded. "I agree. But how does this bail option work?"

Lynne spoke, "You pay whatever bail is set..."

"There is no bail," interrupted Dan.

"I hadn't finished." She snapped. "Someone will approach you to make the arrangements. Perhaps a change of judge, one more amenable, then a prosecutor who may be agreeable. With a will, these things are manageable. The bail is paid, and Mat gets out of the country." She paused, "You may already have been approached."

"Kumat?"

"It's possible. It seems he has the connections."

"OK, so we have to wait, and, in the meantime, we go after the third boy. The other question I have is what Pollard did with the disk. We're assuming it's Mat's itinerary. Who did he hand it over to?"

"We are following up on that. The driver who picked him up at the airport has been located. He can tell us where he took him."

He looked at Dan. "I'm going to speak to Ray now."

He looked at Lynne Kramer. "Tomorrow, we get the first flight back to Chiang Mai. Check out this woman at the Orchid Hotel and see if we can locate the third Boy."

She stood and walked to the door before turning her expression angry. "Anything else you haven't told me?"

They both shook their heads.

* * *

Tavinor called Ray Lancaster, who was in Cooper's office when he called.

"You want to sit down."

"What is it?"

"It was Pollard that brought over Dan's computer or at least a file from the thing. Mat's itinerary. That's how the guys over here picked him up."

"Shit. So..." Lancaster fell silent.

"Yes. This has to be about us, about the explosion – the destruction of the warehouse, and Mat is in this mess because of the backfire."

"Mayer's money? The ten million he wanted from Dan?"

"I don't know how else this plays out. The scumbag will show himself soon enough, I'm sure."

"How did you find out?"

"The agency I used to work with over here pulled some CCTV from the airport. It showed Pollard getting in from Chiang Mai after meeting with the guy who seems to have been involved in Mat's arrest."

"The drug dealer."

"Yes, Chao Thanarat. He's not just any dealer but one of the top two or three operators. He's a serious player and has investments all over the country. Powerful guy."

"I don't get it. Why would he be involved?"

"No idea. Yet."

"So, when Pollard got to Bangkok, where did he go? Who did he meet? Presumably, he had to hand this disk on to someone who set the thing moving?"

"We're locating the driver who took him from the airport and hope to get that information in the next day or so. What progress with the robbery?"

"The car used in the robbery was stolen in Eastbourne on the south coast. The local police are pretty sure they know the two guys who were involved, but there's no proof. It's no big deal to them; I've had to push them all the way. I'm down there this morning. There's a DI who's willing to share."

"OK. Contact me as soon as."

CHAPTER TWENTY-ONE

Tavinor and Lynne Kramer had left to get to the airport for their flight to Chiang Mai before Dan set off to see Mat. He was alone, Nirundorn was in court on another case.

Mat was already waiting in the meeting room.

Dan held him, suddenly realising how thin his son had become. He didn't want to dig too deeply into the conditions behind the locked gates. He had to get Mat out of there.

They sat down.

"We have to talk," said Dan.

"It's about Sucher, isn't it?"

"I don't know what else we can do. I've spoken ..."

Mat interrupted. "Sorry, but before you go on, I want to tell you what I've been thinking. You get a fair bit of time for that in here. Am I right in saying I will only get bail if money is paid?" He raised his eyebrows. "There's no bail in drug cases like mine normally. Is that right?"

Dan shook his head. "Apparently not, according to Nirundorn."

Mat lowered his voice. "So, the right people are paid off,

and then I'm free. Get on a train or drive across to Malaysia and disappear. That's it?"

"That's it," agreed Dan.

"And what then? They put out an international arrest warrant for me. I can forget University because the British Police would be notified, and I'm left with the countries that don't have extradition with Thailand, or I change my identity. Either are life sentences. There's no way out, is there? I mean, I've got it right."

Dan was silent. Mat *had* got it right. He'd tried to brush aside the same thoughts because he'd seen Bangkwang and couldn't cope with the thought of Mat being there.

Mat continued. "There's no way they'll drop the case. That would be accepting that the whole deal was bent. I'll spend my life looking over my shoulder, perhaps with an assumed name and a bent passport."

He paused and licked his lips. "I couldn't live like that. Is there no chance of finding out what the hell happened?"

Dan explained that Tavinor and Lynne Kramer were going back to Chiang Mai.

"I'd rather trust you guys to come up with something than spend the rest of my life hiding away. I'm sorry, Dad. I know you can't bear thinking of me stuck in here or Bangkwang."

Dan couldn't disguise his shocked expression. "I've heard all about it."

Mat frowned. "Bangkwang - have you been there?"

"Lynne took me."

"You didn't tell me!"

Dan leaned across and gripped his son's hand. "I'll do anything to keep you out of there."

"Perhaps I'm being stupid. You may be right. I should be prepared to do anything to get out. But I've not done anything. Why the hell should my life go down the tube? It might be better if, at least, I knew why. But nothing makes any bloody sense." He wiped his sleeve across his eyes. "Dad, I don't know what to do."

"OK. I'll do everything I can to find out what happened and to get you out of this. If I fail, then we appeal, and I'll sell the business and buy the bloody Prime Minister or the King if I have to. Whatever it takes. However much it takes."

"It may be too late then."

Dan lowered his voice as he felt Mat's hand gripping his. "I know. But what else can we do? I also hate the bail option, but at least you'd be out of this place."

"But what sort of life would that be? Years looking over my shoulder. It would never end." He paused and wiped his sleeve over his face again. "Give it your best shot, Dad. I don't want to spend my life running away."

The words sent a tremor of fear through Dan. He tried to smile. Nothing came. "OK. We'll talk some more with Nirun-dorn tomorrow. Think of it as a possible very last resort only."

A guard came into the room. He smiled at Mat. "English, we got to go."

Mat smiled. "There's another inspection today. Have to go early."

Dan held the frail body as he spoke. Mat was trembling. "I'll be in tomorrow. We have to get something ready for trial, whatever happens."

Mat nodded. "Tomorrow." He turned at the doorway, the smile suddenly reminiscent of another time, another place. "I know you can do it." The door slammed.

Dan didn't move for almost five minutes after the door closed. Nobody bothered him. He sat in the scratchy silence, trying desperately to imagine that it was all a mistake and, at the same time, knowing a dread apprehension that Mat could place such faith in him when everything around him was beyond his control. He hadn't told Mat what he had heard about Mayer and Pollard last night. Perhaps he should have done, but what could Mat do? It was for Dan to calm his own anger and remind himself that, above all else, he needed Mat out of this place. If there were feelings of vengeance, they would have to wait until his son was free.

Suddenly, the light bulb in the ceiling cracked, and glass fell onto the floor. The room was in darkness. He grabbed the edge of the table, breathing deeply of the stagnant air. He tried to push himself up, but nothing functioned as he wiped the sweat from his face. It may have been only a few seconds or minutes. He had no conception of time as he sat, unable to move before the door suddenly swung open, light burst in, and an elderly man stumbled in with a broom. He didn't even look at Dan as he started to sweep the pieces of glass scattered across the floor. Eventually, he glanced across toward the table. His eyes were empty. Dan got to his feet and made his way from the unit. Nobody challenged him.

CHAPTER
TWENTY-TWO

Dan had not long been out of the extended shower he liked to take after being at the unit. Scalding hot water would take away the smell and taste of the place, but nothing could rid him of the anguish he felt at leaving his son behind.

He admired Mat's reluctance to accept the bail option and to get out of the prison unit and the country as soon as he could, but at the same time, all he wanted was to have his son free and out of this Kafkaesque turmoil.

The telephone rang as he sat in a bathrobe, staring blankly at the window.

The receptionist told him the *gentlemen* were there to see him. Which gentlemen?

Kumat came on the line. "We need to meet to make progress. Since we met, I have secured the support of important principals in the matter. So, if you have a few moments, we can move forward. We will be in the lobby."

The call was disconnected.

He was not about to tell Kumat that Mat was reluctant to accept bail. That was for another time if it came to it.

The lift doors opened.

Kumat sat on one of the sofas in the lobby. He lifted his hand to acknowledge Dan. The figure alongside him turned.

Dan felt he was anaesthetised. His senses were shot. From the early blast of revulsion at his son's condition in Bangkwang prison and through the surreal pictures painted by Aldrin, he didn't think he was capable of being surprised any further. In truth, he wasn't shocked after listening to Tavinor in the early hours, but the reality in the shape of the individual sitting across from him left him momentarily speechless and motionless – a marionette whose wires had fallen.

Of course, it was about him and not his son. He felt a blast of determination and anger that had been subsumed beneath indecision for too long as he had struggled in this strange place with its unexpected culture. He fell into a chair opposite the sofa where Kumat and Charles Mayer waited.

He looked at Mayer, trying to contain his contempt. He would destroy the man, but not before Mat was free and safe. Not before he'd eaten whatever shit the arrogant bastard wanted to feed him. Not before he'd given him whatever he wanted. There were no limits. Mat's life would not be destroyed.

He waited, clenched his fists, imperceptibly moving shoulder muscles, freeing the tension. This was pressure he could handle. Mayer didn't know him. He hadn't been anywhere close when Dan faced the destruction of their family business. At that time, he was forced to do things that made him feel ashamed even now, when he woke in the early hours of long nights, and those memories still cursed him.

"Colonel Kumat has been telling me about the bail proposal." Mayer's voice gave nothing but contempt.

"It's the only option. Isn't it?" said Dan, looking between them.

Kumat bowed his head in agreement. Mayer settled back in his chair. A waiter served coffee.

Dan continued. "So, there's no choice. I can't pretend to understand what happened, though. Mat isn't guilty..."

He paused and looked closely at Mayer. "He isn't guilty, is he? He wouldn't be stupid enough to try to smuggle drugs at all." He turned to Kumat again. "But Laos!"

"Strange," agreed Kumat.

"Strange indeed. So, what happened?" asked Dan and sat back.

Kumat spoke. "This is Bangkok," he spread his hands as though the words explained everything.

"And so it is," said Dan. His eyes did not deviate from Mayer's sculptured image. The face was suddenly stripped of pretence. Mayer smiled hesitantly.

"Ten million?" asked Dan.

Mayer contrived regret. He gestured to Kumat, who responded. "If only it had been resolved in London."

"How much?" snapped Dan.

Mayer looked to Kumat again.

"I have no interest, but shall we say twenty-five million dollars. Extra expenses, you understand. Payable upon Mat's departure from Thailand? Release and return of his passport at the Thai border."

"I will speak with Mat tomorrow. Everything is ready?"

"Matthew is agreeable to the proposal?"

Dan shrugged. "What is the alternative?"

Kumat nodded. "Everything is ready, although final arrangements will take a few days," he said. "You will excuse me, gentlemen." He turned to Dan. "Judge Vyraj has been allocated the case?" he asked.

"Yes."

"Then he will be removed. On being granted bail, your

son's passport may take a day or two to be returned. I will accompany him when he leaves the country - to ensure no complications. You may, of course, also accompany your son."

Mayer said he was leaving for London that night.

Kumat nodded, stood and marched through the lobby. A doorman ran ahead to open the rear door of a black Mercedes waiting outside.

Dan wanted to grab Mayer. To smash him. Break him. But that was not for here and not for now. This was about Mat. Revenge would wait.

Mayer didn't look at Dan. He shrugged as though trying to dissociate himself from what was happening.

Dan stood without another word and walked to the lift.

As the lift ascended, he wasn't sure whether to feel anger or relief, but neither seemed appropriate, so he settled on thinking of Mat walking away down the steps of the Interrogation Unit. What happened until then could wait for that moment, but he wouldn't forget.

He called Róisín. He assured her that Mat was fine and there was hope. He didn't say at what cost or humiliation it would be bought, nor did he care.

Mat's voice played in his mind: *"I don't want to spend my life running away"* – perhaps there was no choice.

He hadn't heard from Tavinor since they had set off for Chiang Mai - perhaps there *was* a choice.

CHAPTER
TWENTY-THREE

Nobody was playing the grand piano marooned in the heavily shaded wood-lined lobby of Chiang Mai's Orchid Hotel. Statues of four Thai musicians, lit by bulbs sheltering under cumbersome wooden lampshades, dotted an oppressive arrangement in the centre of the lobby.

Nobody did anything much at all. Three waitresses talked quietly to each other next to a small serving area offering coffee and snacks. A desk with a sign indicating *Taxi Service and Business Centre* was situated on one side of the main door. It was unattended. On the other side of the door, a woman sat behind another desk - *World Travel Service.* Lynne moved across and sat at the desk while he wandered around the lobby, photographs lining the walls beside the lifts. Celebrities who had passed through the Hotel: Princess Diana and Prince Charles - in better times - Emperor Hirohito, The King and Queen of Thailand.

Tavinor moved to a sofa in the centre of the dark, over-bearing lobby until Lynne came and sat beside him. She touched his knee and gestured toward two security guards in brown jackets watching from near the entrance doors.

"Let's go," she muttered quietly.

He noticed the *World Travel Service* desk was empty as they passed through the lobby. He saw the woman, who had been behind the desk, sitting on a moped down the steps from the entrance. She nodded at Lynne. The two guards watched from the top of the steps by the doors.

Lynne called over a tuk-tuk and whispered in the driver's ear. They set off behind the moped. As soon as they were out of the hotel approach, she turned to Tavinor and pointed at the woman.

"She knew the boy's father."

Tavinor frowned.

"The third boy. I think."

They followed along a road running beside the moat surrounding the old town, crossing a bridge before doubling back in the opposite direction on the other side of the water. The woman kept looking behind, checking that they were still there as traffic thinned out on what appeared to be a ring road. The moped turned left for a few hundred yards before rolling slowly into the forecourt of a Temple - the sign read *Wat Phra Singh.*

Lynne slipped her shoes off at the base of the steps leading up to the elaborately decorated building as the woman moved into the temple. Tavinor followed. A single bell tolled an irregular beat amongst the chanting of six women on their knees in the centre of a red carpet stretching through a line of pillars supporting a wood-framed roof. Vases of flowers surrounded an enormous golden buddha, their colours lighting up the incense-flavoured atmosphere, stirred only by the desultory attempts of a couple of ceiling fans high in the ceiling.

The woman beckoned them to one side and knelt on the

floor before holding her hands together in prayer, palms together, eyes closed, for almost five minutes. Tavinor made to speak, but Lynne gently touched his hand. The feeling of her soft skin made him jump. He turned to look at her, but her eyes were closed, facing toward the figure of Buddha at the front of the Temple. Her mouth moved soundlessly with the women's chanting. A sense of timelessness hung in the warm air. He also closed his eyes - only for a moment.

He looked about him, at Lynne Kramer, at the women chanting. Warm-scented air brushing his skin.

The woman started talking. Tavinor strained to hear the quiet voice as she stared toward the Buddha.

"Three of them. Boys. Worked in Orchid Hotel and packing station," she paused and looked at Lynne, "before going to Bangkok. Two came back a few days ago."

She paused. Silence reclaimed the moment.

"They died." She stopped again. Her eyes closed. "Bodies found on way to Mae Rim. Hit by lorry." Her head shook slowly as though denying what she had just said.

"The third boy?" asked Lynne.

"Pa Sang." She stood and reached into a pocket in her dress, pulling out a folded map.

There were two crosses on the map. One was just outside Chiang Mai, and the other was on a town called Pa Sang. There was a name, *Chris* and a note in Thai.

"Who's Chris?" asked Tavinor.

"Chris Ralston," said the woman. "Brought up in Pa Sang by his grandparents. Parents murdered." She leaned closer, her voice barely audible, "Chao Thanarat."

Faces turned as Tavinor asked, "Is there anything else?"

The woman paused as she moved silently across the stone floor.

"There must be something," he insisted.

Lynne gripped his arm. "Back off. She's already out on a limb. This isn't her fight."

The woman turned. "They worked at the packing station." She pointed to the other cross. "Global Harvest."

"Is that where the boys were killed?"

"Just outside." The face was sad as she pushed to her feet and trod softly toward the door.

A young shaven-headed monk, swathed in a saffron robe hanging off his shoulder, held together with a broad yellow band at his waist, looked toward them as he glided across the Temple from a side door. He handed a flower, three incense sticks and a candle to Lynne. She moved to the statue of Buddha and knelt, placing a flower in a vase, lighting the candle from another already lit candle, and then igniting the incense sticks, placing them upright in a container of sand. She waited a few minutes before gesturing for them to leave.

"What do they mean?" he asked.

"The candle for enlightenment, so that I may help others; the incense spreads the fragrance of virtue throughout the mind and body; the flower reminds us that life is short and impermanent." She pointed to a saying on a pillar: *"Death is a mirror in which the whole of your life is reflected."* She held out her hand, "Let's go."

She looked at the slip of paper as they slipped on their shoes. "We need to get to Pa Sang. It's about twenty-five miles south of Chiang Mai. I need to have a shower and get some of my stuff. I'll go back to my place, and you need to get a room in case we need to crash out. My place is too visible. Go to the Roong Ruang Hotel and get a room, just in case. We'll rent a car later and get to Pa Sang. We'll meet up at the Westin Hotel, which is on the right side of town."

Tavinor watched Lynne's tuk-tuk engine spring into life,

jerking across the bumpy forecourt. A plume of smoke shot out of the exhaust as it carried onto the main road.

As he watched, Ray Lancaster called and told him he'd located one of the guys who had stolen Dan's computer. He had met the man and persuaded him to tell him who had hired him. It was somebody the guy had met a few years back in Ford Prison. He had followed the man back to his house in Kent, and he was taking Ray there the next day.

He ended the call and got a tuk-tuk to the Roong Ruang Hotel.

* * *

Tavinor listened as Lynne outlined their next moves, sitting in the vast mirror-lined lobby of the Westin Hotel. Chandeliers dotted about the ceiling shone down on ceramic floor tiles amongst brutal air-conditioning. A piano played over a muzak system, competing with a German tour group, just disgorged from a coach parked outside the lobby.

"I've asked at reception for the way to Lampang, which is way past Pa Sang. I've written the address of the Roong Ruang in Thai in case we split up. You've checked in there?"

He confirmed he had. "Why should we get split up?"

She nodded across the lobby. Tavinor recognised the security guards from the Orchid Hotel but without their brown jackets. "We have to get rid of those guys."

She passed another note to Tavinor. "I've taken the details from the map. This is the Thai name of a woman in Pa Sang. Somehow connected with Chris Ralston, possibly his grandmother. It's a little town famous for cotton. The note is in Thai, but the address is Stall twenty-two in the Textile Market, just off the main road. You pronounce the name in English - Anitra. The name Magach is also written in Thai?"

Tavinor remembered Aldrin's photograph: *Chuck, Magach, Chao and me.*

"Chris, he could be Chuck Ralston's son."

She nodded. "OK. Let's go," she said, leading him to a white rental car she had picked up in the city.

The route was lined with tall Yang trees shading the road from the reach of the relentless sun pouring onto the narrow pot-holed road. Small market stalls selling fruits and vegetables studded the dusty kerb. After about six miles, she started checking in the rear-view mirror, slowing down and waiting for traffic to overtake before speeding up again. This happened a couple of times.

"Blue pick-up. Two cars back. Been with us since we left the Westin."

"Are you sure?"

"Certain."

"Shit. How the hell do we lose them? There's only one road. Suppose they know where we're headed?"

"It's possible. That's why I mentioned Lampang. They may have checked."

"They may fall for it," said Tavinor, "but it doesn't solve the problem of how the hell we lose them."

"About seven miles before Pa Sang, we hit Lamphun. We'll have to take a chance to get ahead of them, and you can jump out there. Find a car and driver for the rest of the day. He can take you to Pa Sang and then back to Chiang Mai."

"They'll notice I've gone."

"You can't see with these headrests."

"What about you?"

"I'll take the Lampang Road. It's another thirty-odd miles. By the time I get there, you'll be away."

"And if they work out, what's happened?"

She smiled. "It's not my first rodeo, Tavinor."

They rolled to a halt as a policeman moved to the centre of the road and stopped the traffic. Two lines of monks came toward them, moving slowly and holding a couple of ropes along which, strung behind the monks, were a collection of black-clothed figures, some weeping quietly, unobtrusively. The ropes pulled an elaborately decorated structure carrying a gold and jewel-encrusted coffin. As they passed across the road, two men rushed with long wooden poles to push up telegraph wires lining the road so the coffin and ornate carriage could pass beneath. The procession was followed by a pick-up truck with four musicians wearing straw hats playing a soulful tune. The procession continued slowly up a dusty track leading away from the main road.

They rode in silence for another fifteen minutes before Lynne spoke. "We're getting to the outskirts of Lamphun." There was a crowded bus about four vehicles ahead. She checked in her mirror. "They're three cars back. See the main street up ahead."

"Yes."

"Halfway along, there's a school. See the kids congregating on either side?"

The pavement was crowded with young children in white shirts and blouses, black skirts and shorts.

"The bus has to stop there, in the middle of town. There's bound to be a whole bunch of people getting off and on. I'll pull in front and stop at the traffic lights just beyond." As she spoke, she dragged the wheel over and accelerated past three cars and a battered motorcycle to a chorus of hooting. They ended up directly behind the bus.

"They've got stuck," said Lynne, looking in her mirror. "As soon as I pass the bus, I'll pull in so they can't see your door open. Get out and mix with the passengers. Put your hat on."

She smiled. 'I'll see you back at the Roong Ruang this evening. We'll catch a late flight back to Bangkok.'

"Be careful" was the best he could come up with. He jammed a black sun hat on his head and grabbed the door handle as the bus slowed down.

The bus stopped, and a crowd of people gathered as they passed. Lynne swung in front and halted at the red traffic lights.

"Go!"

He wrenched open the door and dropped just as the lights changed. The white vehicle pulled away whilst he thrust himself into the chaos of the passengers alighting from the bus. He waited a few minutes before looking down the main street after Lynne. The blue pick-up had disappeared in the line of traffic.

* * *

The road was almost empty after Lamphun. A taxi driver had been only too pleased to take Tavinor when he offered him a couple of thousand baht for the rest of the day.

Houses rose on stilts beside a river running alongside the road. Fields led into a wide plain ringed by distant mist-shrouded hills. White cows grazed ankle-deep in thick grassland. The sun poured down, and nothing moved besides an occasional moped and a few chickens scurrying along the road. He stopped to buy a couple of cans of drink from a roadside stall after waking the stallholder sleeping on a bench in the shade.

Pa Sang was little more than a main street filled with quiet, half-open shops slumbering in the afternoon heat. The driver slowed down beside a small indoor market across the street from another dramatically decorated temple. He pointed to the slip of paper Tavinor had taken from Lynne and gestured toward an assortment of food stalls spreading across a forecourt. There was a collection of debris around the stalls: metal cans half-full of water, gas burners, woks, small fridges, mopeds, and women washing, cooking, peeling and shouting with laughter at each other and their customers.

"In there?" Tavinor asked.

The driver gave the note back and pointed to the side of the market. Tavinor wandered through the food stalls and came into a section devoted to textiles. Passing up invitations to examine mounds of brightly coloured sarongs, jackets, trousers, and swatches of material, he came to a stall with the number 22 on a metal support.

The woman was no more than five feet tall with short, thick black hair. Her round face broke into a smile as he approached. She held up a pair of wide trousers, demonstrating how he could tie them with a waistband.

He said her name. "Anitra."

The smile disappeared, replaced by fear.

"I've come to see you about Chris Ralston."

She blinked at the name but said nothing.

"I'm trying to find him."

A younger woman came over. She peered through thick lenses, a long ponytail down her back. "She doesn't speak English."

A burst of Thai came.

"Are you from Chao?"

"No."

The woman turned away.

"She doesn't know anything."

A couple of men approached them from adjoining stalls, waiting silently, threateningly, a few yards away.

"Please tell her I'm a friend of Magach."

Almost out through a door at the back of the stall, the woman turned as she heard the translation and, without hesitation, walked across to Tavinor. She grabbed at his wrist and indicated for him to follow. They moved quickly through the market and across the main street into the Temple he had noticed earlier.

After leaving their shoes by the door, the woman moved to a cushion under a statue of Buddha, put her hands together and fell three times to the floor.

He understood now and waited by the entrance until she gestured for him to come forward. The other woman joined them. They sat by one of the ornately decorated pillars under what he took to be a history of Buddha in brightly coloured pictures in a frieze around the wall and hanging from the ceiling.

The voice was a whisper.

A stilted translation fed into his right ear.

"Magach is good man." As the whisper fell into silence, the woman wrote out a note in Thai on a slip of paper. It was passed across to him.

"What is this?" he asked anxiously.

The round face turned to him, and she pointed vigorously at the piece of paper.

The two figures rose to their feet without another word and moved slowly from the Temple.

The script meant nothing to him. It would have to wait for Lynne. He checked his watch. She would have made Lampang by now. He knew she was resourceful, but Chao Thanarat was ruthless, that's what everyone said. He looked around the Temple, feeling silence he had rarely known. His life had been filled, he had controlled it, and there had been no time for pause. The silence was invigorating and intimidating.

A cough came from the doorway. He leapt to his feet as

though discovered in something shameful before moving to the doorway and holding the map out to the driver wandering about in the forecourt.

"Roong Ruang Hotel, Chiang Mai. OK?"

"OK."

Tavinor pulled the note from his pocket. "What does this say?"

The driver frowned and then looked up. "Patpong. Bangkok." He laughed. "You like girls. Plenty girls in Chiang Mai." He laughed a toothless laugh.

* * *

The driver dropped him at the Roong Ruang Hotel. It was a faint hope that Lynne would be waiting for him. He clung to that hope until he entered the hotel's small reception office. An elderly woman looked up from behind an ancient Imperial typewriter. She shook her head when he asked whether Ms Kramer had checked in. A small veranda ran the length of the building. He sat down on one of the seats outside his room.

A ceiling fan circled aimlessly in his room behind him. At the end of the balcony, a young couple drank a bottle of beer each. They kept leaning forward and whispering to each other, sparking waves of laughter which washed over Tavinor, leaving him untouched.

It was four hours since Lynne had dropped him off in Lamphun. Too long. Culpability was almost too great a weight to carry. More laughter crept along the balcony, and a mist of insects dived frenetically for a small light by the stairs leading down to the hotel office. He picked up a mango in a bowl on a table before him. The smell was rich, the skin soft and smooth. A bird clattered out a bizarre call from the branch of a tree high above him; beneath the balcony, he heard the chatter of two young boys playing checkers.

A taxi came from the road.

The driver ran up the steps.

"Tavinor," he shouted.

Tavinor jumped out of his meditation. "Yes."

"You come," shouted the driver.

Tavinor waited.

"You come. Lady says..."

The driver held out a note. Tavinor read it: "I'm at the airport. The driver will bring you. Bring your bag. Hurry. Lynne."

He grabbed his bag and rushed down the steps.

* * *

The taxi dropped him away from the terminal building. The driver pointed toward a hangar. "Lady in there." Tavinor paid him off. There was nobody around. A few small planes were parked up in the gloomy, cavernous space. A light shone from a far corner. A metal object fell in the darkness. He turned as a blast came from the main runway when a Thai Airlines plane took off. Too many fears rushed through his mind as he pushed at a tight-fitting metal door in the wall. A creak echoed through the hangar. He stopped and waited before pushing again, stepping carefully into the building. A smell of engine oil mixed with the rich evening humidity. He moved cautiously between two small aircraft, stepping carefully around a large open toolbox. Leaning down, he took out an iron bar. A sudden clang of metal hammering against metal echoed through the empty spaces. He knelt beside a plane, sheltering in the wing's shadow. The sound died down. A hesitant silence returned. He moved again toward the light.

Suddenly, an engine burst into life. The sound ripped through the building. It came from the far end, where he saw another large open door. Just in front was a twin-engined plane. One of the propellers was turning, and whilst he watched, the other sparked into action. As he got closer, he could feel the buffeting created by the engines roaring into life, setting the plane juddering and moving forward slightly.

A cough was almost lost in the racket. He whirled around, the iron bar held high above his head. A figure in oily overalls watched, eyes wide in fear as he stared at the bar.

"Tavinor?" came a muted shout.

He frowned.

"You Tavinor?"

He nodded.

"Miss Lynne," he pointed at the plane moving slowly across the forecourt in front of the hangar. "You get on."

As he got closer, a small door halfway along the fuselage opened. He couldn't see who was inside. He looked behind him. The mechanic was gesturing him forward. A small set of steps was moulded into the door. Tavinor pulled them down and got on the bottom step.

"Get the fuck inside, Tavinor."

He signed with relief as he heard Lynne's exasperated voice.

"Get in!"

He rushed up the steps and pulled the door closed behind him.

"Seatbelt," she shouted from the right-hand cockpit seat as the plane accelerated. A Thai wearing a white shirt and sporting four epaulettes on his shoulders sat with his hands folded as Lynne guided the plane to the end of the runway.

"Where the hell are we going?"

"Out of here," shouted Kramer over the sound of the

engines and pointed to a set of headphones on the seat beside him. He put them on.

"Can you hear me?" she asked. He could. "Talk when we're in the air," she said and manoeuvred the plane to the end of the runway before communicating with air-traffic control to advise she was ready for immediate take-off. The order came to hold position. The figure in the left-hand seat touched Lynne's arm and pointed to a blue pick-up speeding along a taxiway toward them.

Lynne spoke on the radio again and said she was ready for immediate take-off.

The same response came, *"hold position"*.

Her fellow pilot looked around. "It's clear," he said.

Lynne looked toward the pick-up. It was about two hundred yards away. Tavinor could see three figures in the rear. They were holding weapons pointed toward their plane. Lynne confirmed again that she was cleared for immediate take-off and thrust the throttle levers forward.

"Runway clear," said the figure in the left-hand seat.

"Hold position", came the instructions over the radio.

"Radio breaking up, cleared for immediate take-off," responded Lynne as they gathered speed on the runway and started to pull away from the vehicle racing down the adjacent taxiway. Just as they lifted from the ground, Lynne wrenched the control column over, and they turned sharply away from the vehicle. It felt as though the wing would touch the runway, they were so low. She levelled off only a few feet from the ground, speed building up quickly until they reached the airport perimeter when Lynne heaved back on the column, and they shot into a dramatic climb. Tavinor left his stomach somewhere down in Chiang Mai as the climb continued until he noticed the altimeter reading five thousand feet when the plane levelled off.

He heard Lynne's voice. "Sorry about that."

"So where are we going?" Tavinor asked.

"You tell me. I planned it this far." She pointed to the figure in the left-hand seat. "This is Captain Joe Senajai. He taught me to fly."

A hand came over the seat. Tavinor gripped it. A laugh came through the headphones. "Didn't teach you to take off like that."

"We've filed a flight plan for Mae Hong Som, but that was only for take-off," said Lynne. "What did you find out?"

Tavinor leaned into his bag and pulled out the note from the woman at Pa Sang.

Lynne read it. She turned to Senajai. "We're going to Bangkok."

* * *

They sat in the small air-charter office as Tavinor Senajai filled in some forms for Tavinor to sign as he worked out the cost of the charter. Angry messages from air-traffic at Chiang Mai were waiting when they arrived. Senajai called them up and shouted and laughed and eventually smoothed some feathers.

Tavinor turned to Lynne as Senajai continued with the forms. "You have to get out," he said. "It's not your fight anymore. This is my fight. I'm one of the reasons Mat's in the shit. I was just too blind to see it."

He was staring at his cup when he spoke. It was a mistake. Only as he finished did he look up and see the fury in her eyes. It silenced him.

"Don't you dare tell me this isn't my fight. Mat is innocent, and you hired me to help prove his innocence. That's what I will do if it's possible." She stood up and walked round the room. "This is my fight. More than you realise." She shouted.

"You understand that. Look, OK, I understand you were trying to do the right thing. But believe me, I have skin in this game."

Senajai looked up, "I've got the invoice." Tavinor drew out his credit card. Senajai filled in another form. "Did you see those bastards at Chiang Mai? I guess one," he looked across at Lynne and laughed, "or both of you must have upset someone."

Tavinor asked. "You know anything about a regular flight from Chiang Mai to the UK carrying fruit and vegetables?"

"Sure," replied Senajai. "Global Harvest. Refrigerated cargo twice a week to East Midlands. I've done it a few times. Good business."

CHAPTER
TWENTY-FOUR

Lynne Kramer and Tavinor barely had time for a shower and a rapid change of clothes after rushing from Don Mueang airport to the hotel before they got a tuk-tuk across the city.

Keith Richard's bass line in "*Jumping Jack Flash*" hammered from the first floor of a club called *'The In and Out'*. The narrow neon-flamed street in Patpong throbbed with obtrusive and simulated desire; an alley was studded with young boys leaning against the wall in tight shorts; a small group of stunningly exquisite figures dressed in scanty red silk struck poses as they walked past.

"Ladyboys," said Lynne, waving them away.

Tavinor pushed aside a pimp asking if they wanted to come to a club. "No entrance fee. Plenty sex, you join in."

"Take it easy, Tony," said Lynne, taking his arm and leading him toward a street bar advertising Singha Beer on its wooden stools. A wide doorway opposite led into a club called "*Pussy Paradise*'".

Lynne went up and spoke to a doorman.

Darkness was broken by multi-coloured strobe lights

flashing in time with *"Satisfaction"*, definitely a Rolling Stones night, thought Tavinor as the doorman took them past a wide black wooden bar - in front of a wall of mirrors - on which about thirty girls - picked out by spotlights and wearing G-strings, minute bikini tops and numbers round their necks - moved suggestively toward the mass of tables hidden in the immediate gloom.

A figure in a Hawaiian shirt, who had long ago given up trying to contain his massive stomach, gave a slip to one of the waiters. A moment later, two girls came rushing over and sat at the table. They grabbed at thick thighs, laughing and kissing the man's cheek and rubbing his chest. A bottle of champagne, the cork removed, arrived at the table just after the girls arrived.

A German voice came from a figure pushing past them. He looked about fifty, a girl on each arm - both aged about four-teen. Tavinor watched as he barged through the club and into the street.

He cursed into the chaos.

Lynne sat at a round table, indicating that Tavinor should sit beside her.

"He's gone to get her."

She pointed to the doorman disappearing through a door in a rear corner. A waiter came to their table. Lynne spoke to him in Thai and pointed toward the door. The waiter moved away.

About ten minutes later, the door opened.

According to the note from Pa Sang - that Lynne had trans-lated - Buppa Suwanno was the Madame of the premises. She was dressed almost entirely in red. A bright silk red dress covered by a long red jacket trailed onto the floor with her neck swathed in a loose black scarf. A tiny red purse was balanced delicately on her wrist. As she emerged from the door, she stopped, took in what was happening and whispered to a tall, heavily built bouncer alongside her, who leaned down to listen. He turned and followed her finger, pointing to a table of four Japanese businessmen who sat with solemn propriety as they gazed at the girls on the bar. The bouncer called a waiter, who took a tray of beer to the table.

Eventually, her gaze fell on them. She didn't move as the scrutiny continued for over a minute before waving away the bouncer and coming toward their table.

Suspicion stained a bitter expression on a face coated in thick makeup, a mask concealing what would no longer be sold to the highest bidder. She stood beside the table. The voice was harsh. It was hard to hear her above the sound of yet another Rolling Stones number: *Brown Sugar*. He knew that although the lyrics were about slavery, the link to heroin was too strong, and he wondered whether the woman had asked for the number to be played as she sat at the table.

"You want Chris Ralston?"

Lynne answered. "Yes."

There was no response as the figure looked silently about the crowded club. Mick Jagger's voice spat into the expectant fantasy.

I'm no schoolboy, but I know what I like

You shoulda heard me just around midnight

"He's in danger. Two of his friends were killed," continued Lynne.

The song ended. A hand emerged from beneath the long red sleeves of the dress and waved away the explanation. Each finger carried at least a couple of gold rings. Her eyes turned to Tavinor. He felt the mistrust. It seeped from her pores. "Why you want him?"

'He's the only way we can find out what happened to our friend."

A young girl shrieked in false laughter and made a show of licking a grey-haired customer's ear. He pulled her closer, curling a hand around a breast.

"Mat Cooper. Dumb falang. That's what happened."

Tavinor fell silent with surprise.

Her eyes narrowed. "You think I don't know what the hell happening." She clapped, sat at the table and beckoned a waiter. A bottle of champagne was brought over. The cork had been removed. Three glasses.

"We think Chris may be with someone called Magach. You know him?" asked Lynne as Suwanno took a delicate sip from the glass.

"Good champagne, Mr Tavinor?" she asked, the smile signifying contempt. He sipped at his glass. Cheap, fizzy cider. He didn't reply.

She spat out a burst of Thai toward Lynne.

"She doesn't remember. It was too long ago."

He looked across. Her eyes were taunting him. He understood.

"How much?"

"Two thousand dollars," came the sharp response.

He placed his credit card on the table, his hand resting on a black American Express card. "Put it on that," he said.

Ring-encrusted fingers came across the stained wooden surface. Tavinor didn't move his hand. "What do I get for my money?"

"You get Magach," came the angry response as she pushed his hand away and lifted the card toward the bouncer, who rushed across the room and listened to the instructions.

Music hammered through the packed club as Tavinor looked around. Cider, the price of vintage champagne was drunk with angry realisation that the minimum price of satisfaction was humiliation. His fists clenched, and he accidentally knocked the table. Glasses smashed to the floor, the champagne bottle twisted round and round, and a patch of liquid grew on the stained wooden floor. A few pathetic bubbles made a forlorn effort. Faces turned toward them. The dancers on the bar momentarily ceased their writhing ersatz eroticism. His anger led nowhere. It was as absurd and hopeless as the expensive fake orgasms that the club could have added to the menu.

The bouncer stood with a slip of paper. He righted the table and wiped it dry. Suwanno placed one of the menus on the wooden surface and put the credit card slip on top. She held out a pen. He leaned over and signed the $2,000 voucher on the club's list of services.

Thai massage - oil - body to body - make you dreams cum true - high class models - special services ...

He turned away and shouted across the table whilst holding the voucher, refusing to hand it over. "Somewhere to talk. Not here."

Suwanno nodded and moved to a door in the corner of the club.

It led down a narrow corridor into a small room. In the hot and airless space, a bed covered in brightly covered cushions was pushed up against a wall. A bottle labelled *massage oil* stood on a table alongside a small black sofa.

Suwanno lay back on the bed. Pushing up the cushions, she leaned against the wall and held out her hand. Tavinor passed the voucher and sat on the sofa alongside Lynne. The bouncer waited at the door until Suwanno waved him away. The door closed, shutting out the frantic sounds. It was almost silent except for an air-conditioning unit cranking somewhere in another room. Lynne turned a switch by the door, and a ceiling fan stirred the stifling air. Tavinor wiped his forehead, sweat trickled down his spine.

"Magach was a bastard. Still is..." started Suwanno.

"I want to know where Chris Ralston is," interrupted Tavinor.

Suwanno looked at him through hooded eyes. She paused and waved the voucher at him. "I know what you want."

Tavinor sat back and waited.

"I got to know Magach sixty-seven. Here. In this room." She smiled. For a moment, the makeup cracked, and suspicion fell from her eyes. Tavinor saw her as one of the young girls dancing on the bar - laughing, hopeful, contemptuous of a future which promised nothing.

Suwanno continued. "He was one of the secrets. That's what we called them. They weren't the GIs in from Vietnam - they mostly scared young kids." She shrugged. "We helped them make journey to body bag a bit easier. The secrets were crazy bastards. From Lao. Didn't care if they lived or died as long as they had a pipe of opium, beer and fuck, and as many of each as possible."

"Where does Chris Ralston come in?" asked Tavinor.

She didn't answer immediately. When she looked up, she wiped away a tear carving through a dark line of mascara down her cheek. "Chuck Ralston, he save Magach. He was as close as anyone got to the bastard. They came through the war together and survived. Chuck married one of the girls from here. She made it. Got out..."

Lynne Kramer interrupted. "You knew her well?"

The smile was sad. "She was my sister."

"You were from Pa Sang?"

She nodded and continued. "Chuck got a job with US Government. Chris born eighty-one. Moved back to US for four years. Chuck with DEA. Came back to Chiang Mai. Murdered eighty-six."

"How?" Lynne's voice was sympathetic.

"Both shot leaving house Saturday morning. Chuck and my sister." She paused. Patting her forehead with a tissue. "I see Magach again at funeral. He said he owed Ralston and would look after boy. Chris went back to Pa Sang. Brought up by grandparents and friends." She looked crestfallen and gestured out of the door. "I couldn't have him here. Magach sent money ever since. To me. Every month, a bundle of cash delivered, he never missed. I know who from. I send it on to Pa Sang."

"Who shot them?" asked Tavinor.

Lynne asked quietly. "Chao Thanarat?"

"Of course. Fucking bastard," said Suwanno. "Chuck got too close to bastard."

Lynne continued. 'Where is Magach?' she asked.

"He love Lao. Last to leave when yanks quit in seventy-five. Moved across border to Udon Thani. Ended up in a village near Sangkhorn and Wat Hin Maek Peng on the Mekong. Used to sneak back to Lao across the river. Disappear into hills for months at a time. Still got Lao friends."

"So, he's back there now?"

"Now, Luang Prabang."

Suwanno reached into her bag and pulled out a well-worn photograph of three men. Tavinor could smell her perfume when she handed it over to him. He recognised Magach and Ralston from Aldrin's picture.

Lynne stared at it as though transfixed when he passed it over.

"What is it?" he asked.

The reply sounded like an echo of something important she alone could hear - but would not divulge. "They look so young," she eventually whispered. 'So young.'

There was a pause.

"Who's the other guy?" Tavinor asked.

Tavinor thought he heard Lynne whisper *'Edward'* as Suwanno answered.

"I only knew him as Ed. He was a good guy. Worked for Aid Agency in Xieng Khuang Province. Killed at Long Tieng."

'How did he die?' he asked.

Lynne turned away, staring at the photograph.

"Fucking bastard Chao shot him. That was the story."

She eventually took the photo from Lynne, who gave it up reluctantly, slid off the bed and made her way back to the bar.

They followed.

"I get you a drink," Suwanno said as she called over a waiter and shouted in Thai when they re-entered the bar. A table was cleaned, and a bottle of Johnny Walker was placed in the centre with three glasses. "Scottish Johnny Walker, not Bangkok Johnny Walker," she laughed and poured three glasses. As she spoke, and as the fierce liquid brought a bizarre respite to Tavinor's uncertainty. Suwanno let out a burst of Thai toward the bar. She lit a cigar and laughed while looking over at Tavinor.

He shook the thin hand, feeling the heavy rings scrape his skin as they left the club.

'What did she say?' asked Tavinor.

"Asked if we could tell her if we find the boy," said Lynne. Her voice was distracted. She didn't speak until reaching the hotel.

She looked at her watch. "It's three o'clock. I'm bloody tired. Let's get together for breakfast early tomorrow. There's a midday flight to Luang Prabang."

"The agency are meeting tomorrow morning with the driver who picked up the guy who came down from Chiang Mai after meeting Chao. I want to get over and meet up with him."

"OK," she yawned. "We'll sort it in the morning.

CHAPTER
TWENTY-FIVE

Dan had spent the journey to the unit in silence. He didn't know whether to tell Mat about Mayer, or that he may have agreed to bail without discussing it with his son, or to raise possibly false hopes about Chris Ralston.

He had no chance to speak. Mat was already in the meeting room. As they came in, he gave his father a hug and shook Nirundorn's hand. He looked between them.

"I've decided." He paused and looked between them. "I think I've decided. I am not taking this bail deal. It's corrupt and only means I serve a sentence somewhere out there," he waved toward the small window in the corner of the room, "instead of in either this or another stinking prison." He looked at his father. "This whole deal is bent." He leaned toward them. "I did not do this. Someone set me up. I have no idea how or why, but it happened, and I'm in here, and it's for you," he pointed to the two figures sitting silently, "to get me out."

Nirundorn started speaking. "Matthew, I beg you, I *can* get you out of here..."

Mat tried to interrupt, but Nirundorn raised his voice.

"No. No. You must listen to me. This is Thailand, and you are in the hands of police, the hands of Major Prisit, and the hands of a system that doesn't care about whether you are guilty or not, because you have been caught carrying heroin. Therefore, you are guilty, and I can't defend you. Your father can't defend you," he was almost shouting.

"Nobody can defend you. Take bail. Get out. Please," he subsided into his chair.

"Please, I beg you."

Mat looked toward Dan, who spoke softly. "I agree with Mr Nirundorn. Maybe it's time to end this any way we can."

They turned as the door opened. Prisit looked in, his eyes went from one to the other, and then, without speaking, he closed the door.

Nirundorn started again, his voice softer now. "Matthew. I believe you are not guilty. I have clients in Bangkwang the same. So, walk out of here. Out of Thailand. Forget Bangkok." He breathed in deeply and looked between them, his expression declaring that he had said everything that could be said.

Footsteps clattered by outside.

There was silence.

Dan suddenly realised he was holding his breath. Mat touched the bruise on his cheek. But then he seemed to summon all his strength. Eventually, he spoke. "I couldn't, though, could I? Not forget it. I'd be looking over my shoulder all the time."

"Better than life in Bangkwang..." started Nirundorn, but Mat interrupted.

"I understand. Perhaps I'm being stupid, but what sort of life would it be? Karen Sucher is on Interpol's top ten wanted list..."

Dan turned to Nirundorn. "Still? Is that right?"

"Perhaps. Possible, but not relevant."

"It is to me,' said Mat. 'One of the guys here told me." He shook his head. "I won't do it."

Nirundorn stood. He extended his hand to Mat. He looked defeated and didn't say a word as he left the small room.

"Here's the thing, Dad. I want to live my life. I don't want to spend my days skulking in the shadows, hoping nobody checks me out. That's not a life. I don't think I could do that. It's not who I am."

In retrospect, Dan wasn't sure why he told Mat about Mayer.

"You said you had no idea why it happened. Charles Mayer is why."

"What." Mat frowned in confusion. "Mayer. That banker. What the hell. The guy who was after you for a few million after the warehouse went up?"

"Yes."

"How?"

"We don't know. Tony Tavinor is trying to find out how it happened."

"Has Mayer got contacts out here? I mean Prisit, and all this comes at a price. So does taking my daypack apart and filling it with heroin." He put his hands on his head. "What's behind this, Dad? What have you got into?"

"I should have paid him."

"No, you fucking shouldn't," Mat paused. "Sorry, Dad. I didn't mean to swear, but how could it be right? Those land-mines were going to East Timor. From what I understand from Tony, they would have caused devastation and more suffering in a place that had already had enough of that. You did the right thing. Me being in here is not your fault. Look elsewhere for that. To Mayer, this guy Chao and whoever is behind it."

"You talked about filling your daypack. Tony and Lynne think they may have located the boy... "

"There were three of them."

Mat fell silent. There was no way he was telling Mat about the two boys murdered in Chiang Mai. How could Mat deal with that in this place? "They found one of them, you mentioned an Amerasian boy."

"Sure. I remember now, his name was Chris. I think he tried to warn me."

"We're hoping he could help."

"Hope," laughed Mat. "That's what we have, isn't it?"

The door banged. A guard looked round the door. "English. We go."

"Will you at least think about it?"

Mat nodded. "OK."

CHAPTER TWENTY-SIX

Tony Tavinor had left the hotel before Lynne had moved. He made his way to the agency when he got the call that the driver who had picked up Pollard from the airport a few weeks ago had eventually shown up. The man was nervous and looked ready to flee at any time. They agreed to pay him one thousand US dollars to take them to where he had dropped Pollard. His misgivings were understandable as Chao owned the vehicle agency he worked for, and he had found out that his passenger had met up with the drug dealer in Chiang Mai. Even after the money was handed over, he remained terrified. The name Chao inspired dread, and the driver, who was about twenty-five years old, was not immune to that fear.

One of the agency guys drove while Pollard's driver gave instructions in nervous staccato bursts of Thai punctuated by long silent spells staring through the windscreen, anxious shallow breaths coming as the road unfolded past the airport and then the Alpine Golf Club.

He asked the driver to slow down as they passed along a quiet two-lane road, occasional stalls lining one side of the highway with grebes pecking at the mud at the side of a narrow-disinterested river on the other side.

"There. Turn there."

The car turned down a narrow road that came to a dead end at a pair of elaborate electronic gates before the start of a long drive leading to a substantial property standing white and imperious in the middle of a wide expanse of dark green lawns. Tavinor could see a swimming pool protruding from the rear of the house and a large field with equestrian fences dotted about.

A high fence encompassed the estate on either side of the gates, securing land spread with an expanse of trees, partially obscuring the drive ahead.

Tavinor jumped from the car and made his way to the gate. He pressed a button on a keypad attached to the wall beside the gate. A call issued through a speaker. Nothing happened. He tried again. A voice answered in Thai.

"We need to speak to the owner of the property."

The line was disconnected without a word.

He asked the driver to come over. He shook his head. One of the agency guys came out. "I'll try. I speak Thai."

He pressed the keypad.

The call was answered, and a burst of Thai came over the speaker.

"There's no one here. I asked who lives at the house, but he cut the call. We'll check back at the office who owns the place, and we can come out here and ask the locals what they know."

"OK," said Tavinor. "I have to get back. Find out what you can. Watch the place in case someone shows up. I'll be back later."

* * *

Dan Cooper made his way into the lobby after returning from the unit. Lynne and Tavinor were waiting.

"Magach could be in Luang Prabang," said Tavinor without preliminaries.

"You know this, how?" asked Dan.

"It's complicated," said Tavinor.

"What isn't? So, tell me."

Tavinor ran through their trip to Chiang Mai, ending up at Patpong and Buppa Suwanno. He ended up saying he was going back to meet up with the agency guys waiting at the estate."

"Still no idea who lives there?"

Tavinor shook his head. "None of the locals has seen whoever it is, the windows of any car are blacked-out and there's often a police escort to discourage curiosity. It's owned by a trust based in Caymen with nominee trustees."

"So how would you identify whoever, it is even if they do show up?" asked Dan.

"The agency guys have got a lorry. They'll block the gate, say it's broken down. Force whoever it is out of the car rather than sit there for a few hours."

Lynne laughed, "And you think that will work."

Tavinor nodded. "They can't get a recovery truck in there. They'll just have to walk a few yards through the gate and get in a vehicle coming down the drive from the house. That's all we need."

"We need to get to Luang Prabang asap," snapped Lynne.

"I'll get back this evening."

"Where is Luang Prabang?" asked Dan

"On the Mekong about a thousand kilometres north of here. There's a flight at three this afternoon," said Lynne, "I need to move."

Dan gestured to the concierge and told him to get two seats

for himself and Ms Kramer for the three o'clock flight to Luang Prabang.

Tavinor shook his head. "It could be difficult. Even if you find Magach and the boy."

Dan stood. "The unit is closed for a couple of days. I'm going." He turned to Lynne as he got to his feet. "I'll get my stuff. We need to be off to the airport."

* * *

The plane banked over extravagant layers of rice paddies terracing down to a wide brown stain winding beyond the horizon.

"The Mekong," said Lynne, sitting in the seat in front of Dan, looking from the window of their small plane as it descended into Luang Prabang.

They descended the steps into blistering sunlight, across a deserted airfield to a modest white terminal. The formalities were mercifully smooth. An immigration officer even smiled when Dan wiped his forehead to clear the sweat breaking out in the heat.

The terminal was almost deserted apart from the ten other passengers who had left their plane. Most seemed to be locals and were picked up on mopeds or an occasional motorcycle bumping off down a dusty road. A couple of tuk-tuks remained. One of the drivers was fast asleep in the back of his vehicle, while the other driver came and took their bags.

"OK, where you go?"

Lynne checked in her bag. "Auberge Calao."

"OK."

"How much?"

Dan knew Lynne couldn't get in a vehicle without demanding the price.

"Ten thousand."

"How much?" Lynne seemed affronted.

"Ten thousand kip."

"How much is that?" asked Dan.

"OK," said Lynne. "About two dollars."

They set off down an empty road, leading over a wooden prefabricated bridge spanning a narrow river. They passed a few cyclists and one or two mopeds. A couple of children sat on a makeshift seat on a moped behind their parents. The children waved as the tuk-tuk passed the moped, Lynne waved back, and the children laughed.

Nothing much happened.

The road remained quiet. A small market down a side street tried to bustle. Temples shone down almost every dusty lane. Monks walked by in saffron robes, carrying black umbrellas to shield themselves from the sun. There were a few small shops, mostly deserted, and one or two cafés amongst distinguished buildings on wide avenues fringed with trees.

They pulled up outside a stunning mansion. A plaque by reception stated that it was built in the Nineteen-thirties and was occupied by a French merchant for many years before being restored in the early '80s.

Dan dumped his bags in a room overlooking the Mekong and came down to wait for Lynne at one of the tables in a terrace restaurant. She appeared and sat down after ordering two coffees.

"How the hell do we find him?" asked Dan. The coffee came in two glasses with thick milk at the bottom. "This coffee's good," he said.

"Some of the best coffee in the world, Lao coffee." She laughed. "I guess you know a bit about coffee. This was a French colony, remember. You can get baguettes and croissants up the road," she said, scooping a spoonful of the milk. He watched her quizzically. "Condensed milk. I love it."

"Good for your teeth, I guess," he laughed and did the same. "Delicious."

Lynne finished her coffee. "Look around."

The road was almost empty. Another sleeping tuk-tuk driver, two monks sitting on a wall talking, and an old woman passing by carrying a couple of bunches of bananas on a yoke across her shoulders.

"What do you mean?"

"You see any falangs?" She paused. "That's what they call pale people here. Like you."

A moped came slowly past. Two empty wooden boxes were strapped on the passenger seat. A boat meandered along the Mekong.

He didn't reply.

"They'll be a few backpackers about, but that's it."

"What are you saying?" he asked.

"Don't you get it? Your rules don't apply here. When and if Magach wants to find us, he finds us. He knows we're here."

"How?"

"If you have to ask, you don't understand this place." She smiled and turned her head in amusement. "The crazy son of a bitch belongs here. He has for the past thirty-odd years. You heard what Buppa Suwanno said. He can't keep away. Even before the borders re-opened, he was back in. This is his home. We've no standing here. We wait."

He leaned back and began to wait.

* * *

Waiting was the cruellest time.

Dan had another coffee with Lynne. She was heading out of town to Kuang Si Falls.

The sun hovered mercilessly above hills lining the valley. He walked slowly down a wide row of white steps leading to the Mekong, almost four hundred yards wide at that point. A dozen novice monks were swimming, laughing, and washing themselves in the brown water. Diving off the bottom step, they shouted, yelled, shampooed their hair, and cleaned their teeth whilst one of their group scrubbed a bucket of the distinctive robes before laying them on the steps in a patch of bright saffron.

A long boat came quietly along the river, the boatman sitting in front of the narrow structure as it cut through the waters, making slow progress upstream, the river piercing a range of dark hills fading beyond a distant horizon.

Along the river, several fragile craft floated with the current, fishermen lying on their decks holding lines thrown into the water, waiting for a bite.

He would wait.

Magach would contact him when ready.

So he had been told.

He walked along the riverbank, trying to calm the impatience that ate into him. Pausing, he looked at the waters flowing through wild swathes of deep green vegetation hanging over the rushing brown current. An older woman stopped and brought her hands together in front of her face. He returned the gesture. Deep lines illuminated the shy, smiling face shielded by thin fingers. The road was completely silent, a child played along the path, flicking a towel toward a group of scraggy chickens. They darted away and then returned, unconcerned, pecking again at the barren soil.

Nothing happened.

He waited.

He walked into one of Luang Prabang's many Temples. Entering the Sim - which Lynne had told him meant something like Chapel, he encountered another world, another age. Elaborate golden Buddhas dominated the front part of the building. A wooden roof came down to the floor, where it met with a world of golden pictures on ebony walls. Pillars decorated in golden patterns on a red background dominated the centre of the building. It was a glimpse of something timeless. The patterns and beauty mocked any arrogance. Two fans stirred the desperate humidity. Sweat soaked his body. A saffron-robed monk moved slowly past one of the doors - a cockerel crowed in the grounds outside, and children shouted somewhere unseen.

A young novice monk about Mat's age unwrapped some incense sticks and lit two enormous candles - he turned to Dan and smiled, head shaved, robe thrown carelessly about his shoulders, before leaving him again to silence and desperate expectation.

He left and walked slowly along the main street of Luang Prabang. Quiet. Almost empty. Signs in shop windows:

Fruit shake 5000 kip
Croissants
Coffee Lao

Time passed.

As he reached the road leading back to the hotel, a line of about twenty monks turned from a Temple, each carrying a silver bowl slung over his shoulder, except for one older monk who could barely walk. He supported himself by hanging onto the shoulder of a younger monk. The line moved at the shuffling pace of the elder figure. There was no impatience, just a calm acceptance. He waited as the line wound past him until the older monk came alongside. The line stopped. Total silence gripped the scene - apart from the noise of the rushing river. An ancient, lined face turned to Dan.

The eyes of the monk looked into him in the silence. Dan tried to hold the eyes. The compassion he felt almost lost him. He switched his gaze in a desperate escape. The other monks looked directly ahead, not one of them catching his eye.

He remembered Lynne's comment.

Death is a mirror in which the whole of your life is reflected.

It was his own life reflected in the calm eyes which seemed to be drawing him ever deeper.

A time-worn hand. Veins standing proud on thin skin came from the saffron robe. It gripped Dan's arm, the hold stronger than expected, and then gestured toward a tuk-tuk driver waiting at the end of the street, revving his noisy lawnmower engine, blue smoke streaming from the exhaust. The monk bowed his head, and the line shuffled away.

Dan waited for a moment, then moved across and clambered onto the shiny, plastic-covered seat.

They took off without a word.

The driver didn't look behind him as he drove one-handed, sipping from a battered bottle of water, shouting with laughter at friends as he passed them on the quiet pot-holed road from Luang Prabang. After about fifteen minutes, they passed a blue sign reading *Ban Pong Vane* and started into a small village. Houses perched on stilts, children playing on mats in the shadows beneath the floors, chickens pecking at the barren ground searching for food. A woman peeling the skin of an onion looked over as the tuk-tuk came to a halt. The driver gestured to a house just off the dusty track which passed through the small village. It was made of interwoven bamboo with a patched dry-grass roof. Paddy fields crept close to its dark wooden stilts. A woman planting rice bent over in knee-deep water. He looked back at the driver, turning round and heading back to Luang Prabang. A burst of laughter came as he gestured for Dan to go up the steps at the side of the house.

Wooden steps led onto a veranda overlooking fields fringed by tree-covered hills. Chairs were scattered about a large wooden table. The chairs were empty. It was silent. He sat down and tried to catch his breath in the airless humidity, sweat clinging to his forehead, shirt sticking to his back. He flicked at an insect trying to land on his face, a tiny gecko rushed across the floor, stopping by one of the legs of the table.

A footstep sounded from inside a door leading from the veranda. Voices, whispering behind the bamboo wall, were almost lost as a cockerel screamed into the languid midday humidity.

The door creaked.

The gecko darted across the room, disappearing through a gap in the floor.

An extraordinary apparition emerged as the door creaked open. Dan instinctively moved his chair away from the table, ready for flight.

He was about six foot six tall, pencil-thin, a face criss-crossed with deep scars cutting through unnaturally white skin, eyes obscured with thick dark lenses. A crop of pure white hair was drawn so tightly into a ponytail that the skin seemed to be stretched into a death mask, dominated by a hawk-like nose standing proud and defiant.

A mumble emerged that Dan didn't understand.

The tall figure pulled up a chair and slumped down. Thin legs emerged from a dirty red sarong, words emphasised by long, bony fingers protruding from the fraying sleeves of a once-white shirt.

He ripped off the sunglasses. Dan felt the force of cold, pale, liquid blue eyes.

"What do you want, Mr Cooper?" The accent was American.

"Magach?"

A nod.

"You've got Chris Ralston with you. I want to know what happened with my son."

A grunt came as a response. The long figure leaned back. It seemed certain the chair would fall backwards as he looked toward the sky. "Why should I care what you want?"

"My son has been set up. He's innocent and could spend the rest of his life in prison."

The chair banged down. Magach leaned across the table. "Wrong answer, Mr Cooper. Your son is your fucking responsibility. Not mine." He replaced the sunglasses.

But he stayed.

"Yet here I am." Dan felt a perverted power in the demanding expression. Magach wanted something as much as he did.

"Chuck Ralston saved your life."

There was no answer. No denial.

"So, we both need to save our children." A thin smile broke out on the lean features as Dan continued. "Chao will kill Chris if he stays in Laos or Thailand. Like the two boys that worked with him at the Siam Paradise. The reason you dragged him away from that place. How long can you protect him here?"

Magach leaned down and banged his fist on the floor without taking his eyes from Dan. The door opened to Chris Ralston, stocky, dark-haired, and scared.

"Tell him," ordered Magach as Ralston perched uncomfortably on the edge of a chair.

The voice was quiet and fraught with shame. Chris Ralston stared at the floor. "We were given the photograph, and he told us which train he would be on. We were to offer him the best room at half-price. We didn't know why. I saw him around the hotel with his girlfriend. He was a nice guy. I liked him. We played chess. Then, we were ordered to pack his bag. I refused. I was told I'd be cut if I didn't do it and that it was only to scare him. He would be let go once everything was worked out. I wanted to tell Mat, but they watched me all morning. He was out all night, and I tried to warn him when he returned. I couldn't believe they'd go through with it."

"What do you mean, "once everything was worked out."'

"The army guy and the prison creep. That's all I know. They were at the hotel before."

"Who, Kumat?" came Dan's angry voice. He was incredulous, "and Prisit? "

"I think that was their names."

He looked at Magach. "They work for Chao?"

"Sometimes. I guess," grunted Magach. "Kumat knows him well enough. Prisit is available If the money is right."

'You know why it was done?' asked Dan.

Ralston looked at the floor. He shook his head. "I knew it was wrong."

Magach snapped his fingers. "So, now you know. What difference does it make?"

Dan looked at Chris Ralston. "Will you give evidence in court?"

Magach answered. "Will he commit suicide? You think Chao would let him live long enough to get in the witness box, and, if he did, how long would he survive afterwards?"

Dan stood up and walked to the edge of the veranda. The woman was still bent double, making a slow path through the water, planting rice at regular intervals. He turned and remembered what Lynne had said. "OK. I would never have found you. You sent for me. So, what's the deal."

Magach jerked his head toward the bedroom. Ralston

moved silently through the door. "I doubt his evidence would be enough to get your son off."

Dan nodded toward the door. 'He's all I've got. At the moment."

"Why Chao? Why is he involved? You're in deep waters." Magach leaned back again and put the dark glasses back on. "Too deep for you, perhaps." His fingers rapped on the table. "I don't want to back the wrong horse."

The silence deepened. Dan eventually spoke. Softly. "How long can you protect..." He gestured to the door. "I presume you're OK here." He looked about the quiet village. "I guess you have protection. But how long will he stay? What is it you want?"

"Who's the judge?"

"Vyraj."

Magach paused. "He's honest. You could do a lot worse. Chris will give evidence if he can get out of Thailand immediately afterwards. He's got an American passport."

"How much?"

"One hundred thousand dollars will set him up and give him a life in the US. You transfer it as soon as we make Bangkok. Say nothing to him. Not until later. I control his security *if* we make it to Bangkok and until your son is released, or he is convicted. There are no guarantees in this. If," he gestured toward the bedroom, "his evidence is probably not enough, that's your problem. They've offered you the bail option?"

Dan agreed.

"Then why not take it? He walks."

"Mat has refused. So far."

Magach raised his eyebrows, "Gutsy." He shrugged, "dumb."

"What about you?" asked Dan.

"I don't need money. I've got all I want here, and it's too late for me to return to the States."

"Is there any evidence?"

"He took some stuff from the hotel. There's the photograph of your son used at the station; the details of the train he would be on; copies of his ticket to Vientiane and the false price at the hotel," came the answer.

"It's not much."

Magach gave a dismissive gesture. "If you had anything else, you wouldn't be here." He lurched to his feet and pushed his way back through the door. Dan saw Chris Ralston lying on a wood-framed bed, leaning on his elbow before the door slammed.

Magach's voice filtered through bamboo walls.

A water buffalo sauntered past the house. Two small children ran behind it, tapping its flanks with twigs. A moped threw up a plume of dust as it sped by carrying three young women who shouted at the children and taunted the water buffalo.

The door banged open again.

Nobody emerged.

The gecko sprinted back across the wooden floor.

Magach appeared.

His voice was clear and intimidating.

"We leave for Vientiane tomorrow and from there to Bangkok. Be ready at dawn, I'll pick you up. I'm not risking the airport. Chao will have it covered by now. I've got friends in villages on the way. I'll make the arrangements. Bring your woman, she's got some legal training. She can take the statement." He moved closer to Dan, so close that he could taste the intensity, staring into his eyes. His breath smelled of smoke. "You renege on this deal, and I kill you and your son." He paused and looked over the paddy fields.

"You said if we can get to Bangkok?"

"Chao will know. They'll be obstacles."

The door banged shut again.

Dan wasn't sure whether to be elated or terrified. He settled for both and stopped the driver of a motorbike and sidecar. They bumped along the road back to Luang Prabang.

He rushed up the steps to the hotel and then stopped, remembering Lynne had decided to leave the city until the afternoon. She was at the Kuang Si Falls, about thirty kilometres from the town. The driver who had just dropped him off was sitting on a wall by the river, talking with one of the boatmen.

He gave him a shout.

They bumped off down the road again.

The narrow, dusty road left all traces of Luang Prabang behind as it crept up into hills carpeted with impenetrable dark-green forests rolling beyond the horizon. An occasional solitary figure would wave as they passed in a cloud of dust, the motorbike engine straining as it laboured up steady inclines. After about thirty minutes, they came to a small village. The driver indicated that the engine was too hot. Wooden huts with dried palm roofs squatted in the bare earth. They pulled up. Two children with wide smiles came running across. They stood beside the motorcycle before the driver dismounted and accompanied them into the village. He turned and beckoned Dan to follow along a dried-up track as he started talking with a woman who came from one of the huts wearing a dark purple sarong draped around her heavy body. Dan looked inside the small shelter. A couple of mattresses on rough wooden frames were perched on the compacted earth alongside a large table piled with clothes, glasses and bowls. He turned away as the woman emerged with a wooden chair and asked him to sit as the children came over, each carrying a glass. One glass was passed to Dan, the other to the driver. Two more women emerged from behind the huts. They smiled as Dan looked suspiciously at the pale liquid. The driver nodded his encouragement.

"Lào-Láo," he said, as though it should mean something to Dan. "Rice."

Dan got the picture and followed the driver's example in taking the measure in one gulp. A fierce heat enveloped his throat, and he coughed. The women gently laughed behind their hands, turning away from Dan. The driver clapped with pleasure as the children stood in front of him with wide smiles on their faces.

"OK," said the driver and marched back to the motorbike. He held his hand against the engine and gave the thumbs-up signal to Dan, who reached into his pocket and brought out some Laotian money. The little group that had silently followed them to the road turned away.

"No." The driver muttered and shook his head.

Dan felt diminished. He instinctively turned and brought his hands together in front of his face. The women returned the gesture. The driver nodded and kick-started the motorcycle into life.

The remainder of the journey skirted round slopes, passing through occasional paddy fields - water buffalo struggling through waist-high water hauling wooden ploughs across terraces trailing down at harsh angles - small villages floating in a hazy distant backdrop.

Eventually, they slowed down on reaching a gate alongside a small hut inside, which had a few tables scattered about - an elephant tethered to a tree looked bored with life. The driver pointed along a path which ran beyond the locked gate. "Falls," he said.

Dan reached into his pocket.

"No. I wait," said the driver, sitting at one of the tables.

After about five minutes, as he walked round a bend, roaring water suddenly cut off all other sounds. Tables were spread in front of a few rough kiosks selling drinks and packets of sweets. A young girl smiled from one of the tables as she leaned her chin on her hand and watched his progress.

A couple laughed as they floated in a pool of bright turquoise waters, sheltered from the bright sun by thick lotus trees. He gasped as he came into a clearing just beyond the pool and saw water crashing down limestone tiers which stretched as high as he could follow the fierce flow before it passed from sight into forests high above, from where the falls emanated.

Lynne was nowhere to be seen. He crossed a narrow bridge spanning another pool formed at the bottom of the falls. The roaring crescendo was exhilarating as he took the trail leading up the side of the waters, the effervescent spray spinning a damp web in the bright sunlight, suddenly throwing a rainbow across one of the tiers, brushing two trees clinging at bizarre angles on the rock face. He stared in astonishment at the colours shining with intense clarity through the dark green habitat. Dragging himself away, his feet began to slip on the damp slope as it rose alongside the incessant cascade until a curve in the path brought him beside another small pool sheltering under an enormous overhanging rock. He continued toward another tier, clinging onto trees and bushes beside the rough, sodden trail. The light was reduced by a burgeoning ceiling of branches and leaves high above the trees. As he turned another corner, the trail narrowed with a steep bank on one side and a broken fence on the other. He clung to broken fence posts until the path came to a dead-end, and in front lay another larger pool into which the ferocious cataract smashed down into the centre of the bright waters.

Lynne was shouting and yelling with pleasure as she stood beside the gushing water, occasionally dipping her head into the flow and throwing back her head in delight. She was wearing a t-shirt which clung to her tight body. She looked over and saw him staring.

"Come on."

Dan smiled. He stripped off most of his clothes and pushed them into a crevice by a rock in the bank before easing his way across a narrow boulder slippery with spray thrown out from the waterfall. A tree had somehow bent its branches into a protective barrier around the fall. As the sound of the plunging water rose to a crescendo, he grabbed the damp wood and eased his way beneath the cascading flow. He shouted with a mixture of excitement and fear. The sound was lost, water hammering onto rocks a few inches from his head, leaping into a fine spray, showering his almost naked body. He turned his face to the flow, feeling a cold shock as the remorseless torrent scoured his flesh. Closing his eyes, he was lost until a hand grabbed him and pulled him into the pool. Lynne's face came through the mayhem, her voice lingering amongst the fierce nature washing over him. Her dark hair was plastered to the side of her head, white teeth shining in pleasure.

"I've seen Magach," he screamed.

Her eyes were wide in shock. "And?" she yelled.

"We have the third boy, Chris Ralston is with him. He'll give evidence. If we can get him to Bangkok."

"We will," she shouted, touching his hand before moving quickly away.

He didn't move. Water hammered down beside him, spray enveloped him, and desire subsumed him. Their eyes caught. Lynne shook her head. She pursed her lips as though in sorrow.

"Another time," the comment was almost swallowed in the crashing water.

He gasped as he lifted his head into the relentless surge.

They didn't speak as they eventually waded through the water and pulled clothes over their wet, warm bodies before slipping down the slope and ending up at one of the tables by the food kiosk. The little girl who had smiled at Dan as he made his way toward the falls brought them each a cold Coke.

"Dan." Lynne stared down at the table. She looked up, her face determined. "We can't carry any baggage. You can't worry about me." A smile came like the sun breaking through. "My Dad took me to the Ton Te Falls down toward the Malaysian border just before he died. I can remember them now. I was so scared, but they were just too beautiful."

"You must have been young?"

"Nine. We went back to the States the next year."

"But you still remember?"

She pursed her lips. "We carry our memories around with us. They damn us and inspire us." She shook her head as though shrugging the thoughts away. "'Tell me about Magach."

Dan replayed the meeting with Magach and Chris Ralston. "He doesn't think it'll be enough."

"It's better than anything else we've got," said Lynne. "And it confirms that Mat was set up and who was involved. Mat's hesitation about bail wasn't expected. They're flying blind. You have to move carefully. Nobody's thought it through beyond the bail option. So, who did set it up?"

Dan shook his head. "That's what I have to find out. Let's get back; we're leaving for Vientiane first thing. There's a motorbike waiting at the gate."

CHAPTER TWENTY-SEVEN

The sun was peering through the mist, blanketing the hills behind the hotel as Dan Cooper walked along a path overlooking the Mekong. A line of monks moved silently away from the Temple, silver bowls hanging from their shoulders. They paused as a woman came alongside and emptied rice from a cellophane packet into one of the bowls. The line started up again, turning a corner, moving from sight.

A grey minibus swung into the road. Dan looked over at Lynne, sitting alongside their bags on the steps leading down from the hotel. Even after yesterday - especially after yesterday - she was still a mystery to him despite their time together. She smiled across at him as the minibus made its way slowly along the road, throwing up traces of dust. The sun began to burn its way into the quiet stillness. Her gentle expression hid more than it revealed, her wide brown eyes concealing a sadness she would not explain. A pair of light blue trousers and a white tee-shirt emphasised the soft olive tone of her precise features. A multi-coloured shoulder bag she had bought in Luang Prabang lay on her lap.

The minivan came between them.

He breathed deeply and started back to the hotel.

Lynne threw their bags into the back of the vehicle. Magach drove alongside Chris Ralston whilst Dan sat beside Lynne on the second of three rows of seats, his feet resting on one of four sacks of rice. They set off as soon as the door closed.

"Chris will come into the back later. Can you take his statement?" shouted Magach as they bumped between market stalls lining the side of the rough road.

Lynne stared at the back of Magach's head. She didn't answer.

"Miss Kramer, isn't it? The lawyer's meeting us if we get as far as Bangkok?" he asked Dan, who confirmed that Nirundorn would be at the Shangri-La.

Lynne leaned forward close to Magach. "You're right. It is Miss Kramer. But you know that, don't you. I'm sure your memory is good enough."

She paused. He didn't respond as she continued. "We'll be on the road for about eight hours?"

Magach nodded.

She turned to Chris. "We'll make a start on your statement in about an hour."

Dark hills were silhouetted against the bright sunlit sky, clouds resting on crests as the road rose and fell in a flamboyant series of switchbacks, from dramatic peaks down to deep green valleys. Magach let out a continual series of unintelligible profanities at the few vehicles they passed and at animals wandering along the narrow, pot-holed road. They swept through the occasional small village, bamboo houses resting on tall stilts. In the valleys, the rice paddies stretched across to foothills. Water buffalo fought through thigh-high mud, dragging ploughs behind them to prepare fields for rice planting. Other fields were bright, shining vivid green where the rice harvest was already poking its way toward the sun. Villagers struggled through knee-deep water, weeding between the precious life-giving crop. Magach levelled another volley of abuse at a secret target as they came up behind an old lorry with two lines of seats tacked onto the rear. The seats and floor were packed with passengers squeezing into every available space. The roof was piled high with luggage tied down under a tarpaulin, and two young faces peered out from under the tarp. They smiled and waved at the minibus. Magach cursed and waved back.

The bus struggled up a winding slope into a village. A small group of villagers dressed in black outfits with colourful waistbands waited at the side of the road. Three little girls, wearing headdresses made up of brightly painted beads, played in the dust. The bus stopped momentarily, the driver shouting through the door before rolling forward again with a flurry of dust and a crashing of gears, leaving the villagers by the side of the road.

Magach pulled over. He gestured for Chris to sit with Lynne and asked Dan to join him in the front. He then got out and opened the rear door, indicating that the villagers who hadn't been able to get on the crowded bus should squeeze into the back seat and the luggage space. Dan stared in amazement as four adults, three children, a few sacks of rice, a couple of bags of cucumbers and a box of corn crammed into the small space at the rear of the vehicle. Magach spoke in Lao, and the group burst into laughter as he returned to the driving seat and pulled away without saying another word.

They set off again. A slow haul up hills, then speeding down into valleys. An excited murmur broke out from the children as they overtook the packed bus, crawling through a village clinging dramatically to the side of a hillside, dropping almost vertically into a steep valley. A waterfall crashed down the opposite slope. Magach pulled up in the next village. He shouted to an old man dressed totally in black who walked across and greeted the American, hands closed together, a gentle smile on his brown wrinkled face. Magach slid open the side door and threw out the four bags of rice. Almost twenty children appeared from beneath the houses where they had been playing, and a group of villagers moved closer to the van. The children grabbed at Magach while he struggled to unload the last two sacks, leaving most locals still packed in the rear of the vehicle. He cursed and laughed as the screaming children clung to his arms. Suddenly, he waved his arms and lifted one little girl above his head. Dan smiled at the terrified and delighted face, shouting with pleasure, pulling at Magach's ponytail whilst the rest of the children clung to his baggy black trousers. The elderly man spoke quietly, and the children immediately fell back as Magach leaned close and muttered in his ear.

They shook hands. Magach returned to the van and drove slowly, waving through the window to villagers who returned the gesture. The children ran screaming alongside the van until it pulled clear of the small group, waving frantically as the vehicle disappeared round a corner, ascending a steep slope above clouds spread across the valley floor far below them.

"Nobody will get past the village if they're not friendly," Magach murmured to Dan as the minibus picked up speed upon hitting the valley floor, where they made steady progress for almost an hour. There was a steady murmuring from the locals crammed into the rear of the van as Lynne sat with a notepad whilst Chris quietly related what happened with Mat. Dan tried to overhear, but the words were lost in the straining of the engine.

The road was virtually deserted, apart from a few cows being pushed slowly along in the oppressive heat. Occasionally, a moped would pass by, and a couple of lorries came in the opposite direction.

Just beyond a bridge spanning a river tumbling down from the hills, they pulled up by a small store built primarily of corrugated iron alongside which a small cafe had spread its chairs and tables beside the dusty street. Dan jumped down, and the back of the minivan emptied with gestures of thanks to Magach.

One or two diners looked up from bowls of noodles and rice as Magach shouted in anger whilst stooping down to listen to a barefooted, toothless old man dressed in a cut-off pair of denim shorts and a stained t-shirt with the logo: *'Its the real thing'* emblazoned across the front. Magach took a banana from one of the tables and shoved it into his pocket before gesturing to Dan. Lynne joined them as she emerged from the rear of the cafe.

"There's trouble ahead. The road's blocked by Chao's goons."

A battered taxi came from behind the café. Four men emerged. Magach moved across and spoke quietly. He came back to Dan. "Five hundred dollars." He held out his hand.

Dan was well prepared. He moved to the van, extracted the cash from his holdall, and handed it to Magach.

"They'll clear the road. I'm too old to fight."

They drove for about four miles, the taxi bringing up the rear, before stopping just after a trail led off the right-hand side of the road and across a small hill.

Magach opened his door, "Wait for thirty minutes," he said to Dan and Lynne, pointing at Chris. "He may be your son's escape route." Delving into a battered suitcase under the driver's seat, he pulled out two handguns. "I suggest you keep him safe."

"I thought you said you were too old."

"To fight, not to watch," said Magach as he joined the four men on the trail leading over the hill.

"You know how to use that?" asked Lynne.

"I was in the army, territorials. And you?"

She snorted in contempt and didn't bother to reply.

He pulled out the magazine, checked it was loaded, and, sliding it together again, released the barrel and slipped off the safety.

"Nice. A browning nine millimetre."

Lynne replicated his actions.

'FBI?' said Dan, watching.

"Police, San Diego." She replied and turned to Chris. "Get in the back seat and keep well down."

Nobody spoke. Dan kept an eye on his watch as he felt Lynne's hand slip into his. They didn't look at each other as he held onto her. He was in a crazy dream, only one scene of which he wanted to bring to an end. The remaining sequences were too full of beauty, where senses he had almost forgotten had sprung into extravagant life.

After thirty minutes, Lynne started the engine. They passed a series of paddy fields before the road rose a steep incline. They completed a fierce U-turn, approaching a small village on the other side of the hill over which Magach had started. A river ran alongside the village in a series of small rapids, white water crashing over rocks, directed at intervals into the paddy field's intricate irrigation system. They lost sight of the village again as the road took another sharp turn over a bridge, crossing the tumbling river. Exiting a final corner, Lynne slammed on the brakes and skidded to a halt at a dead cow lying in the centre of the road.

A black 4WD Toyota waited on the other side of the lifeless animal. Two figures posed on either side of the vehicle. Dan recognised the waiter from the Siam Paradise. The man waved contemptuously and laughed as he turned to his three colleagues. They moved forward, each holding an AK47, pointing directly toward their stationary vehicle.

“Get down,” shouted Lynne as a volley of shots rang out across the valley, the sounds bouncing around the empty landscape.

Dan looked up cautiously, just as Lynne did the same.

Magach emerged from thick scrub at the side of the road. An Uzi machine pistol hung from his hand as he moved to Toyota and leaned on the bonnet. The men from the taxi followed. Four bodies lay just beyond the animal in the road. They were thrown into the black 4x4, while the cow was dragged to the side of the road as Magach signalled for one of them to drive the Toyota back the way they had come. He shouted instructions in Thai.

“He’s told them to take the car back toward the village, torch it and dump it down one of the hills with the bodies inside,” said Lynne as Chris Ralston emerged slowly from the floor behind them.

Magach peeled a banana and slowly ate the flesh

“Let’s go,” said Magach, throwing the banana skin into the river. “They won’t try again. Not yet, anyway. There’s a plane waiting at Vientiane to get us to Bangkok.”

CHAPTER TWENTY-EIGHT

The evening had arrived when they made it back from Vientiane. Nirundorn was waiting in the lobby and accompanied them to Dan's suite and he handed a document to Nirundorn.

Magach sprawled full length on one of the two sofas. His eyes were closed.

"This is Chris Ralston. It's his statement," said Dan, gesturing toward Chris Ralston, who was staring from the window, before moving away to the dining area with Lynne.

Tavinor was still with the agency guys waiting at the house the driver had identified. The owner hadn't showed yet.

The lawyer's smile broke out as he shook hands with Ralston. He then sat in one of the chairs scattered about the lounge. The solicitor stared at Ralston for a few minutes before he turned to the statement. Sitting stock-still, he read through the pages, pausing twice to scrutinise the evidence attached to the statement.

Nobody spoke. Dan could barely take the tension as, eventually, Nirundorn looked up when he finished reading. He stood and walked to the window alongside Ralston before returning to the chair to read from the first page again.

Finally, he placed the papers on the small table alongside his chair and turned to Chris Ralston, who hadn't moved.

"You are Christopher Ralston?"

The boy turned and nodded as Nirundorn indicated for him to sit on the sofa alongside his chair.

"This is your statement?"

Ralston nodded.

"Is it the truth?"

Chris Ralston nodded again.

"I see. So, you were given heroin and told to unstitch and refill a daypack with heroin."

"Yes."

"Did you know whose backpack it was?"

He nodded.

"Answer me, please."

"Yes. It was the English boy. Cooper."

"I see," Nirundorn waited. He remained silent.

Dan had moved back into the room. He started to speak, but Nirundorn waved him to silence.

Ralston began again. His voice was shameful. "I had no choice. He would have killed me."

"Who?"

"The manager - Makok. I protested. He held a knife to my throat."

"You were on your own?"

He shook his head. Nirundorn raised his eyebrows.

"There were three of us and two of the guards as well. We were scared. We knew what would happen."

Nirundorn waited before he spoke. "What would happen?"

"We had to do what we were told."

"What would happen?"

Ralston's voice rose. "You know what happened even though we did as we were ordered. They didn't want any witnesses." He held his head in his hands. "Suchinda and Arthit were killed in Chiang Mai."

"Who are they?"

Ralston looked about, and then Magach. "It's in the statement. Chao Thanarat owns the hotel, and Makok managed it."

"Thank you." Nirundorn stood and then turned back to Ralston.

"How much are you being paid to give this statement?"

The boy looked confused and then angry. "I'm telling the truth. I don't need to get paid to tell the truth."

Cooper looked across at Magach. The man's eyes remained closed. He didn't even seem to have heard the exchange.

Nirundorn turned to Dan, who asked. "You suppose it's enough?"

Nirundorn didn't answer. He walked over to the window and looked over the river.

"It's not just the statement there's the evidence," said Dan. "The photograph of Mat handed over by Makok; the details of the train he would be on; copies of his ticket to Vientiane and the false price at the hotel. All of these back up the statement.'

The lawyer let out a nervous laugh. "It is an interesting statement."

"Interesting!" echoed Dan.

Nirundorn continued. "What does the judge make of it? That's what we need to consider. Judge Vyraj is a very fair man. An honourable man. That's our advantage. However, it means he has to be convinced by the strength of our arguments and the evidence we present."

He placed the various pieces of evidence on the table in front of him.

"Mr Makok threatened the boy. I understand he is employed by Chao Thanarat. Is that correct?"

"Yes."

"What happened to the two boys?"

"They were murdered just outside Chiang Mai," said Dan.

Nirundorn looked toward Lynne. "Is that the conclusion of the police?"

"No. It's being treated as a traffic accident," answered Lynne.

"Yes," said Nirundorn.

Lynne raised her eyebrows and shook her head.

Nirundorn looked up from his notebook. "Let me see. We have Mr Chris' statement." His expression as he glanced around the room was sceptical. "An air ticket, a photograph, some details of a hotel room." He moved to the window before turning round. "You will forgive me." He turned to Dan. "Your son would still have difficulties."

He picked up his notebook. "Where is Makok?"

Magach grunted, "Not available."

Dan frowned as Magach looked away.

Nirundorn continued. "The boys were not murdered as far as the police are concerned. What is the judge to make of this statement? He is from Bangkok. He may have doubts, but he is a judge, and he decides based on evidence. The facts available to him are the heroin and the possession. The statement is persuasive and helpful but not sufficient on its own. I go to court with Mr. Chris and this evidence, the statement, and I think Matthew has a chance, but," he took Dan's arm and led him to the window. "I think he is found guilty."

He turned to Dan. "I do not understand what has happened, and I am certain of Matthew's innocence, but I am also certain that," he hesitated, "'should he go to trial then..." he paused and looked back at the statement on the table, "he would be found guilty, and he will be sent to Bangkwang for most of his life."

The lawyer paused. Dan felt the hope and expectancy of the last few days fall away. He had deluded himself to survive. He had indulged himself.

Nirundorn spoke again, his voice softer. "It will help. It is not enough. I will use Mr Chris as a witness." He fell silent. Dan felt his intense gaze.

Nirundorn moved through the room and looked across at Chris Ralston.

"More important. You realise that Chao Thanarat will hear about this statement when I deliver it to the Judge's office. You understand me?"

Dan frowned.

Nirundorn made his way toward the door. "Don't underestimate the resources that Chao Thanarat can call upon. That would almost certainly, be a fatal mistake. If there is no defendant, there is no trial, no statement and no witness. Chao would not be named."

"What do you mean," said Dan. "You think Mat could be at risk."

"Of course, he is at risk, as I said. No defendant, no trial, no statement."

"Can you hold on to that statement until tomorrow," asked Dan.

"Of course. I will release the statement to the court when you advise."

Dan moved to his bedroom. "Please wait a few minutes." He moved into his bedroom, took a notebook from beside his bed and began to write. Ten minutes later, he re-emerged into the lounge.

"I intend to make clear that even if there is no trial, what has happened to Mat will not be swept under the carpet. I want to find out what happened. How Mayer set it up. Everyone involved. If this goes through, it's not the end of it. If it's Chao Thanarat or Mayer, I don't care. I'm going after whoever set my son up."

"What do you propose."

He held up the note he had written. "A press conference and press release stating that Mat is an innocent victim of Thailand's corrupt collaboration between major drug dealers and the police and the failure of the British Embassy to give any support. I will name Chao, Kumat, Prisit, the Ambassador and Fairbrother at the Embassy."

He gave the note to Nirundorn. Who read it before looking at Dan. "This is dangerous, Mr Cooper."

"I hope so. My son is already in danger."

"What help would it be to hold such a press conference before the judicial process is completed."

"A process you say will lead to his conviction and a lifetime in prison."

"There is an alternative."

"The bail option? He has already rejected that."

Nirundorn walked to the window. He stood alongside Lynne Kramer, who had remained silent.

"If you threaten this action, you will become a target."

"That is the point."

Nirundorn held up the statement. "This is a threat to Chao. It would be public shaming. Humiliation. He will demand that you and Mat are eliminated to resolve that humiliation."

He paused and handed the handwritten copy of the press release back to Dan. "When this is released, both you and Mat are at risk – Mat will no longer be the primary enemy, but you will be."

Dan nodded and smiled.

"OK, Mr Cooper. I prepare for trial. We have Mr Ralston's statement and the exhibits. I need to speak with Matthew again and take his statement for the court."

He looked across the suite to Magach.

"I suggest you keep Mr. Chris safe."

The solicitor left.

Magach stood. "I've arranged a place." He gestured to Chris, "Let's go."

"I'm typing this up," said Cooper, holding the press release. "I'll get a few copies done and see where it gets us."

CHAPTER TWENTY-NINE

Dan sat in the back of the hotel car as it made its way through the inevitable traffic jams. As they approached the unit, Tony Tavinor called to say he was still waiting outside the address Pollard had visited. Nobody had shown up yet, and the place was closed off.

"That's not why I called. I've had Ray on, and he's just found out about a UK Minister coming to Bangkok next week. I thought you might like to know in case the embassy is willing to get him to talk to the Thais about Mat's case."

After the call ended, he called Kumat and asked if they could meet at the hotel in two hours. Kumat agreed.

As he entered the unit, he recalled what Nirundorn had told Mat - *take the deal and get out of Thailand* - Dan couldn't help but agree with the sentiment while he also understood his son's hesitation. But after today, there would be no turning back. Mat had to understand that.

A guard was smiling as he led Mat into the interview room.

Dan held his son, who was becoming frailer by the day.

"You look spaced out, Dad."

Dan took a deep breath. "No kidding." He laughed.

"So, what is it?"

"We found Chris – the third boy. He's prepared to make a statement..."

Mat interrupted with a relieved shout, "That's good, Dad - isn't it?"

Dan nodded, hesitantly, "Nirundorn doesn't think the statement will be enough."

Mat's head dropped to his chest. "Surely, though. If he admits packing my backpack and the rest." He looked perplexed. "Why would that not be enough?"

"Nirundorn could be wrong, but he thinks we need more."

"What more is there?"

"There is the heroin, and you were carrying it. That's the evidence, and a single witness may not be enough to allow the judge to dismiss that fact."

Dan nodded and paused for a moment. "I intend to put out a press release that names everyone involved in the case: Mayer, Chao, Kumat, Pollard, the embassy. So they all know you've been set up, and we're fighting your case, whatever happens. That is...? He hesitated... "if you're sure."

"Sure?"

"Sure that you want to dismiss the bail option. That is still possible - even now."

"You heard Nirundorn. Sucher still on the Interpol list six years after - I can't..." His voice rose, "No, I won't do that."

"OK. Then I threaten to put out this press release."

"And you'll be a target, Dad."

"I hope so."

Strained laughter came from Mat as he leaned across and gripped his father's arms. The laughter, tinged with hysteria, spread between them until the door opened, and Prisit stood looking between them. His expression was confused as he saw them laughing. He slammed the door, and the laughter became louder and even more frantic.

The door opened, and a guard indicated that time was up.

The laughter ceased. Mat grabbed his father.

"Do it, Dad. All in. Let's go."

He moved through the door. It closed behind him. Dan could hear his son's chains dragging along the concrete floor.

* * *

He instructed the driver to get him to the British Embassy.

The traffic jams seemed to be getting heavier.

It was the same receptionist as before. He noticed a security guard move quietly beside the door leading into the offices.

"The Ambassador is engaged, and Mr Fairbrother is out. Nobody else is available. You'll have to make an appointment." The words came with a malicious smile before Dan had even spoken. However, Henry Fairbrother exited a taxi by the gate as she finished speaking. Dan moved toward him.

"Mr Fairbrother."

There was no sign of recognition.

"Dan Cooper."

"Of course." Fairbrother moved toward the Embassy. "If you'll excuse me."

"I would like a word."

The diplomat looked at his watch. Dan felt the exasperation as he spoke. "I hear there's going to be a visit by a Minister."

Fairbrother raised his eyebrows. "We've only just been notified."

Dan gritted his teeth. "It may surprise you, Mr Fairbrother, but my company has good contacts in Government."

Fairbrother gave a self-deprecatory smile. "Of course. It is easy to get sidetracked." He held out the folder in his hand. "We're all pretty tied up with last-minute arrangements."

"Can you mention my son?"

There was no response. Fairbrother gestured toward a bench in the garden. "Please sit, Mr Cooper."

He placed the file on his lap as Dan continued.

"If the Minister could bring it up with the Thais, it would indicate the Government's concern," said Dan.

"Concern," the voice had an ironic edge to it. "The visit is primarily about trade. Most of the meetings are scheduled with trade officials."

"There are meetings with the Prime Minister and Foreign Secretary."

"You *are* well-informed, Mr Cooper. They will be essentially ceremonial in nature."

"Will you raise the matter?"

Fairbrother paused and looked directly at Dan. "I will ask the Asian desk and the Ambassador. There's no guarantee it will be possible to fit it in. You understand?"

"Yes", he hesitated. "No. I don't understand. My son is entitled to the protection of his country's representatives."

Fairbrother eyes narrowed. "I understand your lawyer has made you aware of a possible resolution."

"How would you know that?" Dan demanded.

Fairbrother leapt to his feet. "I do have to go."

"I'm sure you do." He pulled a copy of the press release from his pocket. "This is for you, just as a matter of courtesy."

Fairbrother gave a cursory glance and then sat down again. He finished reading and looked at Dan.

"What do you think this will achieve?"

"As I said, a matter of courtesy. I'm not discussing it with you."

He left the Embassy grounds. As he reached the car, he saw Fairbrother standing by the entrance and watching him.

* * *

Kumat was waiting in the lobby with an empty espresso cup on the table before him. He was bristling with purpose. He stood as Dan arrived and began speaking before Dan sat down.

"Good news, Mr Cooper. Arrangements have been put in place. There will be no objection to bail being granted."

"Mat will not accept the bail option."

There was silence. Kumat's face seemed to tighten. Muscles tensed, eyes narrowed, almost imperceptibly. The result was menacing and the voice cold. "You must prevail upon him to reconsider."

Dan said nothing.

The voice acquired an even harder edge. "Nothing more can be done for him. You realise you are allowing your son to be incarcerated, certainly for the remainder of your life, possibly his.'

"He does not want to spend the rest of his life on the run."

Contempt assumed prominence. "So, he prefers Bangkwang. An American prisoner died in the *Big Tiger* a few months ago. You know that description?

Dan nodded. He had heard the name given to the prison.

"He was screaming through the night. Eventually, another prisoner persuaded a guard to open the cell. A large growth had appeared just here." Kumat touched his head just above his ear. "It was moving. The prisoner sliced it open. It was a nest for maggots. They squirmed out. A cockroach had crawled into his ear one night as he slept in his cell. It laid its eggs. His brain had been eaten away. He died."

Kumat paused. Dan couldn't speak.

"Nobody from Thailand will want your son back. Nobody will care where he is. You must speak with him again."

The soldier stood. Anger took over.

"I have worked hard to make the arrangements. People will feel betrayed if I say their efforts have been rejected. You understand, Mr Cooper. I have done all I can to help your son. Every decision has consequences."

Dan stood alongside the man. He brought a copy of the press release from his pocket. "This is for your attention."

He moved to the lifts. When a door opened, he turned. Kumat was focused on the document. He looked up at Dan as the lift door closed. There was no expression on his face as he drew his hand across his throat in an unmistakable gesture even as he spoke on his telephone. Dan watched as Kumat turned and marched through the foyer. The black Mercedes was waiting outside. A doorman opened the passenger door. The vehicle slipped away.

He called Nirundorn when he reached his room. "Send the statement to the court," he instructed.

CHAPTER THIRTY

Mat lay on his bed in his cell for the afternoon. His four cellmates were out of the cramped space they shared. He had been given a dog-eared copy of *The Quiet American* by Graham Greene, and the words helped the time pass as he joined the author in the opium-fuelled confusion of Saigon a lifetime ago.

The images took him to that day as he arrived at the airport. The anticipation and excitement that lay ahead. A few days in Laos: Vientiane, the Plain of Jars and the secret campaigns of the CIA during the Vietnam War. Strange men who stayed behind with the hill tribes. An adventure hailing from back in the sixties.

However, the words from the page couldn't take away the hope that had sustained him following his father's visit. For the first time, he felt that there was a chance he could get out of this bastard place.

He paused and heard a metal door crash against a wall and boots marching on concrete floors. They moved fast, angry, unyielding - closer.

His door was thrown open. Three guards, Prisit hovering

behind shouting. He was grabbed by the hair, hauled from his bed and wrenched along the floor, his protests ignored. Eventually, he was thrown into the room where he had met with his father. Nothing had been said, no words except for the frantic shouts from Prisit as he urged the guards to move faster.

The room was empty. He was alone. The door to the yard was open. He turned as a guard screamed in fury and slashed a bamboo cane across the back of a skeletal figure squatting in the dusty enclosure. The prisoner brought his hands together in supplication. The gesture seemed to arouse greater fury, and the cane came down again and again. An angry gash rose on the skeletal face as a futile appeal was muttered and ignored. Mat had no idea what offence the prisoner had committed. He had ceased to attach any reason for the violence which permeated every day in the unit - it just was, and there was little point in trying to understand. What he did understand was the fear that accompanied every moment - the fear that, at any second, it could be directed toward him.

He felt a tap on his shoulder.

Prisit! The man had appeared in the room. The sunglasses gave nothing away. The expression a flicker away from the fury that characterised his existence.

Mat shivered in fear as he saw another slashing blow strike the prisoner lying full-length on the ground. Prisit guided him to a chair. A vicious smile emerged as he strutted around the room.

"You don't want to leave, English. OK. You big boy now. You think you tough enough to survive."

He came closer. "Tough enough to survive me." A desperate scream punctuated the silence that followed the sudden switching off of the smile. Mat turned and looked through the open door. The prisoner lay still. A patch of blood soaked into the dust as the guard launched another blow, both feet leaving the ground, bringing the cane down, splitting the skull, a sudden spurt of blood leaping upward like a fountain before spraying an abstract sadness across the silent scene.

It was a dance choreographed for him. He felt sick. Suddenly, Prisit grabbed his neck and hammered his head down on the table.

"You think you tough enough to survive me." The laugh that followed was obscene. Prisit took a gun from one of his two holsters. It looked like something from a Western or Clint Eastwood in *Dirty Harry* - Long barrel, round chamber. Prisit rotated the chamber and took out the single bullet. He rolled it in his fingers as he spoke. "Dum-dum bullet. Little hole as it enters. Rips your brain apart and blows your head to pieces." He laughed again as he put the bullet back into the chamber and spun it round in an exaggerated gesture. Mat saw a glimpse of what lay ahead - he suddenly understood - as he felt the barrel of the gun pushing into the back of his head - as he saw the body lying in the dust - that there were no constraints. Prisit could do whatever he wanted.

Too late to flinch.

"You understand English. You're mine."

His hair was grabbed, and he was jerked up. Two trustees dragged the lifeless body across the yard, leaving a trail of blood in its wake.

"You're mine."

The barrel pushed harder into his head. Prisit pulled the trigger. The hammer fell. Nothing happened.

Prisit laughed.

"Next time, English." Another burst of excited laughter.

The guard stood at the door. He tapped his blood-soaked cane against the step. Mat followed and was ordered to gather up his belongings from his cell.

"New home," said the guard and then smiled. His teeth

were stained. He leaned closer, put two fingers against Mat's head, and whispered. "Bang, bang."

They passed down long corridors and through clanging gates to a different part of the unit. The guard pushed his cane against Mat's legs, causing him to stumble and almost fall, but he refused to give the bastard the pleasure.

The smell hit Mat at the door. A wall of excreta, dried piss and frightened sweat coating every movement, every sound. Whatever paint may have been applied to these walls many years before had long peeled away. A hole in the corner of the room gave off a vicious aroma which scoured the back of his throat. A single bucket stood beside the hole. It was empty.

Silence fell as he walked through the door.

Faces turned toward him as the guard punched the back of his head and sent him sprawling across one of the forty-odd straw sacks that passed as mattresses and were laid side-by-side across wooden floorboards with no room between. A few had been piled against the wall in one corner, making enough space for the small group whose frightened faces watched the guard turn away and move down the corridor.

Mat struggled to his feet and took off his shoes. He brushed the dust from his clothes and rubbed the bruise developing on the back of his head.

A few voices sprang up again, and attention shifted away from him. The group were looking down a small hole in the floorboards. Mat slumped down on one of the sacks. Why the hell had he passed up the deal? So he would have had to change his name. So what. Anything would be better than this. Anything. Prisit had lost it completely. It wasn't a question of getting by anymore. It was survival. He remembered the words: *"You think you tough enough to survive me." "Dum-dum bullet. Little hole as it enters. Rips your brain apart and blows your head to pieces as it leaves."*

He wasn't tough enough to survive, but he had no choice.

One of the group looked over at Mat. He had been in one of the adjoining interrogation rooms at the very beginning, at the airport. A smile came as he beckoned Mat across to the small group. One of them was dropping small pieces of rice from one of the bowls in which they were given their usual meals of rice with a spurt of flavoured liquid, which tasted of nothing Mat could identify and which always came with a few insects crawling through the tepid offering.

As he came closer, he saw a writhing mass beneath the floor. Cockroaches! In a rusted can. The biggest cockroaches he'd ever seen. The biggest he ever wanted to see. As he drew back, he suddenly felt a biting pain shoot through his foot. He stared with horror at the obscene creature hanging onto him. He'd heard about the sewer rats but never seen one until now. It was the size of a small cat with a long snout and fangs for teeth that dug into his foot, ignoring the blows as some prisoners thumped their shoes and sandals against the thick, slimy coat. Mat kicked out in terror, lifting his foot and smashing the vile, struggling thing against the wall. It still didn't let go. Pain shot through him, he was screaming. He hammered the brown figure against the wall, again and again and again, until a shriek echoed around the cell - a baby screaming - and the teeth released him. The creature fell and ran through a gap in the wall. Mat collapsed, shaking, sweating. The prisoner he had recognised held out his hand. Mat gripped it, hanging on a life raft in a storm.

"OK now, English. It go." He laughed. "Until tonight."

One of the other prisoners leaned into the hole in the floorboards. He came up with a plastic bag full of squirming cockroaches. Mat turned away. Across in another corner, a prisoner was burning the end of an empty biro tube around a hypodermic needle, blowing on the plastic whilst waiting for it to cool and harden. When the compound had solidified, a small quantity of white liquid was poured into the end of the tube, and the prisoner beckoned one of the group across to him. He slipped his trousers down and examined the skin around his groin before thrusting the needle through the skin. The other prisoner bent down and blew into the tube, forcing the liquid into a vein. After a moment, the prisoner fell back, the needle still hanging from his groin. He closed his eyes and smiled.

Mat turned away. The cockroaches had been dropped into an empty can. One of the prisoners poured a small quantity of oil and a few grains of salt into the can, then picked up a spoon and started crushing the writhing mass into a paste. He lifted out a spoonful of the paste and ate it. Mat fell back in horror as each of the prisoners ate a share. They looked toward him, a spoonful was offered to him. He stared.

"Protein, English. You want to live?"

He started to speak but couldn't find any words as a shadow fell across the door. He felt the fear tremble through the group as it huddled into itself, sheltering against the wall. There were certain prisoners Mat had been warned about. You didn't go near them. They ran their own affairs. Even Prisit didn't mess with them, or he'd have bits of his body chopped off when he was outside the walls, just as the story had it that another officer who had tried to get tough had been left at the gates with broken arms and legs, all his fingers chopped off and castrated.

A bleak face looked at the group and then turned to Mat.

"Cooper." The gesture indicated for him to follow. He looked back to the group. They turned away.

The voice was more insistent. "Cooper."

He followed through the door.

CHAPTER THIRTY-ONE

The press statement Dan had crafted lay on the table as Lynne Kramer and Tony Tavinor read copies of the document.

Tavinor spoke. "So when do you propose releasing this?"

"If Mat gets found guilty or someone like Prisit decides he's expendable."

"No fucking euphemisms, Dan. You mean if Prisit or another psychopath kills Mat?"

Dan nodded.

"Who have you shown this to?"

"Kumat and Fairbrother."

"So that will be with Chao, through Kumat. What about Prisit? Are you assuming Kumat or Chao controls that idiot?" He paused. "Because they don't."

"The unit is Prisit's domain. Even Chao's grip has limitations where Prisit is concerned, and no government official would dare challenge him, said Lynne.

"Then Chao will get Mat out of there," said Tavinor.

"How the hell...?" Dan's words stuttered to silence.

Tavinor held up the press release. "This will crucify Chao. It will expose the facade he's been cultivating. The patriotic businessman who cares deeply about the country would be shown as bullshit. He'd be out there as a cheap crook. Mat's safe while this is not released. If you release it, he's finished." He paused, "but you knew that when you spread it about. You've made yourself the target to take the heat off Mat. You're hoping Chao has enough pull to get Mat out, and then you can bin this."

Dan nodded.

"Interesting. One thing you've misunderstood. It involves trust. That Chao will trust you not to release this if Mat is freed. Believe me, that man doesn't do trust. He will find a way to silence you and ensure this," he held up the press release, "never sees the light."

A sudden commotion started outside the door of his suite.

Dan opened the door.

Four policemen moved toward him.

"Cooper?" said a thickset figure in a grey uniform.

He nodded.

"You come with us."

"Why? What's going on?"

The policeman was tugging at his arm. "You come with us."

Lynne spoke in Thai. After receiving a reply, she turned to Dan. "He's been sent to take you to the Interrogation Unit. He doesn't know anything. You'd better go. It's probably just another piece of bureaucracy."

Nirundorn was waiting in his car parked at the hotel entrance. A policeman touched Dan's arm. He held open the passenger door of the vehicle.

Nirundorn smiled and pointed ahead at a police car. "We have an escort."

The siren started blaring. They sped into Bangkok's traffic chaos.

"What's this about," asked Dan as they juddered to a halt only a few minutes from the hotel.

"They called me, ask where you are. Tell me to meet you at the hotel."

Dan was desperate for the lawyer to tell him it happened all the time. He didn't. The smile disappeared. He turned away and looked through the window.

The rest of the journey passed in silence.

Dan's mouth was dry. His heart was beating too fast, and bizarrely, even with brutal air-conditioning, he broke out in a sweat but also started shivering.

They pulled up at the Interrogation Unit.

Prisit stood at the top of the steps, his arms folded. He looked down at them through his sunglasses as they approached and then turned without a word. Dan led Nirundorn as they followed along the corridor. Prisit pushed the door of a room with his foot. A contemptuous gesture indicated that Dan should go into the room.

He paused.

Prisit's face gave nothing away.

He moved inside.

Prisit spoke. "Where is your son, Mr Cooper?"

CHAPTER
THIRTY-TWO

Mat was guided through an area of the prison he had not visited. Guards turned away when they saw his companion. They came to the end of an empty corridor. He felt a touch on his arm and was directed toward an open doorway from which the sound of Eastern music drifted into the corridor. He paused at the door and tried to adjust to the gloom. A window high on the wall had been covered over with black material. A single candle threw a dramatic aura upon the face of the sole occupant of the cell. Mat thought about the thirty-odd prisoners sharing his new cell as he looked around at a television in one corner and a CD player giving out quiet music beside it. He felt eyes turn to him.

"Cooper," an arm indicated a chair. He sat down and looked at the silent figure squatting on a mat in a corner of the cell. Age anywhere between thirty and sixty, dark, hooded, staring eyes, body covered in a black full-length tunic, spreading from his waist, lying in folds on thick thighs.

Mat remained silent. He wasn't sure he dared to speak. His chest was gripped in a vice, struggling for breath.

"Prisit," the name emerged like an obscenity.

The silence fell again. Mat didn't know what he was supposed to do. Should he respond? Was he supposed to stay silent? He didn't know the name but had heard the reputation - unrestrained violence and connections that gave whatever privileges were demanded - somehow, it didn't match the silent figure sitting in the gloom, but then nothing was what it seemed in this place.

"He will kill you."

The words came slowly. Like a death sentence. A sombre declaration of intent but with the meaning stripped away as though death was irrelevant, at worst an inconvenience.

"Tonight. You die tonight."

Mat shivered as he heard the words, but they didn't seem to apply to him. The quiet voice sucked the significance from the statement. He believed it, though, after today. After the scene in the interview room.

"This afternoon. You escape."

What! Escape! What the hell was he talking about? This was a Thai prison. He'd turned down the chance of getting out on bail ... his mind stopped functioning, he could only remember: *the barrel pushed harder into his head. Prisit pulled the trigger. The hammer fell. Nothing happened. Prisit laughed. "Next time, English."*

Perhaps he was right. Perhaps the next time would be tonight, and the chamber would stop, and a bullet would line up in the barrel.

"What do you want?" his voice was trembling.

The face turned toward him. There was no expression. The eyes closed, and he lifted a remote control toward the CD player. The music got louder.

Mat felt a touch on his arm. His escort, who had brought him, led him away from the darkened room, along another corridor and into a bare room in the centre of which was a rough wooden coffin with a claw hammer lying on top. The lid of the coffin was prised open. Mat recognised the bloody, emaciated figure he'd seen beaten to death in the yard. He turned, a hand gestured into the coffin.

Mat slumped back against the wall. He whispered, "No."

There was only just enough room between the body and the lid. He whispered again, "No," What if it went wrong, what if he couldn't get out? Nothing was what it seemed. What if ... What if... He whispered, "No".

Prisit laughed. "Next time, English."

He clambered into the coffin.

Hammering reverberated in confined darkness. He tasted decay. A terrifying end. Buried alive. Soil thrown on bare wood. The body beneath him was rigid. He stretched, his hand touching cold skin. He recoiled in horror, a pain shot through his foot, and he remembered the angry fangs of the sewer rat clinging to him as a taste of nausea rose in his throat, and he tried to scream - for release. Even death would be better. No sound came. Nothing came, he grabbed for breath, finding only stale putrefaction. He had to calm down. There was no survival in this desperate agitation. He closed his eyes and tried to search his imagination. To discover memories and pictures that could sustain him, give hope to carry him through. To shut away voices crying of the despair that had become his substance since that bloody day at the airport.

He almost succeeded and then heard voices and felt a movement as the coffin was lifted and then banged down with a violent jolt. A dead hand jolted upward and struck his cheek. He lay still. Eyes tightly closed, trying desperately not to move or make a sound as stiff fingers clawed at his cheek. An engine sparked into life. It sounded like a lorry. It moved slowly. Voices started up. There was a bang as something clattered on top of the coffin directly above his head. Laughter broke out. He tried to brush away the hand that scratched his face.

Shouts, more laughter. A gate opened. The lorry accelerated. He heard the high-pitched tone of a tuk-tuk and the deeper blast of what sounded like the lorry's hooter. Sounds and movement reverberated through his panic as the coffin swayed and cracked against the side of the vehicle. He clenched his fists and screwed his eyes closed, trying to shut away the terror.

Suddenly, the movement stopped, and the coffin was lifted amidst a renewed burst of shouting. A violent jolt came as it seemed to be thrown to the ground. A hand came round, gripping his face. He recoiled, he wanted to scream, he thrust his hands against the lid, but it didn't move. The unexpected silence was worse than the noise that had preceded it.

Nothing moved.

All was quiet. He couldn't stay still and pushed as hard as he could.

Nothing moved. He pushed against dead constraints.

He was trapped.

CHAPTER
THIRTY-THREE

It was early morning when Dan returned to the lobby of the Shangri-La Hotel. He stared about the vast room and heard Nirundorn speaking amongst a flurry of bows and assurances that he would do all he could. All being offered with a vagueness that Dan had come to understand as the lawyer's sincerest intentions but meaning nothing. Voices came from groups of residents and their visitors sitting around drinking, eating and laughing. Faces moved through his sight. Night passed outside the window, alien, ripped from all he knew. Somewhere out there. Somewhere, his son waited. Somewhere or nowhere. Was it too late?

He felt a touch on his arm.

Lynne Kramer.

"I waited in your room."

She guided him to the elevators as Nirundorn left the hotel, promising to make some calls.

They didn't speak. Not until they came into his suite. The space that was a link to horror, sheer fucking horror. The dread of a father. The guilt of a lifetime.

"Mat's escaped."

Lynne poured a glass of cognac.

"Sit. Drink."

She moved Dan to an armchair and placed the glass in his hand.

It was sharp. Warm. He breathed deeply and tried to restore a sense of resolve.

The door banged. Sharp and insistent.

Tavinor marched into the room after Lynne opened the door.

"I heard. I've been overnight at the guy's house who collected the itinerary from Pollard. The house is still empty, but whoever he is, we'll identify him when he shows up. So what's the story? Mat's out, I understand."

Dan sipped the cognac.

Tavinor's voice continued. "Mat's life depends on you now. There's no time for self-pity. Get your act together, Dan." He paused, "have you contacted Róisín? She'll be knee-deep in media shortly, you'd better tell her."

Dan stood up, "I should have thought of that," He went to his bedroom.

Lynne turned to Tavinor, "Take it easy."

"No. There's no room or time for that. We must react, or Mat's flushed down the Mekong and Dan with him. There's some powerful shit going on. Prisit is a tool, a vicious and psychotic tool, but a tool, nevertheless. Some heavyweight actors are running him. I've been sitting outside the estate of one of them tonight. As I talked to the locals, I sensed the fear surrounding the place. We're up against real power, and that has no morality, so Dan hasn't got the time to reflect. He *has* to get his act together, and so do we."

Dan came back. "Thanks, Tony. The media have picked it up, but I got there in time. Róisín is still hoping to come over."

He breathed deeply and walked to the window. After a few minutes, he turned back. "OK, Tony," he asked, "what do we do?"

Tavinor continued, "He didn't get out of there without assistance."

"You sound like Prisit. He's been saying that for most of the night. As an accusation."

"He's right."

"It was as if Prisit was going through the motions, though." Dan pushed his hands through his hair. "As if the words, the accusation, had to be made, but he didn't believe them himself."

Lynne sat back in her chair. "OK. So, someone has helped Mat. That's a certainty."

"Why?"

Nobody spoke.

Silence continued.

"It has to be me, doesn't it?" said Dan, eventually.

Tavinor spoke. "Of course, it's about you. That's why Mat's still alive. He turned down the bail option, then, so he could have had an accident, and that would have ended it. Mayer wouldn't have gotten his money. I suspect he's irrelevant now. You blew it up when you spread the press release about, but without releasing it. That's the unexploded bomb that's keeping your son alive, for the moment. You knew that, Dan. Didn't you?"

Dan nodded and paused. "I didn't think it through, though. It wasn't supposed to be like this."

"So what did you think would happen?"

Dan leaned back and looked at the ceiling. "That they would come after me, and a deal would be struck that allowed Mat to get out, and I'd keep quiet."

"And they would trust you? Dream on, Dan. I told you

these guys don't do trust. You're in the cross hairs now, and your son's a hostage for your silence. He's been taken out of the equation. He doesn't have a say any longer."

"Who are *these guys*?"

Lynne Kramer stood and walked to the window. "What do we have? Chao is one of the major drug dealers in the area. Heroin and methamphetamines. One of his major markets is the UK and Europe. One of the main problems with drugs is money laundering. Own, or control, a respected bank, like Mayers, and you hit the motherload. Buying a brass plate in Vanuatu or the Caribbean is easy, but Mayers has been around for decades..."

"A hundred and seven years," Dan interrupted.

"Exactly. So, the authorities don't look so hard. The question is, who benefits - cui bono? We need Chao's UK contact. He must have a major importer." said Lynne, pausing. "And using Mayer as a figurehead but controlling him at the same time?"

"Finding that out is for another time," said Tavinor. "We have Chao to deal with now." He gestured to Dan, "You've threatened him with Chris Ralston's statement and the press release. He can't afford them to see the light. Either would smash his carefully curated image as a reformed character promoting Thailand, the country he loves, as a true patriot. He would be held up to the light as exactly what he is: a vicious, psychotic killer at the top of a corrupt drug industry that is crushing the country. He will fight to stop that happening, and he has the resources to succeed."

"How does this help Mat," Dan's exasperated voice broke through the analysis. "What do we do?"

"Nothing," said Lynne. "You get out of the way. Chao knows where you are; his goons will be on the way to visit, and it won't be a social call. The press will be after you, UK and

Thai media. There's nothing you can say that will help. One wrong word and Mat is history. We don't know where Mat is yet, so we have to wait. I have someone to see. Tavinor, you come with."

She turned to Dan. "We'll drop you off on the way."

"Where?"

She gestured around the room and shook her head. "On the way. Let's go."

Lynne gestured as they left the lift. The three of them sat in the cavernous lobby crowded with an Australian tour group eating their way through an assortment of Thai pastries and chocolates.

"OK. We've got a few days. I'll get your suite checked out as a precaution. Chao will be coming for you, so we get you out of the way. Chris Ralston is in a safe house in Sukhumvit and," she gestured across to two large men waiting by the exit, "these guys will take you there and stay with you. I know them. They're solid and trustworthy, ex-Aussie SAS. Turn off your phone and take out the battery. When we find out where Mat is, we go get him."

"It's that simple?" asks Dan.

"No. It's not simple." snapped Lynne. "Wherever he is, it will be dangerous for you and Mat. If we fuck up, you both end up floating down the Mekong."

She gestured to the two guards, "Dan, go with them. I'll be in touch either later today or tomorrow. Be ready to move."

She looked to Tavinor as Dan exited the hotel, with the two guards bookending the uncertain figure.

"I've got our ex-colleagues trying to get information from inside the Unit about Mat. Someone will know who's taken him and, with any luck, where. In the meantime, we have an ex-contact of mine to check out."

CHAPTER
THIRTY-FOUR

Lynne gave instructions in Thai to a taxi driver as they pulled away from the hotel after rejecting the hotel car.

"I don't want anyone to know where we're going." She peered through the window and spoke again to the taxi driver before turning back to Tavinor. "It's a club in Silom." She rubbed her face. "An acquired taste."

"Why?"

"I was called. Mat was helped to escape. This guy has contacts in the unit. We're going to try to see him."

"How do you know him?"

She paused, shrugged her shoulders, and opened her hands. "You know how the business works, Tavinor."

She snapped out another instruction to the driver.

"So why are we going to see him?" asked Tavinor.

"I didn't say we were. I said we'd try. He owns the club. It's very exclusive now. We might not get past the door."

They pulled up outside a solitary metal door in a blank brick wall. The street had no lights, the darkness only alleviated by the moon hanging bright above the desolate scene. Tavinor whispered as the taxi pulled away.

"Why would he talk to us?"

She gave a muted laugh. "You were here for a few years; nothing has changed. Self-interest still rules."

Lynne hammered on the door. The sound echoed in the silence.

A tiny gap appeared. Kramer whispered in Thai. The gap closed. Almost five minutes passed before the gap opened again, and then the door slid silently to one side, revealing a dark porch beyond which lay a further metal door. They moved inside and waited until the door closed behind them and the one in front opened, and two doormen dressed in black silk jackets and trousers beckoned them forward. They waited until the second door had closed before carrying out a thorough search. One of the doormen pointed toward a camera in the corner of the room.

Tavinor and Lynne looked toward it. After almost thirty seconds, another door slid open. The doormen stepped to one side, and they made their way into a room the size of a small cinema. About forty couches were separated into individual booths sloping toward a thick glass wall which looked over an auditorium where about five hundred people, men and women, sat in rows around a cage the size of a boxing ring, completely enclosed by heavy metal mesh. A muted roar came from speakers in the corner of the room as the audience bayed at two fighters circling each other in the cage. One of the doormen guided them to an empty couch. Each of the booths had one or two people watching the action whilst young Thai girls dressed in tight red silk mini dresses prepared elaborate long pipes and handed them to spectators who lay back on the couches and slowly drew in the smoke.

"It's opium," whispered Kramer. "One thousand dollars in

here, two hundred dollars down there." She pointed through the glass toward the cage. "Winner takes home twenty thousand dollars. Loser doesn't always go home."

The fighters stalked each other. One was about seventeen stone, crew cut, dark red welts studding his muscled torso encased in long lycra shorts sporting the stars and stripes. An angry face perched on a thick neck, he manoeuvred slowly around the cage, occasionally making a laborious lunge toward a small figure, long black hair tied in a ponytail moving quickly in sudden graceful darts, snaking out a fist, elbow or foot into the body or face of his opponent. He was dressed in shorts, the Thai flag emblazoned on red silk.

"Thai champion," said Lynne. "They bring opponents over from the States. Wrestlers passed their prime."

A sudden dart, a fist flashed into the neck, a mid-air twist - like ballet, thought Tavinor - a heel crunched into the heavy-set figure's groin. He grabbed at thin air and dropped slowly to his knees, looking about as his assailant strode round the cage, taking in the applause as the crowd rose. Tavinor flinched as a foot smashed into the back of the kneeling figure's neck, he slipped further to the floor and then, as another dart brought a slashing blow to the base of his back, he lunged round and grabbed an ankle. Red shorts toppled, the crowd groaned in shock and fell silent as a punch landed on the struggling shape. Screams rang out as a further blow pummelled the slight body. Tavinor saw a hand reach out and grab the thick torso's genitals. An angry bellow rang out as the grip intensified before a further blow landed from blood-covered fists. Another violent twist of the balls and the grip faltered. The red shorts moved in a blur, his face covered in blood. The thick-set figure knelt, rubbing his groin - before he could look up, a blow ripped across his bowed head. He toppled slowly like a tall tree, but before reaching the floor, an elbow crashed against his neck.

The two antagonists paused, each wiping blood from their hands and faces.

Another pipe was prepared to Tavinor's right. A middle-aged falang lay back and touched the breast of the young girl as she kneaded a dark paste and put it in a pipe before lighting the bowl and handing it to him.

The heavy figure in the cage hauled himself upright and pulled up his blood-spattered shorts. He held his arms out to the side and moved across the cage as though trying to trap his opponent in the corner where he waited, squatting down on his haunches and watching the approach with undisguised contempt. As it seemed there was no way out, he leapt up and dug his fingers into the bloodied face. A furious bellow echoed around the auditorium. The red shorts rolled across the floor before leaping again and launching a vicious blow against an unprotected neck with an elbow, followed by a scissor kick which landed against the temple. It looked close to the end. Stars and stripes moved too slowly, and there was almost no defence. He turned as another assault came across the floor. The crowd's roar suddenly paused. A slip on a patch of blood brought the attack to a halt. Red shorts fell, and heavy arms summoned up a supreme effort. They hauled the slight figure from the floor before lunging across the cage and smashing the jerking head against the bars. Tavinor could barely watch as the crowd groaned in pain as the figure fell limp and was hammered again against the bars. The American rose from the floor and dragged up the motionless shape by his hair. He raised his arms in triumph and let the broken figure fall. The crowd fell silent. Tavinor felt sick. He felt Lynne Kramer touch his arm and gesture toward the corner of the room.

They passed a row of booths and waited at the foot of a couch. A silent figure gazed at them through two bright, shining eyes appearing from the shadows of the dark corner. A black full-length tunic hid the man's frame as he beckoned to Kramer. Their soft voices spoke with wary caution amongst suppressed voices echoing from the opium driver booths. Tavinor strained to hear as the two faces turned toward him, and Kramer motioned him closer.

Tavinor barely heard the soft voice. "The boy will be with Chao. In Chiang Rai."

"How do you know?"

There was no response.

"You helped him escape?" demanded Tavinor.

A hand gestured toward the doormen. The eyes had closed.

"Did you help him to escape?"

A doorman grasped Tavinor's arm. He pulled away. Two guards positioned themselves on either side of Tavinor.

Lynne touched his arm. "Go."

One or two faces turned slowly toward them as he was ushered from the room and back into the street.

He was alone.

About ten minutes later, the door opened again, and Lynne Kramer stepped out.

"What was that about?"

"Not here."

"Why did we come here?"

"To hear what we heard."

"You believe him," said Tavinor as they made their way from the quiet street toward a main road. "That Mat is with Chao."

Lynne pulled him over to a street café and ordered two beers.

"So, what the hell was that about?" asked Tavinor.

"He wants you to go to Chiang Rai and take on Chao. That's what this was about, and that's why I was told how Mat got out. Why I was told to bring you here."

"Why would he want us to take on Chao?"

"Because he hates Chao. He used to be a Nak Muay, a Muay Thai boxer. The American in the cage is a Nak Muay Farang, a foreign boxer. My contact was one of the best in the country. Then he set up a gym, built up a stable of fighters, and put on his own shows. Chao saw an opportunity and told the man to fix a couple of fights and pay for "protection. He refused. One of his fighters was seriously disabled in an accident, eventually killing himself. A show was wrecked when the venue was burned down, and other owners wouldn't go near him. He realised he had no choice, so Chao was paid off, and a couple of bouts were fixed."

"So why now? Why this?"

"A few years back, I heard that Chao was going to take over and get rid of him. I warned him, but he had to make a deal with Chao. He organised a tour of Australia, putting on a few shows in Sydney and Melbourne. The deal was he took a few hundred kilos of smack along with the fighting gear they took over. It went wrong, and some of the stuff went missing."

"How?"

Lynne gestured toward the venue they had just left.

"He ripped off Chao? Shit, that takes balls."

"I don't know, but Chao has been after him since then. Today, getting Mat out and getting you to Chiang Rai will repay the debt."

"I don't get it".

"When you get to Chiang Rai, you don't leave..."

"And neither does Mat?"

"Exactly. That's why he asked me to stay. He owes me for saving his neck back in the day. So, he got Mat out and told you where he was. In his mind, that's his part of the deal he made with Chao."

"And when you stayed?"

"He repaid the debt he has to me."

"How?"

"Mat isn't in Chiang Rai with Chao. He's in Hongsa across in Lao with Chao."

"What the fuck..."

"You go to Chiang Rai. That's where his guys will be waiting for you. You will be disposed of, and then Mat will be too. By Chao. He'll a few of his boys over there with him."

His phone rang.

Nirundorn. "Colonel Kumat has contacted me. He is concerned about Matthew and thinks he may be able to help. He's back in Bangkok." He gave Tavinor a mobile number.

Lynne Kramer looked across the car, stuck again in a traffic jam. "It was always going to be Kumat who made the contact. I had someone look at your suite at the hotel again. It has had three bugs installed since the last time we looked. Lounge, bedroom and dining room. Bapit, your valet is from Chiang Mai, Chao's base, remember that. We've left them in place."

She gestured toward the telephone.

"When we get back, you will call Kumat and make arrangements for Chiang Rai."

She paused.

"Then we go to Hongsa."

CHAPTER THIRTY-FIVE

Release when it came was almost too late for Mat.

This was black confinement: death without the dying. The rigid fingers scraping his skin had taken him almost beyond endurance. Beyond even the terror visited in recent horrified memory when he thought he'd reached his limit. The smell of death and decaying flesh brought nauseous despair to every breath he took as he exhausted himself, straining against the coffin lid only to fall closer into the dead embrace of the unknown body beneath him.

He had no dimension of time passed. Minutes, hours, and values shifted as he almost gave way to nagging voices - filtered through desperate visions of cockroaches crushed by the sharp fangs of sewer rats - telling him this was the end. The climax and finality of a life barely started. He wasn't sure if he wept. It didn't matter. Nothing featured beside the horror that embraced and smothered him. He gasped for breath and found only putrefaction.

A single footfall sounded.

Scraping of feet on concrete.

Illusions inspired by what little hope he could summon.

A cough.

Phlegm ejected.

His heart pounded against his chest, tight against the coffin lid, feeling sudden gentle movements as metal braced against wood. Without warning, a fissure of light threw a stray moment of hope into his black despair. Then, sweet freshness invaded his lungs as he covered his eyes from the bright beam of a torch shining into his face as the lid was thrown off. Rough hands dragged him out and threw him on a concrete floor. He rubbed his face just before a hood smelling of motor oil was wrapped tightly around his head restoring the dark embrace, the black fears - hope only permitting a brief intervention.

He was dragged across the floor and lifted into the boot of a car. Brakes squealed. He was flung against a bulkhead as the vehicle accelerated violently and then braked suddenly. The journey was mercifully short. The boot opened again. He was dragged out and thrown onto a wooden floor. A door slammed.

A lock turned.

Bolts scraped closed.

Silence. The hood came away easily. He was in a space about ten feet square. Floor damp. Walls made up of thick wooden slats. He could just see water through a gap in the floor.

Silence

He breathed deeply. Fresh air! So ordinary. So precious.

It was ecstasy.

He felt exhausted. Flopping down in a corner, he closed his eyes and heard the faint sound of a piano. After the terror of the last few days, it sounded like heaven.

CHAPTER
THIRTY-SIX

Kumat was waiting when Dan returned from the Thai boxing. He was shadowed by his bodyguards, who looked suspiciously toward Kumat.

The soldier raised his eyebrows, but the man's smooth face gave nothing away.

"Let us go to my suite," said Dan.

No words were spoken as they ascended in the lift.

Dan nodded at his guards, and they paused and waited by the entrance door as he guided Kumat into his room.

"Why are you here?" asked Dan.

"I merely try to assist." Kumat flicked a piece of dust from the lapel of his black suit. "Nothing more."

"Did you assist in having Mat arrested?"

There was no response. Dan waited.

Kumat held up his hand. "I understand that you would be suspicious of everyone." He gave an ingratiating smile. "I have been asked to assist, nothing more."

"Assist?" asked Dan. "When we spoke last, I advised that Mat had decided he could not take the bail option. Your response was violent and offensive. As I said, why are you here?"

"My behaviour was unacceptable. I apologise. There was no excuse. However, I understand your son may be in danger now. I have contacts. They may be able to intervene. To bring about a solution. You want him back."

Dan didn't respond.

He raised his eyebrows. "You want him back?"

"Where is my son now?"

Kumat shook his head. "I heard he had escaped, but..." he paused and shrugged. "If I can help."

"I have heard that Chao Thanarat may be involved. I do not know the man. Why would his interests be threatened by my son, Colonel?"

Kumat frowned. "I understand that Chao has been offended. Your unfortunate warning that you may release misleading information to the press disturbs him. He is a peaceful man. His reputation has on occasion been called into question, but that is because of the nature of his business, not the character of the man."

He leaned closer to Dan.

He looked around. "Chao feels threatened. It also appears the young man Ralston has made a statement to the court which is seriously flawed. If it were to be believed, Chao would be deeply wounded."

"Wounded?"

"He would suffer deeply - personally. Such lies have a way of creating their own myths, and his business partners may feel obliged to turn their backs on him. Respect is important, and in our culture, it is vital, Mr Cooper. False accusations, maybe, but they still cause scars. They must be retracted."

Dan nodded. "Then I suggest the case against my son is withdrawn."

"Nothing is more important than a man's honour," continued Kumat as though he had not heard Dan.

Dan paused. He looked around the room and made sure his voice was clear. "I am told Mat is in Chiang Rai."

He waited. Kumat uttered a frowning, non-committal sound but failed to answer.

"You have heard that?" insisted Dan.

Kumat nodded. "It seems Chao has been able to intervene and is keeping your son safe," but he held up his hand, "that is pure speculation."

Dan nodded. "Of course not. Why would you."

Kumat continued. "I've merely examined the situation we face. I am trying to assist all parties. I am in no position to speak on behalf of Chao." He stood and moved toward the door. "You have my number, Mr Cooper. Matters will not be allowed to drift."

Dan went out to the corridor after Kumat had left. He moved onto the service stairs and called Tavinor, who was waiting in the lobby. "Kumat has confirmed Mat is in Chiang Rai. Crooked bastard. Is the team ready?"

"Yes. Six guys, all equipped and experienced. They are leaving tomorrow afternoon for Chiang Rai."

"I'll call you back from the room."

Tavinor watched as Kumat exited the lift. He was talking quietly on his phone. Tavinor called Lynne Kramer, who was outside in an unmarked van with equipment from the DEA's Bangkok office after a bureaucratic wrangle that went as far as the new DEA head of station. She had burned some bridges but hoped it had been worth it.

"He called Chao," said Lynne. "A team of his thugs is waiting for Dan at his estate in Chiang Rai. He is in Hongsa with Mat."

"You know the place?"

"I know the area."

"OK, we'll meet up at the safe house. I'll see you there. Magach is still there?" asked Tavinor.

"Just. Straining at the bit. Chris Ralston is quiet. He's a kid wondering what the hell happens next."

"OK. I'll come over later. We need to get organised for Hongsa."

"When do we leave?"

"The team will be in place in Chiang Rai tomorrow evening. They will spend the next day making themselves visible, so we need to get moving tomorrow morning. Are the logistics sorted?"

"They are, but we're reliant on Magach for a tracker. He claims he has the man for that."

"Do we trust him?" asked Tavinor.

"Do we have a choice? He knows the area, and he has the contacts. We don't."

"I'll see you there. Dan's calling from his room."

Dan made sure he was in clear view of the bugs. "Tony, Mat's in Chiang Rai with Chao. Are we ready?" he asked.

"Yes. We'll get up there tomorrow and spend a couple of days surveilling the area. Then, we'll get Mat out as soon as the team is ready."

The call ended.

CHAPTER
THIRTY-SEVEN

Mat felt the sun beating on the battered roof high above his head. The humidity dripped off the rotting walls as he held his head and tried to ease the ache spreading from the egg-sized bruise that had developed just above his right ear. He crawled across the straw-covered wooden floor to a half-empty bottle of water lying in a corner. It was warm but still took the edge off his parched throat. Pushing aside some of the straw, he saw water beneath the floor and, peering through a tiny gap in the wall, glimpsed a woman gently paddling a long-boat filled with fruit. He shouted and banged against the thick wall.

She turned.

The door suddenly crashed open, and a heavy-set figure burst through the entrance. Swinging a baseball bat, he hurled himself across the room. Mat tried to shield himself as the bat swung toward his stomach. His arm took the blow. He yelled in pain as his legs were kicked away. An oil-stained rag was wound tightly around his mouth. His hands were thrust together behind his back. He gasped in pain as his wrists were bound, and he was pushed against the floor.

Not a word was spoken.

The door clattered shut again. He pushed himself on his stomach across to the wall facing the water - uncertain whether it was a canal or the river - a trace of wind trickled through the wood, bathing his scratched face, bringing a moment of relief before he heard a scraping beneath the floor and saw the tiny eyes of a rat emerging from the water. The sodden animal clung to a post sunk into the brown water before slowly hauling itself up the oil-streaked wood, occasionally slipping back down to the water before it managed to pull itself beneath the floor again, trying with frantic energy to force an entrance through one of the gaps in the wood. Its snout appeared in different parts of the floor. Mat tried desperately to ignore the pain throbbing in his arm as he dragged himself up against a wall and then jumped on the gaps as the dark snout appeared.

The door suddenly swung open again. Mat stopped. The guard watched as the rat squeezed through a hole. It paused and examined the room. The guard pulled a gun from his pocket and fired. The rat's head disappeared.

CHAPTER
THIRTY-EIGHT

The safe house – a four-bed apartment - was situated in Lumphini near the park. Lynne and Tavinor arrived with Dan.

Chris Ralston was nowhere to be seen, but a computer game could be heard playing in one of the bedrooms.

Magach was sprawled over a large sofa. He looked between the three of them.

"So we go to Hongsa?"

He suddenly leapt up as Dan moved toward the kitchen to make coffee.

"Sit," he shouted. Dan paused. "Sit the fuck down, Cooper." The man's fists were clenched, and an atmosphere of violence hovered over the intimidating figure.

Dan looked around and then sat down.

"You've seen Kumat? Colonel Kumat..." He shook his head in contempt. "Chao's pet monkey."

"He confirmed Mat is at Hongsa," offered Dan, "and that Chao has his team of thugs waiting for us at Chiang Rai."

Magach strutted around the room. His eyes were wide with tension, his expression cynical. "And we know this because your fight boy," he spat the words out. He turned to Lynne Kramer, "told you," he raised his fingers in quotation marks," in confidence, that was the case?"

"Kumat's call to Chao..." started Kramer.

"Of course, the call," responded Magach with contempt. "And that was real. Are you sure? Not a show put on for the naïve?"

Tavinor watched the scene. He knew Magach's uncertainty. They could be being led into a carefully organised trap. Even though he recognised the man's concern, he knew, in the end, that there was no alternative but to be ready to be betrayed and to survive the betrayal. But Magach was all bristling aggression, and he had to find a way to express that aggression. Tavinor had known people like Magach. At times they were useful, at other times they were dangerous. Only time would tell with Magach, but now he and the rest needed him for his local knowledge and contacts. So he sat back and waited. He knew there was more to follow.

"And if that is bullshit, and we have been fed a crock of shit." He looked at Lynne, "to help your fight man out of a hole with Chao?"

Nobody spoke.

"What if Chao is sitting in his estate in Chiang Rai and his thugs are mob-handed in Hongsa?"

Nobody spoke.

"I don't trust your boy. I'm putting my own life, and Chris's on the line on the word of a guy who's been turned over once by Chao."

He picked up his phone and pressed redial.

"Speak to him," he demanded, handing Kramer the phone.

She looked confused as Magach pressed the speaker.

"Yes," she said hesitantly.

"Kramer?" came a strangled angry voice.

"Yes."

"What the fuck does that crazy bastard want?"

She looked at Magach, who shrugged his shoulders and answered. "The truth you creep, then you go back to playing in your little cages ..."

"Where are you?" interrupted Kramer.

"Hog-tied in a shitty little apartment watched over by two old scumbags. Dragged here..."

Magach interrupted the angry outburst. "OK. We heard you. Now, all I want to hear is one thing, and then you go back to your little games. But be clear, if you lie to me, I will know, and we will find you and kill you. Slowly and painfully. You understand me?"

"Fuck you."

"I'll take that as a yes. Is Mat Cooper in Hongsa or Chiang Rai?"

"I told the woman."

"Now tell me."

"He's in Hongsa."

"Thank you."

He disconnected the call and handed the phone to Kramer before pulling another mobile from his pocket. "Let him loose," he ordered when the call was answered.

Kramer looked at the phone. "What the fuck, Magach. Is this how it goes?"

"You bet your life this is how it goes."

He shrugged aside Kramer's anger. "We've more important things to sort out. We need to prepare for Hongsa."

CHAPTER
THIRTY-NINE

Mat spent his time moving around the room, trying to avoid the sun's rays pouring through narrow slits in the roof. A plate of rice and a bottle of water had been thrust through the door. Eventually, the heat seeped away as evening rushed into dark night and he resumed trying to prise away one of the heavy boards making up the floor. The day's effort produced barely a movement. As he slumped against the wall, crushed with his failure and the realisation that there was no way out, he heard a thin burst of laughter and saw an eye examining him through the wall. He leaned back against one of the damp wooden walls. Exhaustion overwhelmed him. He fell asleep.

The door burst open. A bright beam blinded him, shining directly into his face. He shielded his eyes and pushed back against the wall. Two dark shapes moved toward him, dragging him up and pinning his hands behind him. A fist hammered into his stomach. The pain cut like a knife. He struggled for breath as a rough blindfold was pulled tight about his head, and he was dragged across the damp floorboards. He was thrust into the back of a car and pushed violently to the floor. He lost all notion of time.

The journey, the pain, the despair gripping him were endless – but they would finish. Only then another nightmare would be waiting. The car shrieked to a sudden halt. Hands pulled him out of the car and dumped him onto the road. The sound of a jet engine filled his ears, and the smell of kerosene filled his nostrils. He was pushed up steps, his feet banging on metal rungs, and thrust into a seat. A belt was pulled tight about him. Handcuffs dug into his wrists as they were attached to armrests.

The blindfold was pulled away. He was in the cabin of a small jet aircraft. The sun was just beginning to throw its light across a runway.

He stared at the figure sitting opposite him.

The sunglasses allowed no expression.

He was silent.

Prisit!

The plane accelerated along the runway.

* * *

Fear allowed Mat no rest. Prisit's head dropped to his shoulder a few minutes after take-off. The soft sound of his breathing lent a fraudulent tranquillity to the brutal images that ripped through Mat's memory. The violence was not just indiscriminate. It was pointless - as though all sides expected it but no longer remembered what it was for. He stared at Prisit, trying to understand. He must enjoy it; his pleasure - the satisfaction of perverts in uniform going way back beyond the concentration camps. Mat gave a glimmer of a smile at the irony that he wanted nothing more than to kill Prisit. Always believing in non-violence, never before had he felt such an urge to brutality - it was contagious.

The engine note changed.

"Twenty minutes landing," shouted one of the pilots.

Prisit stirred. He leaned forward and tapped Mat's knee. "Tough boy, English. We see how tough now."

What the hell did that mean? As Mat looked through a window, the sun shot above the horizon, appearing suddenly from behind a range of hills bouncing toward a crystal horizon. The bright light fractured in the plastic window. Mat shielded his eyes as he looked down. The wheels met the runway, and they rolled to a halt by a small control tower, a windsock hanging dispiritedly in lank air.

A burst of humidity flooded the cabin as Prisit opened the door and pushed it outward to form steps leading down to a concrete apron where a 4WD waited. Mat noticed that the flap of Prisit's leather holster was unclipped. He watched the black handle of the weapon as Prisit swaggered over and selected a key from a chain. He paused as he came closer. Mat looked up into the smooth face. He touched the bristles on his own unshaven face and felt the beginnings of a beard.

Prisit unlocked one of the handcuffs. He took his gun from his holster.

Mat had only fired a gun once before. When the school had gone on an adventure weekend, that was a paint gun! He would - if he had the chance. The other handcuff came off.

Prisit held out the gun to Mat.

"You want it, English?"

He waved it in front of Mat.

"No good, English. No balls. No tough boy." The contemptuous laugh was a vicious slash across Mat's anger. He grabbed the gun and pointed it at Prisit. His hand was shaking, but he felt calm, urging himself to breathe slowly. His finger went round the trigger as he looked into the smiling face, sneering at him.

"No guts, English."

He pulled the trigger. The hammer fell - Nothing.

Prisit laughed and then grabbed the weapon.

"No bullets, English," he pulled a magazine from a breast pocket and replaced it into the gun before leaning forward and suddenly thrusting the barrel into Mat's mouth.

"You want it, English?"

Mat struggled as the barrel was forced deeper. He started to choke. Prisit's finger was round the trigger, his eyes wide, sweat forming on his brow. He screamed. "I blow your fucking head off."

"Major Prisit!" The voice was British Army Officer! It resounded from the doorway. "Put your weapon down. *Now*!"

The gun was extracted. Slowly. Mat rubbed his mouth and looked to the doorway. Army fatigues, tall, face shining with self-assurance. "Bring him out here. You need to be moving if you're to get there before nightfall. He's to get there alive." He glared at Prisit. "The consequences would be severe otherwise. You understand, Major."

Prisit tensed. "Yes, Colonel."

He was like an animal. Emotions revealed in movement. Anger and frustration couched in muscles flexed and poised to avenge. He bowed his head, gave reluctant acquiescence, and dragged Mat out of the plane to the door of the 4WD.

"In there," he ordered. The tall figure stood to one side as Mat was handcuffed to two heavy metal rungs fixed to the vehicle's chassis. He called Prisit to him and leaned down. The words uttered with a quiet ferocity sounded like a good going-over for Prisit. Mat cursed. The bastard would be worse when he got Mat alone. He caught a couple of words: *"Cooper," "Chao."* After the rebuke, Prisit saluted. The figure marched away, mounted a Kawasaki motorcycle, and accelerated from the airfield. Prisit didn't move until the motorcycle's deep-throated exhaust had faded. He approached the vehicle, pulled himself into the driver's seat and started the engine. Without warning, he turned and punched Mat violently in the face.

A red-hot pain exploded in Mat's nose as he felt it crunched flat under the assault. His eyes closed, and he tried to absorb the pain shooting through him, tears of anger, fear and torment pouring down his cheeks. Blood ran over his mouth and lips, sweet smoothness trickling down his chin. He opened his eyes as pain eventually slipped from ferocious peaks. A dark red stain coloured his T-shirt. The journey passed in a painful daze, through empty roads, slicing through encroaching rain-forest studded with occasional shacks and small settlements. They pulled off the metalled road and onto a dry track, becoming more potholed and ravaged as they plunged deeper into the forest. Finally, they pulled into a small, deserted settlement. Prisit braked in a flurry of dust, jumped down and waited. After a few minutes, a squat, hunched figure emerged from under one of the broken-down houses, poised on stilts, starting to collapse into the parched earth. Thick scars ran down deep creases on a distrustful expression, staring at the car from under hooded eyes.

Mat didn't hear anything of the short, whispered conversation. Prisit came across and released the handcuffs.

"We walk, English," said Prisit. He put the handcuffs in his pocket and then took out his gun. "You try to escape. You dead. OK, English."

Mat understood. He followed Prisit along the rough track behind the figure who had met them in the village. Mat followed closely. He figured Prisit wouldn't need much of an excuse to use his gun. The guide moved quickly. Luckily, Prisit wasn't as adroit on the narrow-rutted paths running deep into the forest. All Mat cared about was keeping close to Prisit. The sounds of wild animals, waterfalls, and shrieking birds carved into his consciousness, but he dared not pause to acknowledge them. He wanted to survive. Whatever was waiting at the end of this, he *would* survive.

They paused at another deserted settlement for a brief meal of water and cold rice before moving on.

More hills, paddy fields and forest followed as Mat trailed ever more desperately in Prisit's footsteps. He drew on his last reserves of stamina. He thanked God that he'd played Rugby and Squash at school and kept reasonably fit. Still, he was close to exhaustion when they turned a corner on the track as the sun rapidly fell to the horizon.

Four large shacks on stilts were spaced haphazardly around the end of the trail. A smaller brick-built building was almost hidden alongside a helicopter standing incongruously in a clearing about fifty yards behind the shacks. An ancient, wizened figure came from the settlement. He started pushing Mat, who brushed him away as Prisit watched through his sunglasses. Dark sweat stained the armpits of his uniform.

Four more figures moved toward them from the village. Three young men wearing loose white trousers and tops, each sporting a red bandana. One of them kicked the old man to the ground as they came closer. The fourth figure was older, an expression of curiosity flickering on his pock-marked sour face crowned with dark hair cut close to a scarred scalp. He came close, looking Mat over, studying him and staying silent. He turned to Prisit.

"Bring him. We wait to hear the fucking father is dead, then..." he pointed at Mat and drew his hand across his throat.

Prisit laughed. It was a macabre sight and a chilling sound.

CHAPTER **FORTY**

Lynne arrived unexpectedly at the hotel room. His two guards had accompanied Dan when he returned the previous evening. They waited outside the door of the suite.

She put a backpack on the floor. "There's some kit here. For tomorrow."

He looked through t-shirts, thick cotton trousers, a large tube of insect repellent and walking boots.

"You been up that way?" he asked.

"Hongsa?" She nodded. "It's close to Thailand, isolated between the Mekong and the border. Remote mountains and valleys, pretty much impenetrable. It's used by smugglers who cross the border at will. The Lao Army makes the odd foray but keeps pretty clear. There's no law and no roads. I spent some time in one of the Hmong villages up that way a couple of years back."

Dan was silent. He remembered she'd told him before about staying with a hill tribe. He couldn't contemplate what tomorrow would bring. Could he bring Mat back alive? It seemed absurd. That possibility was only made feasible by

Lynne Kramer and Tony Tavinor, who had kept him going through the bizarre ordeal.

When he left the *safe house* the previous evening, Tony Tavinor had made himself a mug of strong tea with four sugars and settled down to scrutinise the maps of the area surrounding Hongsa. He looked relaxed and prepared, even anxious for the following day to dawn. He had hardly noticed Dan leave.

"It will be difficult," continued Lynne.

Dan grimaced. Difficult, if only that were the extent of it! He moved to the drinks cabinet and poured two whiskies. "It looks like Mat's there," he said as he passed a glass to Lynne, "but you don't need to come. I've got no choice. I have to do it."

She closed her eyes. The sense of sorrow that passed across the perfect symmetry of her smooth features took him by surprise. He wanted to reach out and hold her, to take away the grief that stamped its demands on her sensitivity. He remembered the temple in Chiang Mai: "*The candle for enlightenment, so that I may help others; the incense spreads the fragrance of virtue throughout my mind and body; the flower reminds us that life is short and impermanent.*" Where did the pain he saw fit in?

Her voice was quiet. "I have as much reason to go as you." The moment passed. It was as though she brushed away an irritant as she made for the bathroom. "You want me to stay tonight."

He was confused.

Juvenile apprehension flashed through him. He couldn't think of anything more that he wanted, but...

Lynne came closer and gently stroked his face with her hands. "I want company, nothing more. Anything else waits for another time."

She turned and headed for the bathroom.

* * *

Dan woke. He smelled a faint trace of perfume and looked around in shock at the figure lying in his arms - Lynne. His eyes closed again as the first rays of sunlight crept through the large window. The night had passed in weary conversation and gentle tenderness. Nothing more was needed or desired. Not this night. She sighed and pushed closer.

A sudden stab of understanding pierced Dan's momentary pleasure. The day had begun. He didn't know how he could face it. His eyes barely focused as brightness rose slowly through the blinds. His son's face drifted from his view and was lost somewhere in the pain that engulfed him. He had kept talking even when they were both desperate for rest – he didn't want to wake up and have to face this day. Eventually, reluctantly, his eyes had closed, and the anguish stretched into his dreams, reaching anxiety that he had never known before. The pale light grew brighter - he eased out of bed and walked to the window, pulling a bathrobe tightly around him. He craved the dawn to pause and the sun to wait so he could prepare for this. Another part of his fevered psyche demanded that time pass, that the day come swiftly. Whatever he had to face, he would face – and he would bring Mat home.

He heard a rustle of bedclothes. Lynne was sitting up watching him, wearing a black T-shirt, her dishevelled hair framing her face. She smiled and held out her hands. He sat on the bed.

"Mat's coming back with us," she whispered.

They held each other.

"I know," he said, discarding the words which echoed in his mind - *or we don't come back.*

She jumped up and threw her clothes on. "I'll get a bike

back to the apartment and collect my stuff. I'll meet you at the airport."

As she opened the door, the two bodyguards who had kept watch through the night nodded and looked carefully along the corridor before allowing her to pass.

* * *

The driver brought the car to the hotel entrance.

"Where's your favourite Temple?" asked Dan.

The smile broadened, a trace of embarrassment showing on the young, smooth face. He didn't answer.

"Temple... Your favourite Wat?"

The smile got wider. "Ah, Wat? Golden Buddha. Wat Traimit. Favourite."

"OK. Take me there. Then we go to the airport."

* * *

Whilst his guards waited at the entrance. Dan sat on the floor beneath an enormous image of the Buddha - a sign proclaimed that it was five and a half tons of solid gold! He remembered the saying: *Death is a mirror in which the entire meaning of life is reflected.* The meaning of his life had been clear. There had been little time for uncertainty: success, ambition, respect and achievement had been his mantra. Then, suddenly, without warning, everything changed. The words had stayed with him like a nightmare not ending with the waking: *"I apologise for telephoning at such an unsocial hour. I am calling from the Foreign and Commonwealth Office. Our Embassy in Thailand has advised that your son Matthew has been arrested in Bangkok."*

Meaning lost its certainty. Everything that went before was

tainted with the notion that he had lacked the courage to live beyond the small piece of himself that posed no questions and gave no challenges. Fear, he had never known before, reared up and stabbed at him, dragging him to a different place where he was adrift and alone. The experience was terrifying but then gradually, seeping from unfamiliar understanding, liberating. Unknown instinct called him to throw off the restraints that had made him what he was.

A cough came from a figure kneeling on the floor in front of the Buddha - an old man, his eyes closed, hands together in front of his wrinkled face. The flash of a camera came. Two young women knelt and whispered in Thai. There was no order for his thoughts. They slashed at him as reminders of what had passed before, what he had imagined had been rejected but, in truth, had crafted his existence. All the memories that had been pushed into dark spaces he long ago decided never to visit again had flared in the desperate fight to retain some calm; as the scraping clash of manacles surged through his mind, the sight of empty eyes hidden by thick bars disfiguring his view.

He felt a hand touch his arm. The young driver smiled, wâi'd and then pointed at his watch. "Airport, sir."

Gold-framed pictures of King Bhumibol decorated many of the road junctions. Where he wasn't shown in a regal pose, he was holding a camera and taking pictures. Dan looked in sympathy from the air-conditioned car at passengers hanging out of the windows of packed red and cream buses, trying to catch a breeze in the fierce morning heat. They passed by a series of weed-encrusted concrete pillars erected to carry new roads that hadn't survived one of Southeast Asia's regular economic recessions. For a short distance, the road ran parallel to train tracks, cutting through lines of shanty dwellings thrown up alongside the rails, thin card panels for walls, and rusted corrugated iron for roofs. They swept up to a dual carriageway.

The driver turned and smiled. "Traffic OK now, Sir."

Dan nodded and returned the smile.

* * *

Magach looked through one of the windows of the small twin-engine plane as it waited on a taxiway at Don Mueang airfield. He pulled a map of Thailand from his small bag and pointed to the north-east of the country.

"There's a small airfield here at Nan. I've chartered a Bell chopper. It's at the airport," he said. "I've got an ex-US army guy ready. He'll fly in for exfil when it's over." He pointed to the map. "There's a clearing one kilometre away from Chao's camp. He will wait there for a flare. Then he comes in.

"We have to get across the Thai, Lao border into Sainyabuli," continued Magach. "Remnants of Chao's Hmong army dispersed there when the Pathet Lao took over in the seventies. Chao keeps his secure papers there."

He looked at Lynne, "If your fight boy is right, security should be light."

Lynne leaned back in her seat. She wasn't listening.

"Fasten seat belts," shouted the pilot as the aircraft lined up on the runway and then immediately roared up to full throttle, bouncing along the centre line before lifting quickly into a bright blue cloudless sky.

"It's rugged country," continued Magach when the plane levelled off. "Mountains, wild animals, rivers. We'll walk most of the way, although I've asked a guide to get some mules. The best way to travel in that area is by elephant, but it's pretty hard territory if you haven't ridden before."

They stared from the windows as Bangkok's pollution drifted far behind whilst ominous clouds floated past the windows. A flash of lightning burst into the dimmed cabin. It touched the careful terraces of a rice paddy as the pilot began whistling a tuneless song before taking a swig of water from a bottle.

Magach pulled a pile of clothes from a backpack and threw off his shirt and trousers, replacing them with a long black tunic and loose torn cotton trousers. Dan followed suit with the clothes from his backpack. Lynne said nothing. Everything she had bought fitted perfectly.

Tavinor watched in silence, he wore kit he had acquired from some of Bangkok's surplus stores. The plane jolted through heavy clouds, another bolt of lightning lighting up a sky which had clouded over as they climbed above a range of dark green hills. He looked around the cabin. Lynne still staring from the cabin to the landscape below. Magach engrossed in the map. Dan looking through a window with a terrified expression on his face. His first taste of action thought Tavinor- life on a precipice, with his son's survival at risk at the end of it. The man would live or die, as with the rest of them. The day would end – eventually - as all days end. How was unknown, and for that, Tavinor was grateful.

Dan watched as lightning lit up the sky, flashing into thick clouds. He suddenly understood that there was nothing to go back to. What he had become accustomed to was no longer there. It was a time that had passed. A reality that was no longer his. He had no idea where he was going after this day ended, but, as he looked from the window and the engine note changed, beginning their descent overhead a town bathed in strong sunlight - clouds left behind over the brooding hills - a river daubed with the wakes of craft criss-crossing the water - he looked across at Lynne and felt a strange sense of exhilaration he had only rarely experienced before.

The wheels bounced on the runway.

"We've landed at Nan. Move it. We have to get across the border into Lao tonight," snapped Magach, leaping from his seat as the plane rolled to a halt.

Dan dabbed some water from a bottle over his face.

Magach pointed to the cockpit, where the pilot was running through a checklist. "He'll wait to get us back to Bangkok." He laughed. "If we make it."

He opened the door and lowered the steps. The plane had stopped by a large hangar. A Toyota four-wheel drive was waiting on a road leading from the airfield. Magach shook the pilot's hand and took off through the large building cluttered with aircraft in various stages of disrepair. He paused and spoke to a tall figure dressed in fatigues alongside a helicopter at the hangar door.

Magach climbed into the vehicle and talked quietly to the driver as Dan got in the back seat with Lynne and Tavinor.

"OK. If I'm not around when we're at Hongsa, send up a flare when you need to get out," said Magach, pointing across to the helicopter. "Kowalski will be a few minutes away. It'll be a couple of hours before the road runs out, and we meet up with the guide who's getting us across into Lao."

"Why not go in on the chopper?" said Dan.

"We need to get in there quietly." He paused, "if that's possible."

"You know Nan?" Dan asked Lynne as the vehicle set off through a tightly-packed little town, past the usual clusters of young novice monks sitting on walls outside temples and a small street market of stalls selling jewellery, textiles, bamboo baskets and mats.

"Once. I came up to the Orange Festival. It only became a real part of Thailand about sixty years ago, till then local dynasties ran the province."

They crossed a river and left the town behind. The stalls that studded the narrow road fell away as it ran into the encroaching monsoon forest. Seeing beyond the first few yards of dense vegetation became ever more difficult. It was about survival, and Dan knew it would be no accident if he came through the next few days alive. A brooding, insular energy, inured to fear, giving no concession or understanding, seemed to emanate from the undergrowth. Dan felt the power of something he had never encountered: timeless and primordial. Even as fear welled within him, so did the excitement of confronting nature that didn't care and wouldn't offer bland rationalisations.

He looked across at Lynne, staring from the window with the same intensity that was overwhelming him. "It looks pretty rough," he said.

Her voice lost its certainty as though also intimidated by their surroundings. "It's pretty much uncharted territory."

The vehicle suddenly pulled off the road, throwing up clouds of dust as they climbed a series of rough tracks clinging to the side of hills rising from the valley floor. Leaves and giant ferns began to brush the side of the car as the track narrowed and became more unstable.

"We're meeting Kham, the tracker, in a mile or so. Then we walk." Magach gestured through the window as a thick branch scraped along the roof. The driver suddenly slammed on the brakes, throwing them all forward, when two small black pigs rushed across the track, turning and squealing with fear as they saw the vehicle bearing down on them.

A few minutes later, the track dwindled away. A house on

wooden stilts with bamboo walls and a thatched roof sat in a small clearing. Chickens pecked away at the ground beneath the house, sharing the space with a few pans and a fire burning beneath a large pot stirred by a young girl wearing a black outfit covered in intricately embroidered patches, a red fur collar and a blue turban. She looked up and smiled as the vehicle skidded to a halt.

A squat figure emerged from behind the house. He approached the car, pulling two mangy-looking mules who appeared reluctant to move as they were dragged along. The face that peered toward them as they exited the vehicle was disfigured by thick scars down his cheeks. The eyes appeared to have gone into hiding behind heavy folds of brown skin. Dressed in a loose, patched, unbuttoned shirt, flapping black trousers and holed trainers, his skin was taut, carefully carved around bones jutting out in unyielding protest at the ragged coverings.

Dan was overwhelmed by suspicion. He turned to Magach. "Is this Kham?"

"Yes".

"You know him?" The question came as an accusation.

Magach leaned closer. "You brew coffee or some such bollocks." He turned away, dismissive.

Dan grasped his arm. "That doesn't answer the question."

Magach wheeled round, Dan felt a grip that defied the fragility of the long-limbed figure.

"Either you carry on, or you go with the fucking car out of here. You understand," he paused. "Now get moving."

Tony Tavinor moved quietly alongside Cooper, then closer to Magach. "When did you work with Kham?" The tone in the man's voice made Magach pause.

"He knows this area," said Magach, his voice both conciliatory and uncertain. “He also knows which way the wind blows. You have to to survive out here.”

“You worked with him before?”

“Years ago. He was with the spooks.’ He stared across at Kham.

‘How many years ago?”

Magach stared at the tracker and shook his head.

“Perhaps too many. But he’s all we’ve got. No one else was willing to step up when they heard the name Chao.”

Tavinor nodded and gripped Magach’s arm, bringing him close, his voice quiet. “Have some decency when you talk to Cooper. You understand. He’s got more at stake than any of us and less experience.” Magach winced and nodded. He turned to Dan. He grunted something that sounded like an apology.

As Kham approached, the girl under the house looked closely at the figure. The smile had gone. She stared with a strange intensity as an extraordinary croak came from the guide.

Magach spoke in Thai, and the sound of the voice in reply belonged in the jungle, as though it was crafted to communicate with animals rather than humans.

The figure shrugged and pointed to the mules. Chickens continued pecking away at the bare earth. The girl was gone. The clearing was deserted.

Dan turned and looked down a track only visible for a few yards before disappearing into thick, dark jungle. They stood in silence for a moment until a sound came from beyond the house, a scream of agony that cut into Dan like a knife. Two men came from a track. They each held one leg of a pig, blood from its slashed throat soaking into thick dust on the ground. It gave one last sudden agonising scream. Dan gritted his teeth and turned away.

“Let’s go,” said Magach.

Lynne stood on the edge of the clearing, watching everything. She had changed into a long-sleeved shirt and rough trousers; a backpack was slung over her shoulders. She said nothing.

They were entangled in dense green vegetation within a few minutes of seeing their vehicle disappear back along the track. Giant bamboo, banana stalks, and thorny liquorice were all part of the assault that Dan tried to hack his way through with the machete that Magach had handed over as they left the car. The guide was way ahead. At times, all Dan could follow in the damp gloom caused by the heavy roof of thick leaves and branches was the sound of mules' hooves crunching through thick undergrowth. He was exhausted within minutes. On several occasions, a discernible track appeared, and the guide waited. Dan sat precariously on one of the mules for a few hundred yards. The others continued to walk. He tied handkerchiefs around his neck and head. They were soon soaked through with sweat as warm dampness coated his body in humidity and grime.

Lynne appeared untouched, a red headband held her hair in place, and she occasionally sipped from a water bottle.

A noise began to creep up, steadily filling to a roaring crescendo as they turned a corner of the track. They came upon a waterfall thundering down a vertical rock face, which climbed dramatically and suddenly into thick jungle. Dan stopped in astonishment at the sight of a bright rainbow, the colours shining with intense clarity from the dark green habitat. Relentless crystal-clear water dropped down through a fissure in the jungle floor before disappearing.

He turned to Lynne.

She said nothing, staring straight ahead.

"OK," said the guide. "This Lao now. We stop for night. Short time village. OK"

A remote, deserted, hill-tribe village was a further hour along the track. Five bamboo houses resting on stilts were starting to fall back into the earth. Signs of neglected fires lingered beneath the houses but were from long ago. The earth around the settlement looked like it had once been cultivated but was now given over to waste ground.

"The tribe would have moved on when they'd used up the soil," said Magach.

The guide pulled some bags from the packs slung on either side of one of the mules. He gave one to each of them together with a large bottle of water. Dan opened the cellophane pack. Inside was a congealed mass of sticky rice and stray pieces of fat and gristle. The guide wandered away.

"We eat. We sleep. At first light, we set off. Chao's village is about three or four hours away," said Magach.

"Sleep where?" asked Cooper.

"You can select any villa you like. I suggest you find one with a ceiling and a floor. They're called the executive suites," replied Tavinor with an ironic smile as he looked back down the track where Magach was talking to two men. They were carrying Uzi submachine guns and handed over four of the weapons to Magach before they walked away from the angry figure.

Kham was watching from beneath one of the houses.

Magach started shouting.

The two men moved away quickly swallowed into the jungle.

"Who were they?" demanded Dan as Magach came back.

"They were our backup."

"Were?"

Magach remained silent.

Lynne came across. She shrugged, her voice fatalistic. "It

was always going to be just us." She moved toward one of the houses.

Magach stared down the track at the departing figures and then handed a weapon to each of them. "Check them out," he grunted before wandering away.

Dan followed Lynne up the decaying steps of one of the houses. She was squatting on the floor, carefully examining the contents of her backpack. She closed it quickly when Dan approached.

"I'll take this shack," she said, turning away from Dan. The meaning was clear – she wanted to be alone.

Tavinor was standing in another of the derelict structures. He looked across at Dan and nodded before stripping the Uzi and laying the pieces on a cloth he had placed on the floor of the shack.

Dan knew the weapon from his time in the territorial army. But he had never used one. He made his way up the steps of the last remaining broken-down shack.

Dust clung to pieces of rotting grass-matting lying haphazardly about the bamboo floor of another of the houses that Dan decided was as good as any other. A rattan curtain hung down from the roof through which thick branches had forced their way into the room, shedding a thick carpet of leaves. He returned to the clearing watching night arriving in a spectacular show as the fierce sun dropped quickly through an atmosphere festooned with red abstractions played out on a bright blue backcloth. Smoke trickled from under the house where the tracker sat silently, staring into a lethargic fire. Lynne and Tavinor were nowhere to be seen. Magach had moved away into the rainforest. Darkness followed quickly after sunset. The sharp sounds of the day died down. He returned to the hut and gathered pieces of clean grass matting, piling them on top of a mound of leaves. He examined the Uzi.

It was oiled and appeared well-maintained. His limited expertise didn't allow him to strip the weapon, and Lynne and Tavinor seemed distant. He lay down, the matting made a springy mattress, and as soon as his body felt the soft touch, he realised how tired he was. The adrenalin which had kept him going slipped away. He heard a soft snuffling noise from the ground beneath the floor as he closed his eyes. It seemed appropriate and comforting.

CHAPTER FORTY-ONE

Dan woke in a frenzy of scratching at his inflamed insect-ravaged skin. He cursed, having forgotten to coat himself in the insect repellent that lay untouched in his bag. His body felt alive as he stripped off his clothes and threw the remains of a bottle of water over himself. The relief was short-lived. He ran from the room and into the clearing, which was touched by the light of the sun rising above a tall curtain of trees. A large barrel of water stood in a corner. He rushed across, frantically rubbing himself until the irritation slowly subsided, remaining as intense background sensitivity. The tracker sat next to the languid fire. He didn't appear to have moved from the previous night. He stared across at Dan with disinterest.

After scrubbing his clothes in the water, Dan slipped them on. Steam rose from his body as the sun blazed down. Lynne appeared looking crisp and clean as if she had stepped from a room in a luxury hotel. Dan didn't bother asking how she did it. He felt inadequate enough already. He moved back to the hut and gathered his backpack and the Uzi.

Magach emerged and moved across to the fire. Kham poured a dark grey liquid into four plastic bowls and handed them over without speaking. Rice settled into the bottom of the dish, a few pieces of what appeared to be chicken floated in the steaming liquid pungent with the flavour of ginger. Dan looked at Magach, who sipped from the bowl. Dan did the same. It tasted pretty good. Tavinor emerged from the rainforest and grabbed a bowl. He nodded at Dan and ate without comment.

Magach lifted his Uzi and fired into the air. "Check." They each let out a burst of gunfire toward the sky. There was a frantic clatter as animals and birds screamed in panic as they scrambled and flew from the sudden outburst.

The tracker stood and watched whilst scattering the fire across dry earth before moving after them, dragging the two mules standing by a tree, their heads hanging down disconsolately.

"How long?" asked Dan.

"To Chao?" The smile that cracked the guide's disinterested image was disconcerting. It seemed out of place. "Around four hours."

As they began to walk, Dan realised how stiff he was. The previous day's trek had used up muscles long neglected. Each step brought a protest. Nothing cushioned the impact of bone against bone as his joints screamed in pain. The prospect of confrontation seemed absurd. All he could concentrate on was finding the resolution to take the next step. As he did so, a blue snake slid between his feet, disappearing too quickly for him to react. He tried to move a little faster, slithering down an incline on the side of a steep hill. As they reached the bottom, he slipped on a thick glaze of mud and clattered into a tree trunk. He shouted in anger and pain. An answering scream came from the branches of the tree. Three monkeys sat on a branch holding food to their mouths, watching him as though he were an exhibit.

The rest were already down the slope. Dan saw Tavinor watching him as he struggled to his feet and tried to rub the pain from his leg before turning a corner of the track into a small valley bound on all sides by jungle-covered hills. The valley was covered in rice paddies, in two small fields water buffalo struggled with ploughs through waist-deep water. He moved cautiously and slowly along the muddy edges of the fields, continually slipping and almost sliding into the water. His throat was dry, and his body ached like nothing he had known. He didn't understand whether he was feeling anticipation, fear or exhaustion. Each emotion had its place.

The figures waited ahead at the edge of the valley.

"Chao is in a small valley just beyond the next range of hills," said Magach, handing Dan a water bottle. "Just follow me and do what I say."

The tracker shuffled away.

They followed.

Dan moved more certainly now. The reminder of why he was in this beautiful, alien land was enough to hold the pain until later, but another hour of painstaking progress strained his resolve almost beyond his limit. The sun passed overhead and began to fall behind the curtain of trees. He plunged waist-deep through a river, tumbling down slopes covered with a dark, brooding roof of vegetation. Each step became an effort of will until they finally reached a wide, well-trodden track. A grunt and a gesture from the tracker took them to one side alongside a tall teak tree, the width of its trunk as big as a house. As Dan leaned exhausted against the craggy bark, he heard a shuffling and steady rhythmic vibration, intimidating in its power and persistence.

Tavinor turned to Lynne. They had fallen behind the

others. She nodded, and they both moved off down a track leading away from the path they had been following. They were soon lost in a wild rainforest embrace.

Suddenly, an animal call came like an out-of-tune trumpet blast. As Dan turned toward Magach beside the tracker, the trail seemed to burst apart, and an enormous elephant standing at least ten feet high crashed through the undergrowth and moved alongside them. On top of the massive bulk sat a young, black-robed rider wearing a bright red bandanna, a Kalashnikov lying across his lap. As he looked at the extraordinary sight, Dan heard branches snapping as three more elephants emerged from the jungle. Two figures walked alongside the elephants.

He turned to Magach.

His mouth fell open.

He stared in horror and dread.

The tracker, Kham, sat against the base of the tree.

His throat was cut from ear to ear.

Magach held a blood-covered machete. "He sold us out."

Magach gestured toward the last elephant. He spat on the ground, "Chao."

Throwing his machete and Uzi to the ground, he indicated for Dan to do the same. "It's not over."

The rider of the fourth elephant touched the animal on the side of the head with his leg. It slowly lowered itself to the ground, and a stocky figure stepped carefully to the earth. His face was pockmarked, deep pits under dead eyes examining Dan with indifferent curiosity as he walked around him. His hair, cut close to his head, revealed dark scabs on his scalp. Two fingers were missing on his right hand, which resembled a claw. He moved close to Dan, staring him in the face and then spitting on the floor before he turned to Magach and shouted, "Too old, Magach. Stay at home."

"Fuck you," responded Magach.

Chao laughed and climbed back up on the elephant, giving out orders. Dan felt himself pushed along the track.

The elephants began to move along behind. Now, the pain was more than physical as Dan led the line, continually being prodded from the rear. An elephant trunk passed his head and then returned to push him in the back, sending him flying into a mud pool at the side of the trail. A high-pitched vicious laugh broke through the rain forest's chorus.

They walked for about thirty minutes before turning a corner and coming into a small settlement. A human skeleton, lips gaping in a toothless mouth stained red from chewing betel nuts, greeted them. The old man bowed and poked Dan in the chest without speaking. He drew his hand across his throat in an unmistakable gesture.

Chao asked a question in what Dan presumed was Laotian. The wizened old head shook in reply as Chao slid down from the elephant that had slowly, almost sensuously, dropped to the ground.

"Come. Come." Dan was prodded toward a large bamboo hut on traditional wooden stilts. The old man followed, drawing his hand across his throat again, his red-stained mouth gaping in anticipation.

Dan suddenly leaned forward and pushed him in the face, knocking the scrawny figure to the ground. A laugh went up from the steps leading to the hut. Chao pointed to the old man scrabbling about in the dirt, the man looked up and joined in the laughter.

Dan felt ridiculous.

The large hut was dark, with windows covered in black material. The air was still and warm.

His eyes slowly became accustomed to the light. A figure was bound to a wooden chair just inside the hut.

Mat!

A painful smile broke out on his son's face, disfigured by angry bruises around his nose and eyes.

"Dad."

Dan held his son again - at last. A brief moment of intimacy. Desperate relief clashing with sorrow and helpless impotence. He touched the bruised face, his son, the responsibility he undertook when he held the baby, and even if inadequately, nurtured and loved this child. How could it end like this?

He turned to Chao, who was carrying a Kalashnikov.

"What do you want?"

Chao turned to a figure that had come up the steps and stood just behind him.

Prisit! They spoke in Thai.

"Too late, Mr Cooper," said Chao. "Want nothing."

"So, take me. That's revenge enough, isn't it? Whatever you need. To save face, is that it?"

Chao shrugged. "This is Lao, Mr Cooper. You come here, you meet Chao. You play by his rules." The smile faded. "You should have taken your son home. Everybody happy. But you want to be a big man."

He shouted to one of the young men standing around watching. He ran to a small brick hut by a helicopter and returned with a cassette player. Chao turned it on. Dan listened to his own voice in horror: *"I intend to make clear that even if there is no trial, what has happened to Mat will not be swept under the carpet. I want to find out what happened. How Mayer set it up. Everyone involved. If this goes through, it's not the end of it. If it's Chao Thanarat or Mayer, I don't care. I'm going after whoever set my son up."*

"You think we straight out of the trees, Mr Cooper? You

going after me? You." He came over and cracked the butt of the gun against Dan's head. "Where is the fucking woman?"

Dan barely heard the question. His head hammered a desperate rattling pain into his brain, spiking a frantic fear. He slumped to the floor.

Mat started to speak. "No. It was my fault..."

Prisit pulled out his gun and pushed it at Mat's forehead.

"NO!" shouted Dan, squinting through his pain, he threw himself at Prisit.

The gun exploded next to Dan's head. Mat saw the bullet smash through the roof as Prisit shrugged with contempt and indifference. Mat tried to go to the prone figure of his father, but the bindings held him to the chair, and he fell to the floor, crawling across the earth.

Chao pushed Prisit away and turned to Magach, who watched the drama silently. "Where's the woman?" he demanded. Magach shrugged and stayed silent.

"So, she ratted you out with the soldier boy," He laughed. "You're past your time, old man. Should have gone back when it ended."

"Should have left you in the gutter,' snarled Magach gesturing toward Prisit, "and this fuck as well."

Chao laughed.

"Another of the mutants that were drawn to you. You motherfucking piece of shit."

Chao laughed again. He lifted the Kalashnikov and blew Magach's brains across the steps. Blood covered Mat's face. He screamed.

Chao snapped out an order, and Prisit pushed Mat upright and dragged Dan by his hair to an adjacent chair, tying his wrists and ankles with rope.

"Dad."

There was no response.

Mat could barely see through the gloom, but he just recognised the three riders who had brought in the elephants. They lay on grass mats lined up against a wall.

Chao moved across and slumped onto two large black cushions thrown on the ground.

Mat tried to bring his arm up to soak away Magach's blood falling down his face. He failed and grimaced as warm sweetness dripped to his lips.

Prisit laughed and moved inside the hut.

The old man cackled as Mat struggled to ease the bindings holding him to the chair. He came and pulled a knife from his waistband. The point touched Mat's adams-apple as he tried to move away. A trickle of blood ran down his neck. Chao shouted. His father started to stir in the chair alongside. The old man shuffled away, waving the knife in front of Mat's face and laughing.

A burst of gunfire smashed into the roof of the hut.

Dan stared through half-open, bruised eyes as another burst shattered the wall above the group slumped down, watching the action. One of the three men grabbed his weapon. His head exploded. Tony Tavinor stood across from the wall, his Uzi covering the other two men who raised their hands above their heads.

Chao rose with an Uzi at his neck. Lynne Kramer was carrying the weapon.

She gestured toward the old man, waving the gun in front of his face, "Cut the ropes."

The old man danced in a trance toward the chairs, the knife pointing toward Mat's neck. Two shots rang out. He fell. His body was still.

"Cut the ropes, or you're next," she ordered Chao.

He cut the ropes. Mat grabbed the knife and released his father, who looked around in confusion.

"Dad!"

He held his father.

The figures against the wall still hadn't moved. Staring at the drama but not interfering. Mat rushed across and grabbed one of the guns lying on the floor. Lynne watched him. As he turned, a shadow fell across the doorway.

Prisit!

His gun pointed toward Lynne while he gestured for Chao to get out of his line of fire. Chao fell to one side. A single shot rang out. Prisit fell, and a bullet hole appeared on his forehead. Tavinor's gun was poised in case he needed to fire again – he didn't. Chao jumped and started for the doorway.

"Stop," shouted Mat.

Chao stopped and jerked around, aiming a blow at Mat and grabbing for the gun in his hands. Mat jumped back and swung the gun. It clattered against Chao's body, and he dropped to the floor. Mat cracked the butt against Chao's head. Blood poured from a gash on the man's forehead. He lay still.

Dan started to lift Lynne. She shook her head. A trickle of blood ran down her cheek. She wiped it. "I'm OK. It's just a flesh wound. Let's get out of here."

She looked down at Chao. "Bring him," she ordered Mat and started toward a hut behind which, in a clearing, stood a helicopter. A generator was fixed to a concrete pad attached to the rear wall. "That's where he keeps his crap," said Lynne digging into a bag behind the hut. A flare flew into the sky.

The hut was secured with three heavy padlocks. Tavinor stood back and fired into the door. The hinges fell apart. He kicked through into an office.

"Grab the computer," said Lynne, smashing the lock on a

filing cabinet. “Get the files,” she shouted at Dan, who pulled open the drawers and piled as many files as he could into a cardboard box.

Chao started to stir.

The clatter of a helicopter suddenly filled the sky. It dropped down beside the chopper on the helipad.

“Let’s go,” shouted Lynne as Chao’s soldiers gathered at the door of the large hut, but they still didn’t look inclined to get involved.

“Bring him,” said Lynne, pointing to Chao and taking the laptop from Mat.

As Dan began to leave, he noticed a file on the floor. It was tagged *Kumat.* He threw it into the box. Lynne had already reached the helicopter, and she tossed the laptop onto the rear seat. Dan pushed the cardboard box on the floor.

“Get him in,” shouted Lynne to Tavinor, who grabbed Chao and dragged him aboard. The rotors were deafening, churning the air, and leaves on the trees were dancing. The helicopter rose quickly.

Kowalski gestured for Mat to sit alongside him in the front as the helicopter rose.

“Where’s Magach?” he asked.

Mat shook his head as he turned and watched Lynne train her weapon at Chao.

She leaned across and pulled open the door of the craft.

“You remember the aid worker you killed at Long Tieng. You murdered him to save your skin. Do you remember the aid worker?” She yelled at the kneeling figure as they swung in a wide arc and headed down the valley.

Chao turned slowly, holding his head. He shrugged. “You took your time.”

Lynne smashed the gun against his kneecap.

Chao screamed in pain.

“Long Tieng. May Nineteen-seventy-five. You bastard. Remember his face because it’s the last thing you will ever remember.”

Chao’s scream as he was forced from the helicopter was brief and soon lost as his body disappeared down into the rain-forest’s grip.

CHAPTER FORTY-TWO

The chopper skimmed low through valleys carved like deep gashes in the mountains carpeted with rainforest.

Dan looked across at Lynne. She was calm. Her eyes staring out the open door. The wind ripped through the cabin. Tavinor tightened his harness and leaned across, pulling the door shut.

Lynne smiled.

Kowalski's voice rose above the screaming engine as he wrenched the helicopter above another peak, dropping like a stone over rice paddies carved in terraces down the slopes and into a wide valley.

"I'm keeping below the radar, if anyone's watching. We'll say we've come in from Chiang Rai. Then you get straight off to Bangkok."

Dan leaned forward and touched Mat's shoulder. His son's hand gripped his as he stared from the window. The chopper made a steep turn around an escarpment at the end of the valley.

"Lynne. Why didn't you tell me?" said Dan.

She just laughed and pointed ahead. A few lights shone from the ground as the outskirts of Nan came into view.

Kowalski brought them around the town, coming in from the east.

The plane which had brought them from Bangkok was waiting on a taxiway.

"Get the stuff. We're going," shouted Lynne.

Dan and Lynne ran with boxes of files. Mat followed with the computer. Tavinor stayed by the helicopter, checking for any surveillance. There was none.

The pilot was in the cockpit running through pre-flight checks. As soon as everyone was in the cabin, Tavinor closed the door. The propellers started rotating. As they began moving toward the runway, Mat gave an ear-splitting yell. He put his arms around Lynne and kissed her cheek.

"You're my fucking hero."

He pointed at Tavinor and nodded his thanks.

Mat smiled as the plane lifted off.

"Dad"

The single word was enough with the touch of his son's arms around him. A feeling he had stored away because he thought it would never happen, a feeling like nothing that had gone before.

"You did it, Dad."

Dan hadn't the control to speak. Not for the moment. Not yet. He slumped back into the chair. A tear rolled down his cheek.

"I know," said Mat as he fell into the seat beside him, "it's too much. I'd about given up."

Dan found some semblance of control. "It wasn't me." He pointed around the cabin. "It's mainly down to these two," he gestured to Tavinor and Lynne, he paused, "and Magach."

"Who was he?"

"I'm not sure I'll ever know, a strange guy. We could never have got to you without him, though."

"What do we do now?" asked Mat. "I'm still on the run."

Dan gripped his son's hand. "What's been happening? How did you get up there?"

The journey passed as Mat fed them the story of his journey from the prison. As he finished, he turned to Dan, "I'll call Mum as soon as I get to the apartment."

Eventually, Lynne, who had been listening, looked over after making some calls.

"Mat, you go to the safe house when we land. I want you out of sight. Dan, we will go to the hotel. It's not over yet. Transport is waiting at the airport."

Tavinor spoke, "The hotel is clean. All the bugs have been cleared. I'm away to check out the guy who met with Pollard. I think we have an idea who it was."

Dan glanced at the boxes of files. "These might help. We'll get them to the hotel as soon as we land." He said, pointing at the files. The names meant nothing to him until he opened one headed *Kumat.*

"Bangkok, twenty minutes," shouted the pilot.

The engine note changed. Dan cleaned himself up as best he could

Lights spread ahead almost to the horizon.

They started to descend.

Dan could see the runway's glare cutting through a dark patch in the kaleidoscope of city lights.

Bangkok was illuminated in front of the plane as it descended toward the runway lights.

"Wow," exclaimed Mat.

The ground appeared by the side of the plane. They bumped a couple of times before settling on the runway, gently slowing down before turning onto a taxiway. The plane pulled up across from the terminal.

* * *

The two guards who were still shadowing Dan helped him and Lynne drag the boxes of Chao's files into his suite.

"I'm not sure I need you guys anymore," Dan said to the two guards as they finished.

"We'll wait until the trial is over."

Dan nodded. He'd got used to their presence.

"Chris Ralston is in the lobby," said Lynne. "We should..."

"Yes. Of course. Let's go."

Dan stepped out of one of the lifts. He moved over to Chris Ralston, who was sitting alone.

"I've heard," said Ralston.

"I'm sorry."

"I guess it ended in the right place for him. He belonged there. In Lao, the place he loved."

Dan nodded.

"Will you be all right for court?"

"Yes. Of course." He indicated Nirundorn coming across toward them. "The day after tomorrow, I believe. Afterwards, I will go straight to America."

"I'll arrange tickets," said Dan. He knew that Ralston had no idea he would have one hundred thousand US dollars to take with him.

"Thanks. Now Chao's dead, I can go on my own. My father has relatives in Florida. I'll try to find them."

Without another word, he got up and wandered off.

Lynne stood up and indicated Nirundorn bustling across the lobby.

"It's finished for me here. Chao's gone. It will be time to

move on." She paused and smiled. "After we get Mat out. I'll come over tonight. Mat's OK, don't you go over there." She kissed his cheek and looked at two obvious plain-clothes cops standing in the corner of the lobby. She nodded at the lawyer as she exited the hotel.

Nirundorn launched himself before he sat down. "You have Mat?"

"He's safe."

The lawyer leaned forward and offered Dan his hand. "I am happy for you. He is in Bangkok?"

Dan didn't reply.

"The court has contacted me. There is a hearing the day after tomorrow. Ten-thirty."

"Who is the judge?"

Nirundorn frowned. "Vyraj." He hesitated. "Why do you ask?" Dan didn't reply as Nirundorn continued. "Your son will be in court?" he asked.

Dan nodded.

Nirundorn's expression didn't waver. "And what am I to say? I am his lawyer. We hope the Judge will accept Ralston's evidence, but there is no guarantee."

'You said yourself it wouldn't be enough.'

Nirundorn nodded and then stood. "I need to prepare. Tomorrow, we speak again." He gestured toward the plain-clothes officers. I understand you would not want Mat picked up before the hearing. He will attend of his own choice, not be dragged by officers, but I must speak with him before the hearing."

Dan agreed.

CHAPTER FORTY-THREE

Dan Cooper answered the phone. Tony Tavinor had returned from keeping watch at the estate Pollard had visited. Lynne was working through a pile of documents they had extracted from Chao's files.

Dan checked his watch. "Two o'clock in the morning, Tony. What's happening?"

"The place has come to life. Gardeners, builders, and cleaners are going over the place. Whoever lives there is on the way. I've returned for a break. The agency has a few guys keeping watch." He looked across the floor, which was covered with papers. "Anything?"

"Kumat." He held up a file. "He's in it up to his neck. I'm going over there."

"I'll come with you," said Tavinor.

* * *

Dan banged on the Oriental Hotel room door, pushing past Kumat as soon as it opened.

Tavinor followed and moved close to the man.

The soldier stood tall in a light blue silk dressing gown. His expression quickly disguised his surprise. Dan walked to the window and looked at the river. An empty long-tail boat pulled up alongside the Oriental Pier. Memories of Bangkwang Prison flashed across his memory. He turned to Kumat, who carefully lifted a stray hair from his dressing gown.

"What is it you want, Mr Cooper?" said Kumat, crossing the room to a refrigerator beside the bathroom door. Taking a glass, he filled it from a half-empty bottle of Hennessy Cognac.

"My son's freedom."

Kumat dismissed the notion with a wave of his hand.

Tavinor took the glass from Kumat's hand. "What..."

"Sit down and shut up."

Kumat leapt up, Tavinor grabbed him by the throat and held him. The man's eyes widened as he gasped for breath when he was dumped in an armchair.

"Be quiet," said Tavinor, his voice almost lost it was so low.

Dan waited until Kumat stopped struggling for breath.

"You knew Chao was holding him. I'm afraid your childish game didn't work. He was at Hongsa."

A stray note of concern crossed the smooth face as his voice croaked.

"Was?"

Dan moved back to the window and ignored the question. "You were Chao's gofer, Colonel. How did that happen? Educated at Cambridge and Sandhurst. Destined for the top. All the right connections, and you end up running errands for a drug dealer."

Kumat took a deep breath.

"Chao trusted you..."

Kumat looked up, "Trusted," he paused, "past tense."

Dan turned. He pulled the papers from his pocket. "Chao is

dead. Prisit is dead. You're the last man standing. Chao trusted you as much as he trusted the rest of the world."

He tossed the papers from the file onto Kumat's lap.

The soldier scanned through the accounts and accompanying notes.

"All the access codes, passwords and account numbers are there." Dan laughed softly. "I presume Chao opened the bank accounts for you and then claimed to need the details to pay money in."

Kumat didn't reply. He didn't need to. His alarmed expression was sufficient eloquence.

"Unless you agree to make arrangements for my son to be released," he checked his watch, it was past four in the morning, "tomorrow, every one of those accounts will be emptied. Five million three hundred thousand dollars and change is what I make it."

Kumat shook his head. His voice was distracted. "I'll have to consult."

Dan sat in an armchair opposite Kumat. "So consult."

"Vyraj is in charge of the case..."

Dan interrupted... "then Vyraj must be removed. I think that's what you said."

"What can I do at this time?" The voice wavered between anger and capitulation.

"Wake people up."

"It will cost money."

"You've got almost five and a half million," he paused, "at the moment."

Kumat pulled over the telephone. He made a call. It seemed to ring for almost five minutes before he spoke. There followed a ten-minute conversation in Thai. The call ended.

"There is a hearing at ten-thirty tomorrow morning. I don't

know which Judge yet. Mat should present himself at the Central Criminal Court before the hearing."

Dan smiled. "How does that help Mat?"

Kumat spread his hands. "What do you need?"

"The charges dropped."

"How am I able to achieve that?"

"Why should I care how? Perhaps the truth of how he was set up. By you. By Chao. By Charles Mayer."

For the first time, Dan saw the smooth façade shatter. "Chao is dead, you tell me. Mayer is not in Bangkok."

"I guess that leaves you. I'm told you have influence."

"I will do all I can."

"I'm sure you will." Dan moved toward the door, Tavinor stood alongside.

"I'll come down to the lobby with you. May I first go to the lavatory?"

Dan raised his eyebrows as Kumat slipped his mobile phone into his pocket and crossed the floor to the bathroom.

Five minutes later, the door burst open. "You bastard!" snarled Kumat, "the accounts are empty."

"Did you think I'd trust you any more than Chao did? The evidence of your involvement in drug trafficking will be with the police, the Bangkok Post and the US Drug Enforcement Agency if Mat isn't released."

"What about the money?" Kumat's voice was desperate.

"When my son leaves Thailand, the money will be returned to your accounts."

"How do I know I can trust you?"

Dan turned to Tavinor and laughed. "I don't do trust, but my son is worth more than five million dollars." He leaned forward. "And you've got no choice. You screw me around anymore, your money is gone, and what reputation you have will be destroyed, and that'll just be the start. I'll hound you, frame you, and blacken your name, and I promise I'll see you in Bangkwang, where you tried to put Mat. But it won't end there. I'll buy whoever I have to so that your life in that place, or any other shithole you end up in, is a living hell. You get the picture."

He leaned close and whispered. "If my son walks free, so do you. If he doesn't, whatever he suffers, you suffer ten times over."

Kumat leaned back on the sofa before pouring himself another brandy. He spoke quietly. "I need to make more calls."

"I imagined you might. Call me at the Shangri-La when you've made the arrangements."

As they were leaving, Tavinor got a call from the Agency. He should get back.

"I'm knackered," said Dan. "I'll get back to the hotel and see you later."

CHAPTER
FORTY-FOUR

Judge Vyraj was wearing a black cap - the executioner's mask. He banged the gavel. His glasses slipped down his nose. Mat fell to the floor as Prisit pulled at the chain holding his manacles. Dan couldn't move, blood trickled down his legs as insects crawled over him, gouging at his flesh, rendering him helpless.

The gavel banged again and again.

He opened his eyes. The light was still on beside the bed. The ink from his pen had stained the sheets. The door banged again. He rubbed his eyes and tried to brush aside the confusion. The banging echoed in the room as he dragged himself from the bed and looked through the security peephole.

Lynne.

He felt wiped out. She looked fresh and ready for anything.

"I thought I'd better get you moving,'" she said, moving past him.

He rubbed the tiredness from his eyes. "What's the time?"

"Just gone eleven."

"Shit. I didn't get back from that scumbag Kumat until after five."

"And?"

He picked up the phone, ordered coffee and then told her about Kumat.

"He wants his money." He told her what happened with the Colonel.

"You think he's got the clout?"

He paused. "I don't know. What he's fixing now is to lay bare a corrupt system. Bent police tied in with major drug dealers. Think about it. The Thai establishment wouldn't want that highlighted."

"He's desperate for the money," said Lynne. "I've had a couple of guys looking a bit closer. He's into a couple of casinos in Macau. Owes over two million dollars and is under serious pressure. He's been trying to recoup his losses but just gets deeper into a hole."

"He had over five million in a Swiss account."

"Yes, but he's also committed to buying a condominium in KL for about four million. And remember, he doesn't have Chao anymore. That money tap has been switched off."

The valet appeared with two coffees.

"Nirundorn's coming over shortly. Let's see what he says."

"Perhaps we should just get Mat out."

She smiled. "I guess you'd better talk to your son about that. It would be easy, though. And it wouldn't cost anything now. We could get him across the border."

"If it comes to that, I have to speak with him again."

"Be careful. You'll be watched. Don't go near the safe house."

"Why didn't you tell me about your father?" he asked suddenly.

She turned away, "It wasn't your business, and you'd have tried to stop me. It wasn't just what happened to my father.

That was over twenty years ago in a bloody stupid war. People do crazy things. But Chao hasn't changed."

"Is that why you came back to Thailand?"

"Partly. My mother died in a car crash. I was undercover with a police unit in San Diego. I think it was a mistaken identity. They thought I was driving the car." She paused and took a deep breath. "But I wanted revenge."

"Against Chao?"

She nodded.

"You knew about Magach? That he was there?"

"Tried to find him many times. He was in the helicopter with Chao. He didn't stop him and afterwards said nothing."

"You suppose he knew who you were?"

"I guess so." She stood up as though to dismiss the subject.

As Lynne left, Dan got a call. Kumat. He told Dan that the prosecution would agree to a police witness testifying that Mat had been forced to escape and he had been held against his will. If he turns up in court, of course. Dan put the phone down without a response. It was no great help as far as he could see.

* * *

Lynne stood up and indicated Nirundorn bustling across the lobby. "Tony's guy in the UK has more information on your stolen computer, and I want to start clearing all my stuff."

"Why?"

"It's finished for me here. Chao's gone. It's time to move on." She smiled. 'I'll come over this evening. Mat's OK at the apartment." She kissed his cheek. "And I don't want to be alone."

Dan frowned as he watched her across the lobby. She paused and spoke briefly to the lawyer on her way out.

Nirundorn launched himself before he even sat down. "You

have Mat? Still." He gestured toward the police in the corner of the lobby. "He is safe?"

Dan nodded.

"The court has contacted me. The hearing tomorrow is confirmed for ten-thirty."

"Who is the judge?"

Nirundorn frowned. "Vyraj." He hesitated. "Why do you ask?"

Dan felt a tremor of uncertainty as Nirundorn continued. "Your son will be in court tomorrow?"

Dan nodded.

Nirundorn's expression didn't waver. "Mr Cooper, I have expressed my concern, so now we need to plan for the hearing."

"Kumat has told me a police witness will give evidence that Mat was forced to escape and was held against his will."

Nirundorn's voice expressed his scepticism. "I'm not sure how that helps with the charges." He paused. "A police witness?" His pen was poised over a notebook. "His name Mr Cooper. Where do I meet with this witness to take his statement."

Dan shook his head, "I don't have that."

"You say that Kumat is involved?"

Dan nodded.

"He is not omnipotent. An innocent tourist having his backpack filled with heroin and facing a lifetime in the Bangkok Hilton, as it is commonly known, is not the finest advertisement for Thailand as a tourist destination. Almost ten million people visit Thailand every year." He spread his hands. "Who would risk that? Therefore, he is not innocent. You understand. Larger issues are at stake. Powerful forces will be aligned against your son."

"What choice do we have?"

Nirundorn raised his eyebrows. "You have heard my advice. The situation is even more favourable. The borders with Malaysia or Lao are just a few hours away."

Dan nodded. "Mat..." His words stuttered into silence.

"Of course. I have enormous respect for your son." He threw his hands up in frustration. "Let us hope the Judge will accept Ralston's evidence and that it carries some weight."

"You said yourself it wouldn't be enough."

Nirundorn sighed in exasperation. "We can only hope. But if we are betrayed and your witness does not confirm what Kumat claims he will say, the Judge may see Mat's escape as confirmation of guilt. I will speak with Mat tomorrow morning before the trial at the courthouse. You must be there. The hearing is at ten-thirty. I will be there at nine o'clock. Please have Mat there at that time."

He paused. "Whatever Kumat's intentions, the authorities may have their own agenda, Mr Cooper."

"You think Mat could be locked away again."

"I am lawyer, not soothsayer. You know the answer to that question."

Nirundorn leapt to his feet and stamped through the lobby.

Dan fell back. He didn't know what to do. He stared at the scene that had almost become a part of him. The Chao Phraya River. The lobby of the hotel. It was over, he could do no more.

He wanted to go and see Mat but had agreed not to. The last thing his son needed was to be dragged into prison because an alert cop had followed Dan to the safe house. Tomorrow, his son would walk voluntarily to the court, not be driven and manacled in a prison van. He returned to his room and started to flick through Chao's files. He read a few names, but they meant nothing.

He called his ex-wife, Róisín. Her husband was out of intensive care tomorrow. She would come over then. He tried to disguise his unease but failed. He couldn't fail her.

CHAPTER
FORTY-FIVE

Tony Tavinor had checked the photographs at the agency. It was good work. The guys had great contacts in the major hotels and, in this case, had yielded an unexpected result.

As he was leaving, Lynne Kramer had arrived. She had taken over an hour to reach the safe house for what was only a ten-minute ride on her moped. As he left, he heard her talking to Mat about how easy it would be to get him out of Thailand. Tavinor knew that discussion would go nowhere. He had already spoken with Mat and knew he was adamant about his innocence. The boy was willing to face trial and the consequences rather than spend a lifetime running.

He presented himself at the Embassy's reception.

"I'm afraid Mr Fairbrother is unavailable."

Tavinor smiled. "I assumed he would be. My name is Tavinor. Please let him know I am here to discuss the trial tomorrow of Matthew Cooper and Mr Fairbrother's relationship with Major Jaran Prisit."

He sat and waited.

Ten minutes later, a door opened onto a corridor, and the receptionist showed Tavinor into a meeting room.

He sat.

He waited.

Fairbrother entered exactly sixteen minutes later.

He stood by the door. “I am extremely busy,”

Tavinor remained seated. He looked over at Fairbrother. “Of course you are.”

He fell silent.

Eventually, the man spoke. “So, this about Prisit?” His voice expressed outrage. “Should I know this man?”

“I’m here on behalf of Dan Cooper. He thinks it is right to bring to your attention a number of factors which will be canvassed in the proceedings tomorrow.”

Fairbrother sat opposite Tavinor. He didn’t respond.

“Let me tell you a story.”

Fairbrother thrust himself out of his chair. “I don’t have time for stories.”

Tavinor gestured to the door. “Please. Fuck off. That would make my day. I think Cooper is being too tolerant in your case. I have encouraged him to hang you out to dry.”

He gestured again – toward the door.

Fairbrother sat.

“A few months back, two hundred thousand landmines were shipped from a Ministry of Defence facility in Cumbria to a warehouse in Kent, supposedly for onward transportation to Italy for destruction under the Ottawa landmine convention. As you know, the UK signed the Convention in late 1997.

“However, these landmines were to be diverted to East Timor to assist the illegal suppression of the Indigenous people, of whom about thirty per cent have been murdered in the past twenty-five years by the Indonesian occupation. This illicit deal was an inducement for the completion of a five hundred-million-pound arms deal between the two countries."

He paused and pointed toward a table with a jug of water and two glasses.

"Get me a glass of water."

Fairbrother passed the jug and a glass. Tavinor carefully and slowly filled a glass, took a sip, and resumed.

"The main arms deal between the two countries was negotiated by a special advisor to the defence ministry. His name was Charles Mayer. Mayer is also the chairman of the bank Otterburn Fuller. That bank financed the landmine transportation."

He paused and looked up at Fairbrother.

The man stared at the table. He briefly glanced at Tavinor as he continued.

"An explosion at the warehouse occurred, and both the landmines and the building were destroyed. Mayer's bank lost in the region of ten million pounds. Insurance refused to pay out because they had documents confirming the landmines were going to East Timor via Rotterdam, which was illegal and rendered the insurance void."

He paused again. "I trust you're not finding this tedious."

Fairbrother did not respond.

"Mayer lobbied Dan Cooper for restitution of the ten million pounds his bank had lost as he alleged Cooper was involved in instigating the explosion.

"A few weeks ago, Matthew Cooper, Dan Cooper's nineteen-year-old son, was arrested at Don Mueang airport on his way to Vientiane. There was a quantity of heroin in his backpack. He faces a lifetime of incarceration in Thai prisons. He has been offered the opportunity to obtain bail, with the condition that he leaves Thailand and that his father pays twenty-five million to cover any costs, which include the amount he allegedly owes to Mayer."

He banged the table. Fairbrother shot up. "But you know this."

The man started to speak.

"Be quiet," snapped Tavinor.

"Over three weeks ago, a person called Craig Pollard came to Thailand to meet with Chao Thanarat in Chiang Mai. I have no intention of restating Chao's details. His career as one of the area's foremost and most violent drug dealers is well known. Pollard brought with him Mat Cooper's itinerary, which had been extracted from his father's computer after the theft of that computer. After Chiang Mai, Pollard came to Bangkok.

"Cooper's itinerary specified the flight he was taking to Vientiane. He was arrested at customs. His father has sent a note specifying the ill-treatment his son had suffered at the hands of a Major Prisit, who was present at the arrest. You ignored that report."

Tavinor stopped and sat back.

Fairbrother looked up. He smiled as though in triumph.

"Is that it?"

Tavinor didn't respond.

Fairbrother stood. "I'm afraid, sympathetic as I am to Mr Cooper's dilemma, that I do not know Mr Mayer. Of course, I've heard of him, and as far as I am aware, his company is a respectable financial institution. Furthermore, I have never had any contact with Major Prisit. As to the report of ill-treatment, I'm afraid that is a frequent and often unjustified tactic of those that are charged."

Tavinor enjoyed the moment. Arrogance seeped out of every pore of the self-satisfied creep. He waited until the man reached the door. His voice was quiet, submissive.

"There is just one further matter that will be referred to at the trial."

He pulled an envelope from his pocket. "These photographs were taken at the Grand Terrace Suite at the Peninsula Hotel when Charles Mayer was a guest."

He pointed to the images. "Major Jaran Prisit, Craig Pollard and Colonel Thaksin Kumat meeting with Charles Mayer. This was before Mat Cooper's arrest when Mayer came over for a brief visit."

He fell silent.

A look of panic crossed Fairbrother's face as Tavinor threw another photograph on the table.

"Joined by yourself seven minutes later," he pointed to a time stamp.

"These photographs show the connection between the participants in this atrocious deception. They will be presented to the court together with a witness who will confirm he packed Cooper's backpack with heroin under the instruction of Chao's hired thugs after being threatened if he did not comply..." he pointed to a photograph. "One of those thugs was Major Jaran Prisit."

Fairbrother eventually looked up. "You will understand I have responsibility..."

Tavinor's voice was hard as he interrupted. He pulled a mini recorder, the same size as a credit card, from his shirt pocket and pressed *play*:

I'm afraid, sympathetic as I am to Mr Cooper's dilemma, that I do not know Mr Mayer. Of course, I've heard of him, and as far as I am aware, his company is a respectable financial institution. Furthermore, I have never had any contact with Major Prisit.

Tavinor's voice broke into the smooth flow, "Don't make any references to what I may understand. I was a soldier, as I'm sure you have been informed..." Fairbrother bowed slightly as though in agreement, "As much as possible, I understand decency and integrity. You have neither. You have deliberately confused self-interest with the country's interest and betrayed both. That's why I wanted Cooper to use this photograph. You don't deserve any second chance. You have dishonestly contrived to incarcerate a young man for the rest of his life. That is inexcusable."

He banged the table again. "Do not say another word, or I may ignore Dan Cooper's wishes and destroy you in any event. The *Bangkok Post* and the *Daily Mail* would be only too pleased to use these."

He took a deep breath. "If Mat Cooper is not released," he gestured to the table, "these will be released." He paused. "This is what you will do."

CHAPTER
FORTY-SIX

Night rushed in, followed by another glorious sunset over the Chao Praya River. Dan Cooper wandered from the vast window overlooking the city. He tried to erase dark thoughts of what the next day might bring and chose instead to believe Mat would be free and the nightmare over.

As he turned, a shooting star blazed past the glass, and he braced himself for the time ahead. This was no time for melancholy. He had to find the strength to support his son, whatever happened. He laughed ironically as he sat in front of the papers they had extracted from Chao's building. So far, it had been Mat who had been strong – Dan was amazed at how his son had handled the agonies that he had faced. The boy had become a man - and what a man. Dan feared he could not have endured and survived all that Mat had tolerated, but tomorrow, it was for him to be there for his son.

He started to read from some of the papers he'd extracted from one of Chao's filing cabinets.

There was a knock at the door.

Lynne was dressed in a bright purple silk dress. A purple

orchid was balanced on her right ear, held by her hair, pinned up in a loose bow.

He held his breath. She looked too delicate to touch.

She moved close. They held each other. Words had dried up.

Eventually, Lynne spoke softly. “It’s over tomorrow.”

He closed his eyes and then felt her lips touch his cheek. A tremor shuddered through his body.

He related the discussion with Nirundorn.

“Do you trust Kumat?” she asked.

“I trust him to want his five and a half million back. But that’s not the point. What if he can’t pull it off.”

She led him into the bedroom. “Tomorrow will come soon enough. There’s nothing more you can do. Not until morning.”

She pushed him back. He started to speak, but her soft lips felt like silk as she knelt over him. He felt her hands roaming his body, at times stroking gently, at other times pulling fiercely, digging her nails into his skin, causing him to grimace until her lips would touch his, her hands caressing away his anger and pain. She grabbed his hair and pulled him to her. They tore at each other’s clothes, spreading them haphazardly about the floor. Bodies touched, the feeling was palliative and passion, leading them into a world of distraction and beauty. They thrust at each other, becoming one flesh, inseparable, knowing the other’s ecstasy as their own and losing all knowledge of autonomy. The imminence of survival and the demands of mortality brought a fierce desperation to this passion. It consumed them and took them beyond anger and mocking faces, to a sanctuary where love became all meaning and expression.

Tears dropped onto the careworn sheets.

It was quiet.

There was no sound beyond their exhausted breathing.

They lay, sighs subsided, bodies soft and sated - for a time.

Lynne's naked body was stretched out on the bed, the covers disturbed from their frantic, grasping ecstasies in a desperate search for each other. She idly stroked his leg, her hand moving slowly as she leaned on one arm and looked at him while he lay on his back, staring silently at the ceiling. Their hands touched, and they knew the purity of requited desire and the ecstasy of shared dreams. Their eyes caught, they were silent, and for the moment this was sufficient, what they were was what they both wanted. Words were superfluous.

Slowly, truth would be extracted from the deep well of sorrow and rejection that passed as memory. He touched her fingers and felt his dreams again find colour and hope.

"How old was your father when he died?" he eventually asked.

She lay down, her head soft on his chest, "It was Nineteen-seventy-five, I was ten, he was thirty-seven."

Dan stroked her hair as she continued.

"I tried to find out how it happened. Washington wouldn't help. They were too busy protecting the secrets. He wanted to help the refugees. That was bloody stupid. He was supposed to be a symbol, not do anything useful like saving lives."

He felt her head shake, almost imperceptibly, against his chest, "He loved the country. The valleys, mountains and the people. I found some of his writing. He cared about the hill tribes and hated how they were used." He felt her head shake slowly again as she rolled off the bed and walked over to the window. "He wrote about how he wanted to show me what he loved, to pass something on." She turned and moved back to the bed. "He never got the chance."

"Then your mother died."

"I'm sure she was murdered."

“You said.”

Lynne continued. “I earned a degree in criminal justice at San Diego State University. I was just three months into the police academy when I was pulled out. There was a major organised crime op against a Golden Triangle drug cartel, and it was going nowhere. They needed someone inside the cartel. I speak fluent Thai. They put me through a bundle of hoops, and then I went undercover for about fifteen months. I had to give evidence despite being assured that wouldn’t happen. After the head guy went down for life, my mother died in a car crash. I know it was meant for me. I always wanted to find out some more about my father, so I got out and came over here. I changed my name.” She paused, “And don’t ask. No one will ever know, and it’s legal and sealed in Washington. I hope.”

He closed his eyes. Her lips found his, all else was obliterated. Her touch overwhelmed him, her body caressed him. They fell into each other again.

* * *

The telephone rang out in the silent, shrouded room.

Tavinor! “I’m on my way up.”

Lynne shot out of bed. “What is it?”

“Tavinor,” Dan said as they grabbed some clothes off the floor.

The clock read 03.45.

The door banged. Lynne answered.

Tavinor marched in, “The guy who was passed Mat’s itinerary was Khaosai Svetsreni.”

“Are you sure,” said Lynne.

“He arrived back an hour ago. That’s who Pollard met with after he came down from seeing Chiang.” He looked at Dan. “He brought over the details from your computer. The itinerary was about the only thing on there, together with a few photographs of Mat."

"The chief of police!" exclaimed Lynne. "How deep does this go..."

Dan's voice was urgent as he interrupted. "What's his name again?"

"Khaosai Svetsreni," replied Lynne.

"Fuck. There's a file titled KS." He started frantically going through the files spread across the floor before suddenly lifting a thick dossier from the chaos spread across the thick carpet."

"KS." He gave some of the papers to both Tavinor and Lynne.

"See if there's anything interesting."

There was a few moments of silence before Dan spoke again. "Chao has all sorts of information here. Gossip, occasional surveillance from way back..."

Lynne interrupted, "Chao was in trouble in ninety-three. I remember when an extradition request came in from Australia, which named him as being an accomplice with an Australian dealer. The evidence was lost, and it was rumoured he'd paid his way out."

She held up a document.

Tavinor held up another document. "This is dated the day after Pollard was at Chiang Mai. Let's go. We know where he is."

Dan called down to reception and arranged a driver, asking them to send someone urgently to make some photocopies.

As he left, he grabbed some documents from the pile and handed them to Lynne. "Svetsreni and Kumat's bank details. Just in case the wheels need lubricating."

* * *

Tavinor had gone ahead on his motorbike. The driver from the hotel kept up a steady commentary on the route and the landmarks. Dan didn't listen, but he didn't stop him. The sound was a diversion from the consequences of the meeting and whether he'd even get close to the Police Chief. Tavinor called as they eventually cut off the main road and crawled through a jumble of side streets dotted with closed-up stalls before coming onto a quiet avenue with large houses on extensive grounds protected by tall fences.

Tavinor called. "Wait for a couple of minutes. There's a police car watching the place. I'll deal with it."

They stopped.

Dan's phone rang out again. "OK. It's clear."

The driver pulled up opposite one of the biggest houses, standing white and imperious in the middle of a wide expanse of dark green lawns. Dan could just see a swimming pool protruding from the rear of the house and a large field with equestrian fences dotted about. A high black iron fence surrounding the grounds met at a pair of elaborate electronic gates at the start of a long drive.

A police car was stationary in a layby about fifty yards from the gates. Dan looked inside the car. Two police officers were laid out, their wrists handcuffed together, and the car radio smashed.

Tony Tavinor stood by the gates and watched as Dan pressed a switch.

Eventually, an exclamation came from the speaker.

Dan answered. "My name is Cooper. I need to see the Chief of Police."

"Chief asleep."

The line was terminated.

Dan pressed again.

No answer.

Tavinor pointed to the fence. "I can get over."

"Wait," said Dan.

He held his finger over the buzzer until, eventually, the voice answered again.

"Tell the Chief. It is very urgent. Important for him."

"Chief asleep. No see."

The line was terminated again. The driver in the hotel car stared at him through the windscreen.

The air was warm. A humid silence enveloped him.

He had one chance.

"One minute," he said as Tavinor began to scale the fence.

Dan moved back toward the car and made a call.

Kumat answered immediately.

"I assume you have Khaosai Svetsreni's mobile number."

"And, Mr Cooper, I assume you still have my bank account details."

Dan didn't reply.

"Transfer my funds."

"Half a million."

"One."

"I'll call you back in five minutes."

Dan called Lynne. She found the details and made the transfer online.

He called Kumat. The soldier read out a number. Nothing further was said.

A sleepy voice answered. "Svetsreni."

"Chief," shouted Dan, "My name is Cooper. Chao Thanarat is dead. I know about Fang, about UBS."

"Who are you?"

"Dan Cooper, my son is Matthew Cooper."

There was a silence.

"Where are you?"

"Outside your gates."

The line disconnected.

Dan waited. Tavinor was still poised by the fence.

He could feel his heart pounding in the humid silence. The driver continued to look at him through the windscreen. He waited... and waited.

The gate swung open.

They moved back and got into the car, which drove slowly through the gates and along a gravel track, stopping at a set of marble steps sheltered by a portico supported by two heavy pillars stretching the height of the house, leading up to black wooden double doors.

Dan recognised the stocky figure waiting just inside the doors. "I've got this," he said to Tavinor.

Svetsreni led into a library, lined floor to ceiling with what appeared to be exclusively history books and encyclopaedias.

"Why have you come here, Mr Cooper?" Svetsreni asked in perfect English as he pointed Dan to a shining black leather sofa whilst he perched on the edge of a large blue leather armchair. "'Fang is where I was born."

A servant brought a tray with a silver coffee pot and two white china cups. He poured into the silence. Dan topped up his cup from the jug of milk. He sipped and then carefully placed the cup on a coaster on a small table the servant had brought across for him before leaving the room.

"Fang is not just your place of birth." He took the copies of Chao's documents. "I have Chao's records."

A slight inclination of the head was the only response.

"Chao was named in Nineteen-ninety-three concerning an extradition request for a drug dealer."

"The case was not proceeded with."

"Evidence was lost. An Australian was deported without charge." Dan tossed the copy documents onto a table in the middle of the room. "Two days later, one million dollars was transferred into an account at the Paradeplatz Zurich branch of Union Bank Switzerland. The codename for the account is Fang. It's your account. The funds came from Chao."

Svetsreni picked up the documents. Dan sat back. He waited. Each of the pages was studied with intense scrutiny. Eventually, the man spoke. "These are copies?"

"They are."

"You have the originals?"

"I do." Dan paused. "They are safe. It's no use sending officers to my hotel room."

"You misjudge me, Mr Cooper. I'm sure Ms Kramer would protect them even should I do so."

He had been checked out! Was still being checked out! Shock was allowed only a momentary foothold. He didn't respond.

"What do you want, Mr Cooper?"

Dan held up another document. "A further one million was paid to the same account on the day following a meeting between Craig Pollard and Chao Thanarat in Chiang Mai. On the same day, you met with Pollard here."

"What do you want, Mr Cooper?"

"My son's name cleared. There's a hearing tomorrow..."

The voice that interrupted was harder. "I know of the hearing. I have been consulted."

"Consulted?" asked Dan.

"Colonel Kumat has been raising the matter. Your minister raised the case."

"And?"

"Your son will be found guilty."

Dan felt his chest tighten. Nirundorn had been right. He didn't reply.

"The country's reputation is important. Tourism is our major industry."

"Then we all lose," said Dan. A dog barked outside, the sound carried through the thick windows. Svetsreni looked through the documents again.

"We may be too late."

"Too late?"

"There is no advantage in challenging the evidence."

"Evidence!" Dan's voice rose. "There is no evidence. It was a set-up from the beginning."

"You would say that, Mr Cooper. You must appreciate that a case such as this could raise serious questions about the reputation of our country's law enforcement. We have many foreigners in our prisons who claim they were unjustly convicted."

"You're worried about publicity?"

Svetsreni shrugged away the question.

"Then try this." Dan grabbed the documents from the table. "Thailand's Chief of Police paid off by a major drug dealer." Svetsreni tried to interrupt, but Dan brushed aside the intervention. "Son of a leading British entrepreneur set up by a drug dealer with the co-operation of a senior police officer, Major Prisit died with Chao Thanarat if you were not already aware."

Svetsreni's expression didn't change.

"Thai army co-operating with drug cartels in transporting drug shipments from Burma and Lao through Thailand to Europe and the eastern seaboard of the United States. The DEA and US Government will appreciate that." Svetsreni stood up as Dan continued. "I'm not without influence. I'll pursue you. I'll destroy you. I'll blacken the name of your country. I'll drag its reputation through the dirt. Please don't underestimate me. Enjoy this place because you won't have it much longer."

The man appeared unmoved by the outburst. "You make a convincing case, Mr Cooper." He moved across to a window.

"Perhaps your son." He looked out. "Were he not to turn up at court. I doubt we would pursue the matter further."

A burst of anger washed over Dan, much of which derived from his own shame that if it had not been for Mat's courage, he would have got his son out of the country long before.

"You coward. You want my son to have his life destroyed because you're scared of the truth. I won't let him do it."

Svetsreni appeared unmoved. "If the decision were mine." He paused and looked back from the window. "The Prime Minister has touched on the case."

Dan looked at his watch. "My son will be in court in five hours. If he is not released, I trust I have made you aware of the consequences."

Svetsreni nodded.

Dan stood and made his way from the room.

The police chief turned back into the library and closed the door.

Dan's car was waiting by the house. The gates opened as they rejoined the road. Dan looked back. Svetsreni was getting into a car. The gates stayed open as the man's car followed onto the road and then turned in the opposite direction to Dan's limousine.

"Well?" said Tavinor.

"We'll know tomorrow."

CHAPTER FORTY-SEVEN

Dan returned to the hotel after his meeting with Svetsreni and was kept awake by coffee and anxiety. Lynne asked about the meeting, and he had no real answer. He knew what had happened but had no idea what *would* happen.

Kumat called, but he wasn't inclined to talk to the bastard. If he wanted his "blood money" returned, he would have to make his own arrangements. The man left a message saying he would see Dan at the Central Criminal Court.

Tony Tavinor came over two hours before the hearing. He said he had arranged for Mat to be driven to the court in an Embassy car. He explained about the meeting yesterday with Fairbrother. Dan said the UK minister had raised Mat's case with the Thai government.

"Good," said Tavinor. "Now we have to get you to the safe house without any surveillance. They will be watching you, so Lynne and I will clean your route."

He checked that Lynne still had her moped at the hotel and then explained the arrangements to get Dan away to meet with Mat.

Lynne then told Dan that a plane was waiting at Don Mueang airport to get them away should Mat be released. A flight plan was ready for Langkawi in Malaysia.

Dan raised his eyebrows, gave a rueful smile and shook his head.

"Just in case. If it happens, Mat is gone from this place before some jackass changes their mind," said Lynne.

The three of them left the room at eight-thirty. Tavinor led the way, went down a service stairwell, and exited a rear entrance where he had parked a motorcycle. He rode slowly to the road leading up to the hotel and watched as Dan stepped into a hotel limousine whilst Lynne waited back on her moped. Dan looked through the rear window as the car passed Tavinor. A dark blue Nissan pulled out behind the Mercedes, and Tavinor pulled out between the two vehicles. It was slow progress for about ten minutes until Dan's car pulled into an alley just wide enough for the car. Tavinor slowed, and the Nissan blasted its hooter. Tavinor's ex-colleagues had cleared the alley earlier. It stretched for about three hundred yards. He slowed further, and Lynne came past the Nissan and his motorcycle as Tavinor crawled to a halt. The Nissan blasted its hooter again. Angry shouts came from the car, and the passenger door opened. Tavinor watched as Dan's car reached the end of the alley and then turned back onto the main road. Lynne followed. Tavinor waited until the angry passenger almost reached him before he set off down the alley. As he passed the back of a restaurant, one of his ex-colleagues pushed a large waste bin across the route, blocking the passage.

* * *

The Embassy car, a Rolls Royce with Union flags flying, stopped at the foot of the wide steps leading up to the Central Criminal Court. Mat looked across at his father. He touched his hand.

Dan tapped Fairbrother on the shoulder.

"Open the door for my son."

Tony Tavinor stood alongside a senior police officer waiting at the bottom of wide marble steps. Four guards rushed down to join them. They hesitated at the embassy car, at the Union flags. The officer held up his hand.

"I will escort him," said Tavinor as he stood before the police officer when Mat stepped down onto the kerb

They climbed wide marble steps and passed through tall glass doors, the officer ignoring metal detectors and guiding the two men into a small room off a corridor.

Dan followed, looking carefully around the vast lobby.

Police officers stood outside the room. Fairbrother waited a short distance away.

Lynne joined the officers standing guard.

Dan saw Chris Ralston waiting in the lobby. He waved his hand. They entered the room, shortly followed by Kamchan Nirundorn. The solicitor entered and sat at a small desk opposite Mat.

"The prosecutor has come to me with a proposal. It appears that Major Prisit has died in a tragic accident. It is possible that he made an error with the analysis of the drugs you are alleged to have been carrying. Perhaps it was marijuana."

Mat raised his eyebrows, "*Perhaps* it was marijuana? Aren't they sure?"

"It depends if you're willing to plead guilty to that charge. If so, they will only ask for a fine. You will not go to prison."

"A fine for smuggling?"

"It is possible. Marijuana is not considered as serious. The normal sentence would only be a few years."

"And I get a drugs conviction."

"And you walk away," said Nirundorn. "Please, Matthew, I can't do any more. Believe me, they will find the evidence if you oppose them."

Mat looked to Dan.

Nirundorn checked his watch.

"If you refuse, it may go ahead," said Nirundorn, his voice almost a whisper. "It will be adjourned, and you go back to the Unit, under their control." He turned to Dan. "Even without Prisit, accidents have been known."

Mat slumped in the chair. "I don't have any choice, do I? So, what happens now?"

"The prosecutor will state that you are charged with the marijuana offence and that there is another charge pending. You plead guilty to the marijuana, and the other charge is dropped. Plead not guilty, and there will be a short adjournment, and the heroin charge will be brought. It will be adjourned again, this time for a few months." He gathered his papers. "And you will be held in the Unit."

* * *

Judge Vyraj came from a door at the front of the court. He looked down over a pair of half-moon glasses. The face was expressionless as he scanned his court before sitting on a large black chair on a raised dais, arranging papers he produced from a green cardboard file.

The prosecutor jumped to his feet and read from a document.

Dan was sitting alongside Fairbrother, just behind Mat and Nirundorn.

He turned when the door opened at the back of the court. Chief of Police Khaosai Svetsreni came into the room. He wasn't wearing his uniform. He sat at the back next to Kumat. Dan hadn't noticed the Colonel before!

Mat looked around. He stared at Svetsreni and Kumat.

He whispered to Nirundorn, who looked behind him.

Dan saw Mat's fists clench.

"The Chief of Police, Khaosai Svetsreni and Colonel Kumat," said Nirundorn in response to a question from Mat as he made notes while the prosecutor spoke.

Mat recognised the Chief of Police from the airport when he had been arrested! He had been in Chao's pay all along. He recognised Kumat from when the plane landed on his way to Chao's village.

He felt Nirundorn touching his arm.

"You have to stand and plead guilty."

"Do I?" whispered Mat.

He stared to the back of the court. Bastards. He looked at his father just behind him.

"Stand up," said Nirundorn.

Mat stood. He looked to the back of the court again.

"Not guilty."

Dan's mouth fell open. Nirundorn grabbed his sleeve. "No. No."

Mat bent down. "Ask for an adjournment to speak with your client."

Nirundorn started to protest. "Do it!" snapped Mat.

Nirundorn stood and spoke in Thai to the Judge, who looked angrily at Mat.

The lawyer turned. "We've got ten minutes." He walked to the back of the court. Two police officers came on either side of Mat as he leaned over and spoke to Dan.

Mat whispered. "The police chief was at the airport with

Prisit. Kumat organised my escape with Prisit. They were involved from the very beginning."

Two guards pushed Mat after Nirundorn.

Dan felt his hand start to shake. He looked across at Lynne. Her eyes were closed. "Did you hear that?" he said.

She nodded and looked at Dan. "Svetsreni must have thought Mat wouldn't remember."

Dan made his way down the aisle. Kumat had gone. Svetsreni was in discussion with the prosecutor, who was dismissed as Dan came alongside.

"Your son is unwise," said Svetsreni.

"You were at the airport when my son was arrested." Svetsreni didn't respond. The surprise was fleeting, almost imperceptible. "The story is out tomorrow, and the documents are online unless my son walks free from this courtroom. No deals, Svetsreni. No deals."

The police chief's voice was low. Fairbrother joined them. "There is always a deal. Your son's passport may prove difficult to locate. Bangkok can be a dangerous place. You understand me, Mr Cooper?" He turned to Fairbrother with a vicious glance in his eyes. His words were so quiet as to be almost silent. "I go down. We all go down."

Fairbrother was almost contrite, alarmed, "then don't go down." The exchange was unnoticed amongst the commotion in the courtroom.

"If my son does, so do you all, and it will never end for either of you. Don't imagine I do not have the resources to destroy you. Or the will."

Dan left the court. He entered the meeting room. Mat paused as he paced around the walls. Nirundorn was sitting at the table, "Mr Cooper..."

Mat interrupted. "You saw him?"

"Who?" insisted Nirundorn as Lynne came in.

"Svetsreni," said Mat. "He was there when I was arrested. With Prisit."

The lawyer was silent.

Nobody spoke.

Nirundorn checked his watch. "We have to go back in." He turned to Mat. "Are you sure?"

Mat looked at Dan, who nodded. "I'm absolutely sure," said Mat to the solicitor.

"I wish I was," Dan whispered to Lynne as they left the room. The two guards put out their cigarettes and resumed station either side of Mat as he flexed his shoulders and walked back into the court. Svetsreni was in conversation with the prosecutor again. Mat stopped and stared at the police chief before Nirundorn touched his elbow to move him on.

Vyraj made his way back into the court.

He looked down at Nirundorn, who started to rise, but the prosecutor got to his feet first. Lynne whispered a translation into Dan's ear. "The prosecutor regrets that Major Prisit, the officer in control of the case, has suffered a tragic accident and has been killed. His distinguished career is well known to the court. In light of this, it is regretted that the prosecution does not feel it can proceed with the case."

Vyraj looked down at his papers. "He's asked which of the charges he's referring to."

The prosecutor turned to the back of the court as though throwing off responsibility, but Svetsreni had gone.

"All charges."

Viraj shrugged, shook his head and walked out.

Nirundorn whispered a translation in Mat's ear.

Dan closed his eyes. The days of pushing away hope because failure would be too hard to bear left him without the means of response. He opened his eyes.

Mat stood and turned. He held out his hands as though he

couldn't believe what had happened. He yelled in joy. A smile broke out as though it was almost impossible to acknowledge what had happened. He leapt over the seats, pushing aside files and piles of paper and grabbing Dan. There were no words worth speaking as he felt his son holding him, shouting with incoherent elation. He placed his hands on his son's cheeks. They embraced again. The nightmare had passed.

There were no words for either of them. Nothing could equal the moment. The emotions were almost too much. Dan felt his legs might give way. Mat glimpsed the sunlight through the door of the court. He could barely catch his breath.

Lynne joined the embrace. Tavinor nodded to Mat and guided them all toward the exit.

Kumat's perfect intonation broke into the euphoria. "Perhaps we could speak together. I'll be in the meeting room you used before the hearing."

Dan picked up his holdall. "I'll tell you later," he said to Mat. "Wait for me in the car." He looked over at Fairbrother, "The embassy car. I'll be a few minutes. Then we get to the airport." He gently held Lynne's arm and guided her to the room.

Kumat sat at the table.

Dan looked down at them. "Before we start, I want to see Mat's passport."

Kumat placed it on the table. He kept his hand over the passport.

Dan looked at Lynne. "Could you get his transfer ready." He glanced over to Kumat. "At the airport, you'll have your money. I assume we'll have an escort. I've got a plane waiting to take us out. Make your own way."

CHAPTER
FORTY-EIGHT

The embassy car was waiting outside the building.

'We've got a plane waiting at the airport to take us to Langkawi Island in Malaysia. Your Mother's arriving later. I've booked five beach villas,' said Dan.

Mat looked from the window. 'Could we make it six?' He jumped from the car. Dan recognised Tim and Lizzy from the Siam Paradise Hotel together with a young dark-haired girl who grabbed Mat amongst yelps of happiness. 'I guess that's Kathy,' said Dan to Lynne.

'What do you think, Dad? Could we bring these guys along?'

Dan laughed and nodded. He looked down the steps just in time to see Chris Ralston disappearing round a corner through a throng of sightseers at the roadside.

Nirundorn pumped Mat's hand in elation. 'Very brave, Matthew. Very brave.'

Dan took Nirundorn's hand. 'Thank you for bearing with us. I know your children are at school, but the resort in Langkawi has been told to give you the best villas they have for as long as you want. Take your family when it's holiday time. Thai Charter will fly you there. It's one way of thanking you.' He lifted the bag. 'I'd also like you to take on another client. Steven Ross. He's been in Bangkwang for eleven years. Can you look at his case and see if there's any chance of an appeal? When you visit him, could you take these books?'

Mat looked at the titles. 'They're in Spanish!'

Dan laughed and handed the hotel letterhead on which Magach had written the name of the village in Laos from where he'd recruited the bodyguards that eased their route to Vientiane. 'Could you also send ten thousand dollars to the headman of this village.'

Lynne was waiting at the glass doors.

Dan held out his hand. She took it.

'It is over,' she said.

He shook his head.

'For now, it's over.'

He smiled.

'Shall we get going.'

* * *

Kumat hovered by the private terminal.

Dan called Tony Tavinor over. "Are you coming to Langkawi?"

Tavinor nodded. "Penang first though to have a few days with Maria. We'll both be over then. I'll book Mikes Place for an evening."

Dan looked quizzical.

"Long story, good friend, Raguan Rahman – Ragi, the owner of Mikes Place."

Dan looked toward Kumat. "Shall we get this over with?"

Lynne came alongside. She held Dan's arm as they made their way to a small office.

Lynne got out her computer. "Same accounts," she snapped at Kumat. He nodded.

She entered the account numbers and then closed the computer.

Kumat studied his own laptop and then looked up.

He held out his hand to Dan.

"You must be joking", said Cooper as he took Lynne's hand, nodded to Tony Tavinor and left to board the jet waiting across the taxiway.

END

Thank you for reading ***A Bangkok Verdict***. For the very latest information on my books and investigations, please sign up for my newsletter at https://omegafilesquartet.com/go/news letter.

I genuinely appreciate your help in telling the world about my books. Please consider leaving a review on Amazon or your favourite book site.

A Covert Corruption is book 4 in **The Omega Files Quartet** by Mike Kingston. Available 2025.

For release info closer to the launch date, and to download a free companion e-book, please consider subscribing to my newsletter at https://omegafilesquartet.com/go/newsletter.

"IMPOSSIBLE TO PUT DOWN!"
5-STAR REVIEWER FOR THE OMEGA FILES QUARTET
MIKE KINGSTON
AUTHOR OF A CANDLE FOR CONSUELA
ROOTS OF DESTINY
AN OMEGA FILES QUARTET NOVELLA

ACKNOWLEDGMENTS

With enormous thanks to Barney Skinner of Red Nomad Studios for guiding this work to publication with skill and patience. Chech, Kevin, and Ermal, thank you for your critical input. To Robbie Garrad for inspiring the work. To Stephen Willis for insight into California policing. To Peter and Jane Jukes and Peter Lavery for their enthusiasm and support. To a great friend, David Benjamin, who continually inspires and enthuses me with wit, intelligence and wonderful late-night laughter and discussion. And to all my readers who always throw fresh light on the words.

ALSO AVAILABLE IN THE OMEGA FILES QUARTET

The Omega Files Quartet

A Candle for Consuela
A Flyblown Solution
A Bangkok Verdict
A Covert Corruption

Novellas

Roots of Destiny
Forged in Fire
Shadows of Redemption
Legacy of Revenge

Read more about Mike Kingston at omegafilesquartet.com

FIVE-STAR PRAISE FOR MIKE KINGSTON AND THE OMEGA FILES QUARTET...

'Once I started "Candle For Consuela" I couldn't put it down, initially because the action, plot and pacing are thrilling. However, the real draw of the book turned out to be the drama about what was at stake for the characters, including each main character fighting powerful political, theological and philosophical influences. The risks and forces acting on the characters were gripping.

The book provides a fictionalized presentation of events in England in recent times. Those recent events in England resulted from brutalities that actually occurred in El Salvador in a twelve year civil war in the 1980's. Among the past atrocities were torture and murder of civilians and the cold-blooded murder of six Jesuit priests. Thankfully, we are spared witnessing the atrocities. Instead, we are treated to intricately woven repercussions of those atrocities involving money, power, corruption, justice and The Catholic Church. Some characters wrestle mightily with their consciences, while others apparently have little, if any, conscience. All of these events are spiced with romance and sexual scenes that never seemed gratuitous, but instead advanced the plot and themes.

"Candle For Consuela" reminded me of some great and provocative books, such as those by Dan Brown, Graham Greene, Thornton Wilder (The Bridge Of San Luis Rey) and Morris West (The Shoes Of The Fisherman, etc.), while also being a page-turner like some by James Paterson and Tom Clancy.' ***David – San Francisco***

'A wonderful book that really makes the reader think how random our lives are! I look forward to reading more books by this Author and particularly to the next one in the Omega Files Quartet.' ***Hadleigh, Amazon 5-star reviewer***

'"A Candle for Consuela" proved to be a page-turner of a book. I was engrossed. Mike Kingston's extensive experience as a global investigator has provided him with a wealth of resource material for this incisively written story.' ***Angela Thomas, Amazon 5-star reviewer***

'A superb book. Clearly the author has lived the story and has conveyed the heightened emotions experienced during the brutal civil war in El Salvador and its desperate consequences. The underlying tensions between passion and religious dogma serves to add a dimension which makes this a brilliant read.' ***Mark K, Amazon 5-star reviewer***

'Riveting ...and reminded me of Graham Greene. A real pleasure to read. It is a thriller, but the subject matter is thought-provoking, and the characters are believable creating a frustration at the injustice and a hope for resolution. I will be purchasing the next book in the quartet and looking for more information on El Salvador.' ***Nicholas Goodwin, Amazon 5-star reviewer***

'Where fiction takes over from fact. The themes of revenge and redemption are familiar territory for novelists, but Kingston has brought a very fresh eye to them. Not least because he has created the setting effectively with lots of convincing detail which obviously comes from personal knowledge of the civil war. The storytelling is pacey, and it builds to an exciting climax. The background of real events gives a deeper sense of authenticity, too.' ***Peter Bartram, author***

'What an excellent book! It combines a very good story, compulsively told with a terrifying background of appalling criminality, murder and torture in El Salvador at the highest levels of government, supported by the USA who ignored it and the UK finance community who accepted the participants. Written by someone with close experience of the background, it is a very good and easy read and I look forward to the other books in the quartet.' ***Hugh, Amazon 5-star reviewer***

'Mike Kingston is an author who guarantees a good read - epic tales with detailed research and knowledge. "A Candle for Consuela" is a dramatic story based on a terrifying historical setting; it will horrify, engage, and move you in equal measure. Highly recommended.' ***Peter Jukes, Amazon 5-star reviewer***

ABOUT THE AUTHOR

Mike Kingston has spent much of his career carrying out investigations throughout the world for many organisations – from worldwide media companies to multi-national corporations and global law firms. He has been reporting on and investigating corruption, espionage and conspiracy for more than 30 years.

His books reflect events he has encountered and the amazing characters, both courageous and depraved he has met along the way.

Underlying his words is an enormous respect for the resilience of the human spirit in surviving heartbreaking situations and managing to live meaningful and fulfilling lives, often in desperate circumstances.

Read more about Mike Kingston at omegafilesquartet.com

Printed in Great Britain
by Amazon

56983897R00208